Walker Lane

Published by Walker Lane, 2021.

Copyright © 2020 Walker Lane
All Rights Reserved.

Scripture quotations taken from the (NASB®) New American Standard Bible®, Copyright © 1960, 1971, 1977 by The Lockman Foundation. Used by permission. All rights reserved. www.lockman.org.

This is a work of fiction. Similarities to real people, places, or events are entirely coincidental.

A NOTE FROM THE AUTHOR:

Dear Reader,
 Thank you for choosing my book. I hope you enjoy reading it as much as I enjoyed writing it for you. If so, it would mean so much to me if you would drop me a line and tell me your favorite part of Jack and Lily's story, or leave a review if you think others could benefit from it.

Sincerely,
Walker Lane
walkerlane55@gmail.com

DEDICATION:

I dedicate this book to my mom who passed before I was able to finish my final draft, but who after reading my first few chapters decidedly did not like Damien.

To my dad who passed so many years ago. Without him I would have no work ethic. I hope you're proud of me, Dad.

To my husband, who has continually supported and encouraged my writing endeavors and who actually read one of my earlier drafts with great interest.

To my son, who has always shown excitement in my successes and applauds every time I find my way out of technical difficulties.

To my lifelong friend Linda, who spent days helping me establish my website and blog. Thank you for your patience!

To my former students who urged me to finish this book. I apologize for beginning sentences with conjunctions. It just seemed to work.

And especially to God, who I promised no smut. I hope He is pleased with this work of Christian fiction even though it reveals the reality of such imperfections in His children.

REMEMBER ME

Last but not least, I wrote this book for you, my fellow imperfect Christians, who try so hard to follow God's word, and often end up failing, so that you know you are not alone in your sin. We all struggle in this world full of temptation, but He still loves us and picks us up when we fall.

God bless and stay in the Word,

Walker Lane

ABOUT THE AUTHOR:

Walker Lane graduated from Sam Houston State University with a Bachelor's Degree in English, minoring in History. After teaching for fifteen years, she decided to pursue her love of writing which stemmed from a childhood full of daydreams. As a teacher, she learned to organize those daydreams into stories. Her writing career began as a small child with her first poem titled "A Friend" (written on a "Hello Kitty" notepad), and continued on through high school writing articles and poems for the school newspaper, and on through the debut of her first novel. Today she continues writing a Christian Blog and is currently working on her second novel. She is a devoted wife, mother, and Christian residing in Texas. Visit her website at Walker-Lane.com, on Facebook at

facebook.com/walker.lane.73, or
https://www.facebook.com/Walkerswritings, on
Twitter at Walker Lane @WalkerLane1.

Prologue

Tears welled up in Lily's eyes again. How many times had she cried today? She looked around at the mourners all dressed in their Sunday best, amazed at the throngs of people who came to pay their respects. She turned and gazed at her mom. She looked so pretty this morning. She had refused to wear black, and instead had worn a dress the color of spring bluebonnets — his favorite flower.

The gray sky loomed overhead as the solemn voice of the preacher brought Lily back to attention. At the words of the Psalms, her throat thickened. She hated crying in front of people. Lily leaned forward and looked down at the green turf, bright against her black shoes. Nearby, a caterpillar ambled toward his destination. How odd that the world had not stopped after all.

Men in dark suits surrounded her father waiting for the signal to lower him. Apropos of the fire and ice roses that sat atop the simple pine box, she felt as if she were in hell, shivering. She leaned her head on her mom's shoulder and the sobs subsided momentarily when a green butterfly flew in front of her and landed on one of the roses in the spray. It hovered there for a moment then fluttered off into the sky as "Amazing Grace" filled the air.

Her mother reached out and took her trembling hand. Her mother — shouldn't Lily be consoling her? But at that moment, her own despair took charge. Though Lily was all grown up, right now she was just a little girl crying for her daddy. She would be strong for her mother tomorrow.

Lily's mom squeezed her hand as the men gently lowered her dad to his final resting place. She said a quick prayer for her mother who would face an empty bed in the night and loneliness in the morning. It was time to come home. Her mother would need her.

Part One

Chapter One

Hope deferred makes the heart sick.
Proverbs 13:12

Lily's throat tightened as she blinked back tears. Nope. She wouldn't give him the satisfaction. She turned away so he couldn't see.

"Not right now, Babe," Damien said, "I mean, we're still young. We have plenty of time."

She stared out of their kitchen window, watching the sun fill the sky with its orange splendor. "I know. It's just that... I think—"

"And that's your problem." His voice flared. "You think too much." He stomped around the kitchen behind her. "Now, can we please stop talking about this?"

"But—"

"Lily, please! Stop!"

She flinched at his loud voice and folded her arms across her chest. Her heart fell. She wasn't just asking him for a baby. She was trying to tell him there might already be one.

"Look, I'm sorry." Damien approached Lily from behind. "I didn't mean to yell. I'm just not ready to upend our lives with a baby." He put his arms around her.

Lily stiffened.

"What's the rush, anyway?" He backed away, continuing with his breakfast preparations. "I mean, once we have kids, the fun is over."

Lily spun around and glared at the back of his head.

He grabbed two coffee mugs from the cabinet and poured them both a cup of coffee.

Lily didn't touch hers. "You mean your fun is over."

"What's that supposed to mean?" He slammed the cabinet door.

"It means you're the one who likes to go out and stay out till all hours of the night. Not me."

He stared at the toaster, waiting. "It's not my fault you don't have a social life."

"Really. Then whose fault is it? We never go anywhere together anymore."

Ignoring her, he walked over to the refrigerator and grabbed the butter.

Lily continued, "But you're always going out with your friends. Why don't you invite me sometime?"

"You don't like my friends, remember?" He glanced up and scowled at her.

He was right about that. They were a little too rowdy for her taste.

"Face it, Lily. You're a homebody. And you blame me for it." He took a knife from the drawer and slathered butter all over his toast. "Well, it sounds like you're the one with the problem, not me, and I'm not gonna give you a baby just to fill your schedule." He leaned against the counter and took a bite, glaring at her. "Sorry, but I don't have time to play house with you right now."

A sharp fissure tore through Lily's heart. "Fine. Go then," she said. She walked into the bedroom and shut the door then plopped down on the bed and hugged her pillow. For the next few quiet moments, her life would hang in limbo. Either her world would be forever changed, or it wouldn't. She knew what her heart wanted, even though Damien's response was not what she'd been hoping for. Ever since Lily had gotten her first doll, she couldn't wait until the day she'd become a mom in a house full of children. That's one reason she hadn't seen the point in sticking with college. She was a hard worker, but career-driven, she was not.

Slam! She heard the back door. Sighing, Lily stood up and braced herself. Well, it's now or never. She advanced into the bathroom with her sole focus on the little stick lying on the counter—that little object that had the power to make big changes. What would it say? She'd envisioned her and Damien reading the results together—joyful together, or sad together. But now she knew on this, they were not together. She stared at the pregnancy test and sat down on the side of the tub and finally let the tears flow.

Chapter Two

An excellent wife, who can find? For her worth is far above jewels. Prov. 31:10

Lily thrust her weight against the back door of The Charlotte House. The old wood gave way suddenly and she stumbled down the step. Hesitating near the doorway, Lily gazed up into the dark midnight sky and took in a deep breath — fresh country air, a balm to the soul. A whispering breeze ruffled her hair that quickly blustered into a small roar soaring through the tall live oak trees, ebbing and flowing overhead. Leaves blew all around as frantic wind chimes clanged from the eaves of the verandah. The grumble of thunder filled the atmosphere and Lily tensed as large droplets began to plop out of the dark sky and bounce off the dirt, muffling the sound of the leaves meandering on the small gale.

Lily decided to make a run for it, but her small purse afforded little protection from the rain as she scurried across the dimly lit parking lot sidestepping little water puddles. Fumbling with her keys, she unlocked her car and slid behind the steering wheel. She turned the rearview mirror her way and brushed back strands of dark hair clinging to her face. Waiting for the old engine to warm up, the storm suddenly passed, raining just enough for the unrelenting dust to stick to the cars remaining in the parking lot of the upscale watering hole.

    Lily pulled out onto the highway and drove toward home relieved the rain had let up. She was wary of driving in bad weather, especially at night. An ambulance sped around her spurring her to say a quick prayer. By the time she reached home, the rain had started up again, and disappointment greeted her as she pulled into the empty driveway she shared with her husband reminding her of the argument they'd had that morning. Absorbed in her thoughts, Lily's eyes followed along with the windshield wipers, back and forth, back and forth, until lightning crackled across the sky yanking her out of her trance. She jumped out of the car and raced to the side door of her quaint, one hundred-year-old house, its red shutters and brightly lit porch welcoming her home. She unlocked the door and quickly stepped inside the mudroom. *Home.*

    Lily plopped her damp purse down on the farmhouse table and locked the door and hung her keys on the hook. It had been a long night. She stretched her arms up overhead, yawning, then leaned down over her right leg— *Pop!* She stretched down over her left leg, *pop-pop...pop.* Her feet hurt, she felt sticky, and the stench of stale beer and cigarettes assaulted her senses. Exhausted, she pulled off her wet shoes and chunked them into the corner.

REMEMBER ME

Baxter traipsed over to Lily and meowed at her feet. "What?" She picked him up and gave him a big hug, nuzzling his soft gray and white fur. He meowed again, louder. "What is it, boy? Do I smell?" She smiled at him, convinced he could understand her. Baxter wiggled out of her arms and pounced to the floor.

She pulled the night's wages out of her pocket: $143 plus change. The coins clinked against each other as she dropped them in an old coffee can then reached up to place it in the top kitchen cabinet. "Not too bad for a night's work," she said to her beloved cat and an otherwise empty house. She made pretty good money waitressing in the grand former plantation home that had been turned into an upscale bar and restaurant. It wasn't every girl's dream job, but her co-workers were great and it kept her active.

The bar had been pretty busy, and Lily just wanted to take a hot bath and slip into her freshly laundered sheets, but she doubted sleep would come easily. Damien wasn't home yet. Their three-year wedding anniversary was coming up soon and Lily wondered if he would remember or if she would have to remind him again. As she was milling about performing her nightly routine, her mind wandered back to when they first met. He was so handsome with his jet-black hair and dark feathery lashes. There was once a time he would gaze at her, love and desire electrifying the air between them. She missed that.

Lily checked her cell phone — no messages. She sent Damien a text then ran the bath water and fed

Baxter. Lily undressed and stepped into the old claw foot tub. Steam rose up all around as the warm water enveloped her removing all the ills of the night. She closed her eyes and relaxed, enjoying one of life's small pleasures. She stayed in the tub until the skin on her toes began to prune then reluctantly pulled herself out and dried off. After changing into one of Damien's old t-shirts, she crawled into bed and skimmed through a cooking magazine with Baxter curled up at her feet.

Lily didn't like the way she and her husband had left things that morning. Cooking something special this week might help them get back on track. Plus, she enjoyed cooking for Damien, especially since he hadn't had much home-cooking growing up.

Just then, lightning shot through the bedroom. The window rattled with thunder. Lily flung back the covers, hopped out of bed, and pulled back the lacey curtains to peek outside. She leapt back with her heart in her throat as once again lightning erupted in the night sky. Baxter zipped under the covers, hiding like a little child, conjuring memories of her own childhood.

When she was little, she would run and jump into her parents' bed, burrowing between them in safety. Oh, how she missed those days—the days when she felt safe. Someday, she would have her own kids snuggle up to her for comfort.

She couldn't wait to have a baby, but unfortunately, that was not yet to be. The pregnancy test she'd taken that morning was negative. Maybe it was just as well since Damien wasn't too thrilled about the thought of having children just yet. But still, Lily couldn't help but feel disappointed.

Time passed while Lily tossed and turned and finally fell into a fitful sleep. The magazine falling to the floor, Lily flinched and quickly sat up in bed startling Baxter. He meowed at her grudgingly. "Sorry, Sweetie," she ran her fingers through his fur. He forgivingly plopped his head back down and closed his eyes once again. She leaned over to the nightstand and checked her phone. Nothing. It had been over two hours since she'd sent the text to her husband seeking his whereabouts. She'd never go back to sleep now. She crawled out of bed and ambled to the fridge for a snack, staring blankly into the chilly abyss. When she finally heard the key unlock the door, she released a deep breath she hadn't realized she'd been holding. He was home.

Leaves blew into the house as Damien opened the door. He rounded the corner banging his shoulder on the doorjamb between the mudroom and kitchen, mumbling expletives along the way. Clothes dripping, he shuffled in, leaving muddy shoes in his wake. He nearly ran smack dab into Lily standing in front of the open fridge. She stared at him with unspoken questions as his disheveled hair fell across a sheepish countenance. Lily's heart sank.

"Oh Lily, damn, you scared me!" His hand came up to his chest as he took a deep breath and let it out. Dark eyes met hers for only a split second before he looked down at the floor and walked around her. "I'm beat. Gonna take a shower and hit the hay." Damien walked past her and headed toward the bathroom. He closed the door without looking back leaving Lily standing there alone, still holding the refrigerator door wide open, cold seeping into her bones.

    It was too late to question him now, she realized, as she heard the spray of the shower. She closed the fridge and methodically checked the back door and turned off the lights. She crawled into bed, exhaustion overwhelming her into a fitful sleep, leaving her questions unanswered.

Chapter Three

Be of sober spirit, be on the alert. Your adversary, the devil, prowls about like a roaring lion, seeking someone to devour.
1 Pet. 5:8

Lily parked behind the Charlotte House on the outskirts of Chappell Hill, Texas. As she got out of her car, she looked up at the gabled roof, marveling at its splendor. Though people claimed it to be haunted, Lily loved working in the old plantation home. It was intriguing, not to mention beautiful. Years before, her boss Charlotte Adams, bought it and turned it into an upscale food and drink venue. Its charm brought in patrons who came not only for its history but also for the wide verandahs and pastoral views boasting a captivating scene of rolling green hills and colorful wildflowers. But occasionally the patrons over-imbibed, and drunk people were still drunk no matter how upscale they might be—as was the case on Saturday night, which had been particularly challenging for Lily.

A well dressed, if not somewhat harrowed-looking, middle-aged man came into the bar and sat in Lily's section. It was hard not to notice his striking good looks or his sullen expression. Looking incredibly dejected, he walked in alone and sat in the corner. Lily scurried over to his table, presented a smile, and introduced herself.

"Hi, my name is Lily. I'll be your server tonight. What can I get for you?"

"I'll have a Bourbon, straight up."

"Yes sir. Would you like to see a menu?"

"No," he answered tersely.

Lily brought him his drink then moved on to her other tables. Her section quickly filled up which kept her busily running from table to table trying to keep all of her customers happy. The people who frequented The Charlotte House were good tippers, and she worked hard to make sure none were neglected. After a while, Lily checked on her sullen customer in the corner. He ordered another drink then returned to his own thoughts. He never ordered any food, and throughout the night the drinks disappeared rapidly. Unsettling as it was, she might soon find herself in an uncomfortable situation knowing she'd probably have to cut him off. It wasn't often that a customer was refused a drink, but when it did happen, it never seemed to be well received.

"I think he's depressed about something," said Anna, the other waitress working that night. Anna leaned forward and folded her arms on the bar looking in his direction, and smacked her gum. Apparently, she had been keeping an eye on him too, albeit for different reasons.

"Yeah, seems like it," replied Lily. She looked at him warily then glanced back at Anna. "Better get rid of that gum, Anna, before Jack sees it."

"Yeah, yeah, yeah — I know, I know. Gum chewing isn't classy, but neither is bad breath," she smacked her gum loudly.

Lily giggled.

Sometime later, after four drinks—four was more than enough—Lily pasted on a smile and approached her unhappy customer. "All set?" Without waiting for an answer, Lily placed his ticket on the table. "I'll just leave this here for you, and I can take care of it whenever you're ready." She quickly turned to go, but he reached out and touched her arm, stopping her.

"What makes you think I'm finished?" he replied with just an edge of belligerence.

"Oh, I'm sorry. Did you want to order something from the kitchen?" She hoped he would reconsider eating something.

"No. But I will have another drink." Lily felt some trepidation at the idea of bringing him more alcohol. After all, she felt responsible for him. If he had an accident driving home, someone could get hurt. Plus, if she over served him, it would fall back on her…and Charlotte. She stood there for a moment gathering her courage.

"Sir, I don't mean to be nosy, but are you okay?"

He looked at her with one eye half closed. "Just get me another drink, and I guess some pretzels." He stared down into his empty glass, dismissing her.

Lily found the manager, Jack, and alerted him to the situation. "Go ahead and bring him one more, Lily. I'll keep an eye on him." He folded his arms and covertly leaned back against the wall in clear vision of the situation. Lily headed back to the bar to order. Anna raised her eyebrows but didn't have time for questions. The bar was packed. Lily wove in and out between the crowded tables and hesitantly headed for her customer in the corner. "Here you go, Sir." Lily reached across the small table to place the drink down in front of him and heard a sniffing sound close to her ear.

"You smell good," he said,

His tone made her skin crawl.

"What are you doin' after work?" he asked.

Lily pulled back and popped her head in his direction, but before she could step away from the table, he reached out and grabbed her arm, his fingers tight on her skin. Her heart pounded. She had a flashing thought of punching his lights out, but she knew she needed to hold her composure.

"Please let go of me," she said with as much self-control as she could muster, but he didn't.

"Why don't you ssssit down here with me for a while, Missy," he slurred.

"Well, I'm not allowed to sit down with customers. You wouldn't wanna get me in trouble, would you?" Lily attempted to mask her uneasiness. "Oh! I forgot your pretzels. I'll be right back." Lily tried to pull away, but the customer's grip grew stronger. He tugged at her arm and hauled her into his lap, ignoring her protests.

REMEMBER ME

    From across the room, Jack watched the scene unfold and jumped to attention. He shifted into high gear with only one objective — protecting Lily.

    Jack barreled toward the table and saw Lily elbow the patron in the stomach causing him to double over. She stood up, but the man determinedly held on. Looking to Jack for help, her eyes widened when she caught sight of him, fiercely glaring and powering toward them. Without a word, Jack grabbed the back of the man's hair then pulled his head backward and slammed his face down into the table. Dazed, the man quickly released her, and she hurried back across the room rubbing her arm where his unrelenting fingers had staked their claim. Facing no resistance, Jack pulled the inebriated man out of his seat by the back of his collar and calmly guided him out to the foyer.

    Anna ran up to Lily. "Hey Girl, you okay?" She gently brushed Lily's hair out of her face.

    Lily looked away, embarrassed.

    "Come with me to the bathroom." Anna pulled on Lily's arm and called out to the bartender, "Hey Bob, will you watch our tables for a minute? We need a quick break."

    "Sure, no problem, Anna. Take your time." Bob stared after them.

Anna led Lily to the employee bathroom to rinse off her face then outside to the staff smoking area which consisted of a bench next to the ramp where deliveries were made. She offered Lily a cigarette, looking astonished as Lily actually put one in her mouth to light it. Anna had offered Lily cigarettes before, but she had always declined. This time, she didn't. Through her tears, Lily blustered out the whole story while Anna listened intently.

"Wow," Anna said, blowing smoke into the night, "your hero."

"What? Who?" Lily looked down at her hands. They were shaking.

"Jack. He's your hero — your very own hero," Anna teased as she nudged her with her elbow.

Lily raised her eyebrows and glared at Anna.

"Granted, he's not tall like Superman, but he's got nice arms," Anna chided.

"Oh stop. You know I don't think that way about him." Lily sucked in the acrid smoke. She felt dizzy.

"Doesn't matter. He thinks that way about you."

Lily coughed and shifted uncomfortably in her seat. "What are you talking about? You're crazy!" In spite of her protests, a pinkish glow crept up Lily's throat to her cheeks.

"Maybe, but probably not. You should see the way he watches you sometimes."

"Watches me? That's creepy. Besides, you know I'm a happily married woman."

Anna narrowed her eyes. "Are you?"

"Am I what?"

"Happily."

"Anna!" Lily looked at her friend, "Have you been sippin' behind the counter again?"

Anna poked Lily with her finger in pace with her words. "Are—you—a—happily—married—woman?"

"Of course I am!"

"Uh huh. Okay." Anna threw her hands up. "Well, we'd better get back up there. I can't believe I got you to smoke," she grinned. "Always knew you had it in you." Anna stood up and put out her cigarette. She reached for Lily's and disposed of it as well.

Lily stood up wiping wayward ashes off her lap, already feeling guilty—not only guilty about smoking, but maybe a little guilty about Jack too? She was floored by her self-confession.

"Yeah well, don't tell anybody! It was a one-time thing."

Anna stopped and looked into Lily's eyes. "Seriously though, are you okay?"

"Yeah, I think so. I just wanna go home."

"If you need to talk—"

"I know. Thanks. I appreciate it." Anna and Lily quickly hugged and rushed back to the floor.

When they got back to the bar, Jack was nowhere to be found. Neither was the inebriated customer. Bob informed the girls that they were sitting outside together on the curb waiting for a cab while Jack played counselor. "Apparently, the guy's wife is cheating on him with his best friend. No more wife. No more best friend. What's a guy to do?"

"That stinks," Anna replied, popping her gum.

"Yeah, poor guy. I guess you just never know," Bob said.

Thoughts of Damien's late nights flashed through Lily's mind.

"When Jack brought him back in to pay his tab, he said to tell you he was real sorry, Lily. I think he felt pretty bad for scaring you like that, and I imagine he has quite a headache from his forehead meeting up with the table. Ha!" He laughed. "If it makes you feel any better, he left you a pretty big tip, and Anna, better get rid of that gum! You know better!"

"Thanks, Bob." Lily cracked a smile. "I guess it does make me feel a little better."

Anna blew a big bubble and it popped in her face, sticking in her hair. They all laughed as she gingerly tried to pick it out, then she finally spit it into the trash.

Lily was wiping down her last table when Jack finally returned. She stopped and looked up at him. He caught her gaze, holding it. When she realized she was staring she glanced down and started wiping again. Jack didn't approach her. She watched him from the corner of her eye as he sat down at the bar. Everyone had gone for the night except the staff. Jack ordered himself a beer. Bob looked up at Lily and shrugged. Jack had never drunk in the bar before.

"Jack, why don't you wait till we get outta here? We can go over to Harvey's and down a couple while we shoot a game of pool."

"Yeah, you're right. Charlotte wouldn't want me drinking in here."

"Charlotte wouldn't what?" Charlotte drifted into the room seemingly from nowhere.

"Nothing Babe. We were just talking about what happened earlier with a customer," Bob replied.

She threw her hands up in the air and shook her head from side to side. "I know all about it. I just ran into Anna as she was leaving. She filled me in. Jack, Lily," Charlotte slapped her hand down on the bar. "Why don't y'all sit down here and have a drink with me. My treat. Special occasion. Bob, pour four glasses of white wine, please." They all looked at each other questioningly, but did as they were told. One didn't argue with Charlotte.

"What's the occasion?" asked Bob.

"The occasion is that I didn't fire you when you called me *Babe* in front of my employees." She smirked.

"Oops. Sorry, I slipped."

She leaned toward him across the bar and loudly whispered in his ear with a gleam in her eyes. "It's okay. I kinda liked it."

"So, you gonna marry me then?" Bob whispered back just as loudly, smirking.

"Not on your life," she laughed. "And don't do it again!" Bob threw a towel at her and sighed.

"When is this woman gonna realize that she's the only one for me?" He glanced at the other two sitting at the bar.

Lily's eyes caught Jack's, but he quickly looked away.

The four of them moved to one of the tables and sat down together and sipped their wine while Bob retold Charlotte the story of Lily and Jack's mishap. As far as Lily knew, workers did not drink with the boss, but after all, it had been an unusual night. The altercation with the customer had been disturbing, but Charlotte was supportive and understanding. She praised Jack and fawned over Lily then walked out arm in arm with Bob leaving Jack and Lily behind.

Jack cleared his throat. "Walk you out to your car?"

Lily nodded her head. "Well, normally I would tell you it wasn't necessary, but I would really appreciate it tonight."

Jack put his hand gently on Lily's back and guided her outside as he cut off the lights along the way. His touch was warm and comforting, yet disconcerting as Lily realized she liked it just a little too much. As they walked to her car, the path seemed darker than usual casting ominous shadows around every corner adding to Lily's nervousness. When they finally reached her car in the employee parking lot, she unlocked her door then turned to face Jack to thank him. He reached out and gently touched her arm. His fingers lingered where red marks had been left behind. His touch was slightly jarring and left her quivering inside. She looked into his eyes as if just now seeing him for the first time, as one soul slowly gaining recognition of the other.

"Your eyes?" she questioned.

"My eyes? What about them?" Jack asked.

"I've never seen eyes that color before." She tilted her head in fascination as she slowly moved just inches away from him. "They're almost gray, with just a touch of green," she said, inspecting them. Her hand started to reach up to his face, but stopped midway.

"Oh, they're hazel. They sort of change colors depending on my mood." He cleared his throat and look down at the ground.

They heard keys jingling, breaking the spell, as the maintenance man walked by. Jack took a step back away from Lily. "Um, are you really okay, Lily?"

"Yes. I'm fine. Thank you for your help. If you hadn't stepped in, I might've had to take down that customer myself, and frankly, my karate skills aren't quite what they used to be," she laughed nervously trying to mask her lingering discomposure. Why was she so nervous?

Jack's eyes seemed to be searching hers, but he didn't say anything, and the moment hung in the air between them. He slowly reached out and brushed away the wisps of hair that had fallen in her eyes. Her pulse quickened. His soft touch sent warm shivers throughout her body.

"Jack..." Lily's heart felt heavy.

"It's okay, Lily," he said, then turned and walked away.

Lily had the feeling that maybe it wouldn't be okay for a long, long time.

Chapter Four

Pray that you may not enter into temptation.
Luke 22:40

He grabbed Lily's hand and led her to the shadows as she willingly followed, her steps struggling to match his. Her dress billowed with the intrusive breeze. Branches reached out as if to stop her, scratching her arms as the two barreled through the brush. He stopped to face her. Beads of sweat trickled down the back of her neck as she wondered what might happen. She stood frozen in time anticipating his next move. Taking both her hands in his, he raised her arms and leaned into her, their fingers intertwined above her head. His heat shingled her own, sending flames throughout her body. She could barely catch her breath. He looked down into her eyes, piercing her soul. Did he know what secrets they held? He gently brushed her forehead with his lips. His warm sweet breath hovered over her mouth, wanting, seeking permission, permission that they knew she could not give, but would not deny.

"I want you," he said.

And she wanted him, but she turned from him and ran into the dark fog, beads of mist heavy on

REMEMBER ME

her lashes, blinding her way. Damp and cold enveloped her senses. She saw Damien up ahead and grasped for him, but he was out of reach.

Lily bolted upright in bed, waking from her distress, realizing she had kicked the blankets to the floor. She looked over to make sure she hadn't woken Damien, but he wasn't there. But Jack was there dangling on the edge of her dreams. She looked at the clock. It was 3:30 a.m.

Holding onto Lily, Jack slowly emerged back into consciousness. He opened his eyes to look at her, but only a pillow languished in his arms. Disappointed, he reached for the glass of water on his nightstand to quench his thirst, knowing that his real thirst could never be quenched. Lily was married — off limits. His thoughts turned to Hailey who had been pressing him to get married. Jack fell back against his pillow in frustration. Guilt overwhelmed him as he realized just how quickly temptation could rear its ugly head. Nevertheless, Jack closed his eyes and sprung a grin as his mind relived the amorous dream over and over until he finally fell back to sleep.

The next morning, the alarm clock blared waking Lily from a sleepless night. Damien rolled toward her and yelled at her to turn it off. Her head hurt, and she wondered what time he had finally gotten home. Nevertheless, she quickly readied for church, and an hour later Lily tripped up the steps as she ran into the Church of Christ just at the start of the opening song. There was no room by her mom up front, so she sat in the back pew next to a young family of three. Damien wasn't a churchgoer.

Brother Tim preached a sermon on temptation, which made her feel guilty after the dream she'd just had. When on God's green earth had she become attracted to Jack? It seemed to have slipped up on her out of nowhere.

She looked around the full auditorium and spotted Jack and Hailey sitting across the aisle. The thought that he looked handsome in his suit and tie did not escape her. She examined Hailey closely too. She was very beautiful. Her long blond flowing hair hung over the back of the pew. Her undoubtedly expensive make-up had been applied with perfection, her skin flawless. She probably has the voice of an angel. Lily grimaced. Just then, Jack turned and caught Lily's eye, breaking into a smile. Great! She had been caught red-handed, staring. Lily nervously ran her hand down her hair and looked away. She giggled, immediately dismissing thoughts of Jack and Hailey, as she noticed the little boy sitting next to her with his finger up pointing forward, moving along the rows.

"What are you doing?" She leaned down and whispered to him.

"Countin' hats," the little boy answered. Lily looked up and noticed the few hats there actually were for him to count. Only the older ladies seemed to still wear them to church. She should have been paying attention to the preacher but now she found herself mentally counting along with the boy.

After the sermon Lily made a quick escape to avoid Jack. She ran down the steps and out to her car and started it, but it was too late. Jack had left Hailey talking with his parents and was headed her way. She rested her elbow on the steering wheel and her chin in her palm and studied him. He was perfect. Not too tall, not too short, strong— but his muscles weren't too brawny for his size. She liked that. His brown hair was cropped close to his head, neat and trimmed. He was clean-cut, sweet, and handsome, as well as—a churchgoer.

Lily rolled her window down just as he approached her. "Hey," she fashioned a smile.

"Hey yourself." Jack repaid her smile with one of his own and placed his hands on the top of her small car and leaned into her window. He aimed his arresting eyes at her, which she noticed were a deep green today.

Her pulse quickened.

"Why are you running off so fast?" he asked.

"Oh, I just need to get home to my husband." She began to fiddle with her dangling keys.

"Damien, right?"

Lily shifted in her seat. "Uh, yeah."

Jack leaned in closer. "Did you tell him about what happened last night?"

"Last night?" Lily locked eyes with his. The butterflies in her stomach danced all around.

He held her gaze. "Yeah...you are okay, aren't you?"

Lily looked at her arm, breaking the spell. Bruises had already formed in the shape of large fingers. "Uh, no, I haven't really had the chance. He got home late from work."

"Right. He works in Houston, doesn't he?"

"Yes. He works for a car dealership."

"Wow. They must be open pretty late, huh."

"Well, no. It's not that it's just...oh, I don't know." Lily shook her head, frowning.

"Hey, I'm sorry. It's none of my business."

Lily spotted a blue jay bouncing on a skinny limb high up in a nearby tree. It's sound reminded her of her mom's front porch swing, swinging back and forth.

"Okay. I won't keep you then." He took a step back. "I just wanted to see how you were."

She looked at him and smiled faintly. "I'm okay."

"Good." Jack leaned in and gently squeezed her shoulder. "Alright. Well, let me know if you need time off or anything."

"Oh, don't be silly. I'm fine." Lily waved him away. She peered over the steering wheel and pointed toward the church building. "I think your girlfriend is looking for you."

Jack looked up. "Yeah. Okay. See ya tomorrow then?"

"Yes. I'll be there with bells on," she said, her voice raising an octave. Lily watched him go, wondering why she was suddenly acting like a silly school girl.

REMEMBER ME

When she arrived home she found Damien still asleep. Her phone rang and she scampered off to the other room to answer it.

"Hey Mom."

"Good morning, Lily. Why did you run off so fast after church? I was going to ask you to lunch."

"Oh, I'm pretty tired. I just wanted to get home." Lily plopped down on the couch and looked for the T.V. remote.

"Did you have to work late again?"

"Yep. As usual." She finally found it between the cushions and turned on the T.V., surfing through the channels.

"I wish you'd get a different job, Honey. One not in a bar."

Lily rolled her eyes, glad that her mother couldn't see her. "I know Mom, but I like my job."

"Well, when you have kids I hope you can just stay home with them and not have to work at all."

"Sounds good to me."

"Any chance that would be anytime soon?" her mother inquired.

"Not yet Mom." They sighed in unison. They were both eager for Lily to become a mom.

"Well, it's none of my business, but I sure would like to be a gramma before I'm too old to pick up my grand-babies."

"Okay Mom—I get it. Well, I need to change clothes and figure out what to fix my husband for lunch."

"Right," her mother replied in a clipped tone.

"Bye Mom. Love you." Lily hung up and quietly went into the bedroom to change into sweat pants and a T-shirt. She fixed herself a sandwich and headed back to the couch. She didn't bother Damien. He'd probably just want coffee anyway once he woke up.

An hour later, Damien staggered into the living room where Lily was watching an old black and white movie.

"Can't we watch something from this century?" He grumbled.

She tossed the remote control to him. "You can watch whatever you want." She got up to leave the room but he blocked her path.

"What's wrong with you?"

"Nothing. What's wrong with you?" Lily squared her shoulders.

"Don't give me that — I know when you're in one of your moods."

"Really? What was your first clue?" She walked around him, heading to the bedroom.

"Lily? What's wrong?" he asked as she walked out, his tone gentler.

Lily ticked off a list in her mind but decided to keep it simple. She turned around to face him. "I guess I just get tired of going to church by myself."

"Your mom wasn't there?"

"Yes. She was, but she was up front and I walked in late. There was no room next to her anyway."

"So that's my fault?" He raised his eyebrows.

"As a matter of fact, yes, it is."

He folded his arms. "Uh huh. I'm listening."

"I was awake all night waiting for you to get home. Where were you?"

Damien blinked. "Out with the guys from work."

"Where?" Demanded Lily, hands on her hips.

"What's with the twenty questions?"

Lily's eyes pierced his, "Where, Damien?"

"Downtown Houston."

"Why were you in downtown Houston?" Lily asked.

"That's where the bar is."

"Okay. Why were you so late?"

"They didn't close till two. Then I drove back home. It's a ninety-minute drive, Lily."

"I'm aware of that Damien, but maybe you shouldn't be going to bars in downtown Houston. Maybe you shouldn't be going to bars at all. In fact, maybe you should start acting your age and actually come home after work."

"You WORK in a bar, remember? You are in a bar practically every night. You don't hear me complaining."

"It's a job. I'm not there drinking." Maybe he was right though. She knew he had a point. Hating all this fighting, especially on what was supposed to be a peaceful Sunday, she took a deep breath and walked over to him, putting her hands on his chest. "Damien, maybe you're right. But I only plan on keeping that job till we have kids. When can we revisit this baby thing?"

He removed her hands and turned away. "We've been over this Lily. I'm not ready for that kind of responsibility yet."

"Damien, you're in your thirties. Why aren't you ready?"

He turned back to face her. "Are you ready? You're barely twenty-five."

"I've been ready since the day we said 'I do.' Just say the word."

"No, Lily. I'm not ready." He shook his head and looked down at the floor. "I honestly don't know if I'll ever be ready."

Lily stumbled back. "What do you mean?" She couldn't believe what she was hearing. "Are you saying you don't want children? Ever?"

"I don't know what I'm saying." His hand flew to his forehead and he looked away. "I don't know. Maybe not. Maybe I really don't want kids…at all."

"I can't…I can't believe this." Lily slumped down on the edge of the couch. She grabbed the throw pillow and squeezed it tight, anger building inside her. She glared at him. "You know I want kids. You know I've always wanted kids. Now you don't want to have them with me?" Lily shook her head. "How am I supposed to stay married to a man who doesn't want children?" She put the pillow over her face and leaned forward.

"Well, I guess that's your choice, isn't it?"

Something snapped inside her. The calm, sweet, understanding Lily vanished. She bolted off the couch, reared the pillow back and threw it at him full force. "Damn you, Damien! Damn you!" It hit him in the face, making his eyes water.

Damien stood there for a moment, staring at her. She stared back in a rage. All her dreams shattered by this man who had promised to love and honor her. Instead, at least lately, he had only bestowed misery upon her, and now, this was the ultimate betrayal. No children? No way. This was too much.

Damien took a deep breath and let it out slowly. His only response—silence. He did not rise to her anger, he just left the room.

The ground beneath Lily crumbled. What was happening to them? What was happening to their marriage?

Chapter Five

The spirit is willing, but the flesh is weak.
Matthew 26:41

It was early Halloween morning and Jack and Lily had been nominated as the decorating crew. They met in the parking lot at 7:00 a.m. She had bought the decorations with Charlotte's credit card, and Jack brought donuts and coffee. She opened the trunk of her car to retrieve the bags, but gentleman that he was, Jack showed up right by her side to help her. His smile filled her heart with sunshine as he handed her coffee and donuts and the key to the back door. She opened the door, turned on the lights, and put their breakfast down on the counter then went back to help with the other bags, but she stopped short when she overheard Jack talking on the phone. He seemed to be arguing with Hailey. She turned back to give him some privacy. When he came back in the sunshine had turned cloudy, and he wasn't smiling anymore.

"Everything okay?" Lily asked.
"Yeah."

Lily ignored his terse response. Side by side they surveyed the room with a critical eye. "Well," Lily put her hands on her hips, "Where should we start?"

"Good question. I'll go get the ladder. Maybe we could start with the spider webs first." He left the room to retrieve the ladder while Lily began to take the decoration paraphernalia out of the bags. She heard a noise behind her and turned to see a gun-wielding masked man enter the doorway. She didn't even have time to panic before he started yelling at her.

"Get down on the floor!" he screamed at Lily. Terrified, she complied.

Jack walked in behind the would-be robber. "Bob! You're gonna give her a heart attack!"

Bob laughed so hard he couldn't catch his breath. He pointed at Lily. "You should see your face," he bellowed.

"Not cool! You're lucky I didn't sneak up behind you and beat you with the ladder," Jack said.

Lily turned her head and looked up at Bob from her position on the floor and rolled her eyes. "Bob! I'm gonna get you for this!" She reached her arm up towards him. "Help me up." He was still snickering as he held his hand out to help her. In one swift move, she pulled him down and had him sprawled on the floor with her knee in his back before he knew what hit him. "Are you done laughin' now, you creep?"

Jack's bad mood disappeared as he doubled over in laughter. "Bob got taken down by 120-pound girl!"

Bob looked over at Jack and back at Lily and grinned.

Lily turned and glared at Jack. "You wanna be next?"

He held his hands up defensively. "No—no. I'm good."

"I'm sorry Lily. I shouldn't have scared you like that—can you get off me? — but you should have seen your face," Bob said. Spasms of laughter overtook him once again.

"Lily, I'm impressed. When did you learn to do that?" Jack asked.

Lily took her knee out of Bob's back and stood up. "After that jerk pulled me into his lap last month I decided to take a self-defense class. Don't mess with Anna either. She took it with me, and that girl's got skills!"

"Thanks for the tip." Bob hopped up to his feet.

"You wearing that robber suit tonight?" Lily asked.

"Probably not. I think I'll dress up like J.J. Watt."

"Good choice. You'll be popular with the ladies," Jack said.

"I've only got one lady in my heart." Bob lifted his hand up to his chest, "but she does like J.J. Watt," he said, wiggling his eyebrows. "I can't stay long, but do y'all need some help with all this?"

"Sure, as long as you put your fake gun in the truck."

"No problem."

Bob stayed for about an hour. In the meantime, Charlotte checked in with the decorating crew and headed straight for her office. Lily stood on the ladder hanging up twisted orange and black crepe paper while Jack held on and handed her supplies. She reached down to take a piece of tape and their fingers touched, sparking her every nerve. Once again, she recognized the magnetic pull from his soul to hers. She tried to ignore her growing attraction to him, but she knew in her heart it was already too late. She wasn't just attracted to him, she liked him. All day long they'd hung spooky spiders, ghosts, and skeletons, and set out tons of pumpkins, laughing and cutting up along the way. They continued on with the decorating until just before opening. Jack helped Lily down off the ladder and held her hand, she knew, a little longer than necessary.

"Thanks Jack," Lily said but made no move to remove her hand from his. Their eyes held each other's for a moment. "I need to go get ready."

Jack cleared his throat. "Yeah, me too. See ya in a little while."

Lily headed out to her car to retrieve her costume then headed back inside to the restroom to change. Jack headed to his office.

That night the bar in The Charlotte House was arrayed in festive orange and black splendor. Feathery spider webs clung from the corners of the ceiling, occupied by little black plastic spiders.

Glistening orange and white lights dimly lit the room, and ghosts and skeletons hung down above the tables in all their horror. All of the staff planned to dress up for the big Halloween bash.

"Hey y'all! The place looks great!" Anna strolled in late in her wicked witch garb.

Bob, who did dress as J.J. Watt, said, "Anna, you're late. By the way, thought you were gonna dress up?"

"Ha ha, Bob. I had trouble with this stupid green nose. Don't worry, I'll just wave my magic wand and get my tables set up lickety-split."

Charlotte strolled in behind her as Glinda the Good Witch of the North and gave Anna a stern look. "Anna, work on your punctuality or you will find yourself working on the baseboards. They need a good scrubbin'."

"Yes ma'am." Anna darted across the room to set up her tables.

"Several cars just pulled in. It's game time." Sporting pointy fangs, Jack turned from the window, a black and purple cape spinning around behind him. His eyes captured Lily in the back of the room talking to one of the singers in the band they had hired to feature live music for the night. He maneuvered his way over to her pretending to check on the band. "Nice costume, Lily." He tried not to stare.

Lily, dressed as a cat, turned at Jack's voice. "Thanks Jack. You look great. Nice teeth."

"Where on earth did you get that tail?"

"Oh…" Lily turned to look at the long black tail trailing behind her. "Online. I ordered it weeks ago."

"Well, you might have to pin it up…so you don't trip."

"Yeah, didn't really think that one through." She laughed.

He loved the way she laughed. "Lemme know if you need any help." He blushed suddenly at his hasty suggestion.

Her eyebrows rose upward. The corners of her mouth curled into a grin. "Okay, sure."

His heart skipped.

Early on, the bar filled to capacity with festive partygoers. The band was a huge success, playing music of many different genres and keeping the patrons engaged all night. To Jack's surprise, just before closing, they called Lily up to the microphone. "Hey everybody, we have a special guest singer, you may know her as your favorite feline who's been serving you dollar zombies all night. Please give a warm welcome to Lily." The crowd applauded.

"What in the…" Anna, Bob, and Jack all looked at the stage, dumbfounded. Charlotte grinned. Moments later Lily's voice filled the room.

"I didn't know she could sing." Bob handed two beers to a waiting customer.

"Neither did I." Jack stared in awe.

Lily looked nervous performing in front of the crowd. Jack wondered why she'd never told him she could sing.

"Whooooo! You go, girl!" Anna called out.

Lily's voice cracked a little at first, but she soon found her bearings and belted out the notes with ease singing a country song about a young woman leaving home. "Don't Forget to Remember Me." She gazed at Jack as she sang the words, their connection undeniable. The crowd cheered and Lily walked off the small stage beaming with gratitude at their applause.

"Lily, why didn't you tell us you could sing?" Jack lightly touched her arm.

"Oh, I just do it for fun. No big deal."

"Well, you were awesome," Bob said.

"Yeah Lily, you are full of surprises." Anna winked at her.

"Thanks Anna." Lily blushed. "Charlotte, thanks for letting me get up there."

"Any time. I may have to graduate you from server to singer though."

"No thanks. Fame will have to survive without me."

They closed up at midnight and began to clean the tables and set up for the next day. An hour later, Lily and Anna and Jack were all that remained.

"Did you hear that?" They all looked up.

"Yep. What was it?" Anna stared at the ceiling.

"I dunno," Lily answered.

"It sounded like something fell upstairs," Jack said.

"But nobody should be up there. Aren't we the only ones here?" Anna looked at Jack.

"I think so. Where are Bob and Charlotte?" Jack asked the girls.

"They said they were going to some party," Lily answered. Just then they heard another crash coming from upstairs, only louder this time. They froze.

"Probably just some kids foolin' around. It is Halloween, after all. I'll go check it out," Jack said.

"No way! You're not leavin' us down here by ourselves."

"I agree with her." Lily pointed at Anna.

"Okay, but y'all stay close."

Lined up like little ducks, they peered up into the dark narrow stairwell that had been used by house servants two hundred years prior. Jack carried a long weighty flashlight that he'd grabbed from behind the bar and they all headed up the stairs. They heard the noise again and Jack stopped abruptly causing Lily to crash into him from behind. She giggled and he turned to shush her, too late to realize his face was only inches from hers. There they were, only inches apart, being magically pulled to one another. He could feel her warm minty breath on his face and the heat radiating from her body. His limbs went numb as he worked to catch his breath. Anna cleared her throat. "What are we doing?" she whispered loudly. The magic of the moment burst like a delicate bubble and they slowly proceeded up the stairs until they reached the second floor. Jack flipped the light switch. Enormous crystal chandeliers lit up the room over the banquet hall floor revealing that some of the stacked chairs had indeed fallen.

"Must have been the crash we heard." He pointed at the fallen chairs.

"WHO'S UP HERE?" he yelled out. Anna grabbed at Lily and she turned around to swat at her.

"I have to peeeeee." Anna clutched Lily's shoulder, sending them both into a frenzy of giggles. Jack rolled his eyes and chuckled.

They looked around the second floor, but no one was there. Jack was in the midst of restacking the chairs when he heard Lily call out to him. She stood by the back window. From there one could see the old summer kitchen behind the house that was no longer in use. Although Charlotte did use it for extra storage, no one had cause to go in there.

Jack peered over Lily's shoulder relishing in their juxtaposition. A light moved inside the kitchen.

"I'm callin' the police," he said, "Let's get back downstairs." He put his hands on her arms from behind and turned her toward the stairs. "Come on, Anna," he hollered across the banquet hall floor. They hurried back down to the bar and locked all the doors while they waited for the police to arrive. They showed up within minutes and searched the premises but found nothing amiss.

"Probably just some kids trying to scare you," the policeman told Anna.

"Well, no wonder people say this house is haunted," Anna told him. "You know, they say that spirits wander on All Hallows Eve." She looped her arm through Andrew's, the policeman who was acquainted with Jack.

Andrew cleared his throat, "Has anything like this ever happened before?" He looked over at Jack and Lily.

"Not while I've been here." Lily shook her head.

"Well, yes actually, only I never saw lights before." Lily and Anna both looked up at Jack, wide eyed.

"What do you mean? What have you seen?" the girls asked.

"Nothing really, I just hear noises sometimes, but I always chalk it up to this being an old house."

"Well, you're most likely right. Tonight it might have been kids trying to scare y'all though. We'll make the rounds a few more times, it bein' Halloween and all."

"Thanks for coming out. I really appreciate it."

"No problem Jack. I'll call ya next time I take the boat out."

"That'd be great! It's been a while since I've gone fishing."

"I like to fish too." Anna clung to Andrew as they walked out.

"Really? Well…" Andrew's voice faded as he and Anna walked outside.

"Oh Jack!" Lily pretended to swoon. "Will you please take me fishing too?" She clung to Jack's arm mocking Anna's flirtatious behavior.

He laughed but her touch ignited something deep inside him, and he realized how much he really would love to take her fishing.

"I don't think that girl has ever been fishin' a day in her life." Lily giggled.

Jack began to turn off all the lights. "Do you ever go fishing?"

"Oh, not in years, not since my dad took me." He remembered that her dad had died a few years ago, and not wanting to invoke sad memories, he quickly changed the subject.

"That Anna, huh? They sure were becoming mighty chummy." He shook his head. "Well, Andrew's a good one."

"Yeah, it would be nice if Anna could find her Mr. Right." Arm in arm, they walked out to the empty parking lot laughing about the night's adventure. "Thanks for walking me to my car, Jack. I always feel safe with you." She hugged him goodbye but seemed hesitant to let go.

He put his arms around her, enjoying the sensation of Lily in his arms. The heat between them was palpable. If she weren't married, he'd be kissing her right now. But she was married, and he was a Godly man, so reluctantly, he let go, instantly feeling the cold where there had been such heat only seconds before. He searched her eyes with his own, finding himself suddenly lost in a deep blue sea of conflicting emotion, drawing him into a place he knew was forbidden. She stepped away and with a glance back, got into her car and drove away. He waved, knowing he would have to back off. He was starting to like her just a little too much.

Lily looked in her rearview mirror at Jack, waving to her. She knew she was playing with fire, but she couldn't seem to help it. She gravitated to him—a magnet pulling her in. Though she had no intentions of cheating on her husband, she really enjoyed being around Jack. It just felt good—right—but how could it be right? It *wasn't* right. As she drove home, she prayed for God to give her strength.

Chapter Six

How long will you go here and there, O faithless daughter?
Jer. 31:22

Damien left early in the morning to deliver a car to Florida. He wouldn't be back for days. Through the years, Lily had tried to convince him to leave his job in Houston to work closer to home, but he'd refused, arguing that he could make more money working in the city. That night, she still had not heard from her husband. They hadn't been getting along very well lately and with her newfound attraction to Jack, Lily worried about her marriage.

Lily and Damien had once been happy together, but distance had wedged its way between them. Their work schedules didn't match up, and they never really spent quality time together anymore. He had a separate life, one that didn't include her, and she just wasn't sure she could trust him. Plus, she didn't know how she would ever get past the children issue. How could she give up the idea of children, her children? To her, they were already set for existence. Giving them up would feel like, like killing them. Her heart ached over it. No. She could not, would not, give up her children. Not for

Damien, not for anyone. She prayed about it, spilling all her worries, and all her sins out to God. She climbed into bed but sleep would not come.

She'd called her husband earlier to check in, but he didn't answer, nor did he call her back. She had a bad feeling, one she couldn't seem to shake. That feeling had crept up on her before and now it settled in the pit of her stomach like a big rock— no. It was more like a giant boulder. She hated it, but an overwhelming urge hit her. Time to start snooping.

She threw back the covers and hopped out of bed. Her heart pounded. She hated being suspicious. She hated looking through his things. What was she looking for anyway, and what would she do if she found it? One by one, she searched through all of his drawers, his side of the closet, and even his jacket pockets. What she finally found made her heart stop.

Minutes later, Lily stood glaring at herself in the mirror, tracing the dark circles under her swollen eyes, knowing her entire life was about to change. Her hands trembled as she picked up the little square wrapper that boasted the likeness of a Trojan warrior. Like her heart, it was torn open and empty.

The week dragged on without resolution. Since Damien was still out of town, Lily had not been able to question him. Plus, this was not the kind of conversation to be had over the phone. She still didn't know what she would say to him anyway, so she let his calls go to voicemail, only communicating with him through brief text messages. And Jack, well, he hadn't said five words to her all week, which only added to her misery. Consequently, her shifts in the bar had been awkward and uncomfortable. Jack often looked her way but didn't approach her. Instead, he talked to Anna.

By Friday night, the emotional stress had physically gotten to Lily. She'd been in a dark pit far too long and it was showing. Lily made the rounds to check on her customers and tried to stay busy, but her attention eventually focused back on Jack, his broad shoulders and strong arms, remembering the way they'd felt wrapped around her.

"Lily?" Charlotte said, breaking into her thoughts.

Lily shook her head, chasing the unsolicited thoughts away. "Yes, ma'am?"

"I don't mean to pry, but you seem a little out of sorts lately. You okay?"

"Yes, well, no. Not really. I'm kind of having a personal problem at home."

Charlotte put her hand on Lily's. "Is there anything I can do?"

"No. There's nothing anyone can do, I'm afraid. I just haven't dealt with it yet, and it's, well…"

"I understand. Well, when do you plan on dealing with it?" Charlotte tilted her head at Lily. She always was straightforward.

"Soon. I promise."

Charlotte patted Lily's hand. "No need to promise me anything. I'm just worried about you."

Lily nodded her head. "Charlotte? Do you think I could cut out early tonight?"

Charlotte looked around at the half empty floor. "I don't see why not. Anna's here, and we aren't too busy." She waved her off. "Sure. Go ahead."

"Thanks, Charlotte. You're the best." Lily smiled half-heartedly.

"Yeah, yeah. Tell that to everyone else, would ya?" She grinned. "Will you be alright to work the Galveston wedding this weekend?"

"Yes. I just need a good night's sleep then I'll be as right as rain."

"Okay, if you're sure."

"I'm sure. Thanks, Charlotte."

"No problem, Sweetie. Get some rest."

Lily walked behind the bar to get her purse. She just wanted to go home and take a long, hot bath and try to forget everything. She glanced at Jack who was staring at her from across the room, then turned and headed toward the door.

Jack watched Lily grab her stuff and walk out. Following, he called out to her, "Lily, wait up." She stopped and turned. "Where are you going?" he asked.

"Oh, so you're speaking to me now?"

Jack knew he'd been ignoring her. "Lily, I didn't mean to...you don't understand...Man! I'm not good at this. I'm sorry."

"Well, why? Have I done something to upset you?"

"No! No, Lily. I can't explain it. I'm sorry. Can we just forget this week and be friends again? I'm an idiot."

Lily softened. "Sure. We can be friends again." She hitched her purse strap onto her shoulder. "Charlotte said I could leave early."

"But why? Are you sick?"

"Um, no, it's not that…" She looked up at him. "I can't talk about it, Jack." Her blue eyes pleaded with him. "Please, just let me go."

"Lily, please, you can tell me." His hand reached for hers, holding it lightly. "We're friends again, remember?"

Her fingers wove through his in response. "I know. It's just that I don't wanna lose it right here in front of everybody." She sniffled.

"Got it." The last thing Jack wanted was to make Lily cry. "Lily, I wish…Oh, I wish I could say what I wanted to say." He let out a deep breath.

"I know. Me too." She squeezed his hand and lightly touched his face then swung around and walked out the door. Leaving Jack bewildered.

An hour later, stepping out of the bathtub, Lily heard her phone ring. It was Damien. She didn't answer but instead waited for him to leave a message. She checked the voicemail he'd left, but only heard music on the other end. The voice of Randy Travis sang from the background, "I Told

You So." It didn't take long for Lily to realize that he hadn't meant to dial her number when she heard a woman laughing and singing with the music. *Who was that?* Lily looked at her phone. She heard her husband's voice and the woman's response leaving no doubt of her husband's infidelity. Lily dropped the phone, sending it flying off to the corner of the bathroom. The lecherous confirmation brought her to her knees. Cold sweat poured down her face. Baxter approached her and meowed in distress. Lily picked him up and held him tight, rocking back and forth. "What am I gonna do? What am I gonna do?"

The bar was closing and all the customers had gone. Jack trudged over to Anna who was wiping down her tables. "Hey Anna, can I ask you something?"

"Sure, what's up?" She kept wiping.

"It's about Lily."

Anna stopped and looked up at him. "What about Lily?"

"Well, what's up with her?"

"What d'ya mean?" Anna replied.

"Well, why did she leave early? And why's she been in such a bad mood lately?"

Anna stared at him blankly for a moment. "Jack, let's sit." She sauntered over to the bar and hopped up on a barstool.

"Okay." Jack looked at her questioningly but sat down. Anna reached for the Vodka bottle and started to pour them both a shot when Jack held up his hand and shook his head at her. She frowned, but withdrew the Vodka and grabbed the soda gun instead.

"Soda okay, Boss?"

"Sure." Jack grinned.

"Can I leave just a little vodka in the glass? To mix with the soda?"

"No." Jack shook his head.

Anna rolled her eyes. "Party pooper." After she poured them both a soda, she asked him straight out, "Jack…what's going on with you and Lily?"

"What?" He turned his head from side to side to see if anyone had overheard Anna's accusation. Realizing that no one was within earshot, he turned back to her. "Nothing, I swear…she's married! Anna, I would never…"

"I know, I know, I know all that!" She waved him off. "I know you two aren't having an affair, okay? Calm down. Don't get your knickers in a knot."

Jack sighed in relief. "Well, what do you mean, then?"

"Let me start over. You two used to be friends, right?"

"We're still—"

"Wait!" Anna held up her hand, cutting off his words. "Let me finish…y'all used to talk all the time, joke around all the time, you were friends. Now you avoid her like the plague, and she shoots daggers at me every time you talk to me."

"She shoots dag—? Wait…you think Lily is jealous? Of me and you?"

"Duh." She rolled her eyes.

"But why would she be…? There's nothing going on between us."

Anna shook her head. "Men are so dense sometimes. Why do you think she's jealous?"

It finally hit him. His face opened up into a huge grin. If Lily were jealous that meant she felt something for him too. Guilty, he looked down and focused on some wine that had stained his shoes earlier in the night. "What am I supposed to say? I don't understand you women."

"Uh huh. Right. Well, I think I'm beginning to understand, so let me pull you out of your stupor of confusion." Jack looked up from his shoe stains and gave Anna his full attention. "It's simple, Jack. You and Lily are falling for each other. She's married. You feel guilty, and of course scared, like every other man in the world, so you avoid her. And that hurts her. Does that sound about right?"

"Anna, that doesn't make any sense. Lily couldn't be falling for me. She has a husband. And why would I avoid her if I were falling in love with her? That's just not logical."

Anna laughed. "Logical? You're too funny." She tapped his cheek with her hand. Jack glared at her. "Oh, you were being serious? Okay, let me try this again. Why would you ignore Lily if you were falling for her? Let me see…" Anna tapped her fingernails. "Let me see. Let me see. I've got it!" Slam! She slapped the bar. "Because that's what men do." Anna climbed down from her stool. "And in case you haven't figured it out yet, Lily married the wrong guy. And since when are men logical about love anyway? Logical?" she repeated and walked back to her tables, waving her rag through the air, laughing all the way.

"Wait!" Jack slid down from his barstool and followed her. "What do you mean she married the wrong guy?"

Anna looked at him like he was the stupidest man in Texas. "Damien isn't a good husband. He cheats on her all the time." Jack looked at her blankly while he processed this new information.

"Does she know?"

Anna shrugged. "We've never talked about it, but half the town knows." She stopped and looked him square in the eye. "Lily is a good person. He doesn't deserve her." Anna picked up her rag and wiped the table enthusiastically. "Face it, Jack. She cares for you. You care for her. We all see it." She put down her rag and looked at him, asking him point blank, "Now, whatcha gonna do about it?"

Jack was dumbfounded, but deep down he knew Anna was right. He had to talk to Lily. He grabbed his keys and finally knew what he had to do, and he had to do it now. He ran out of the restaurant and hopped into his pickup truck. He followed the directions Anna had given him to Lily's house, driving down the street looking for the white house with the red shutters and a large front porch. He should have known Lily would live in such a traditional home. He slowed his truck as he approached it, letting the engine idle. *What am I doing here?* He asked himself over and over as he stared at a lamp shining in one of the windows. Maybe she's still awake then, but he couldn't go up to the house, could he? This is another man's house, another man's wife...*what am I doing?* Just then, he noticed the curtain moving to the side, and he saw her peering out the window and, was she crying? Jack didn't know what to do, but he couldn't stand to watch Lily cry. He reached for his cell phone and dialed her number. Feeling like a voyeur, he watched as she answered her phone and turned away from the window.

Lily recognized the number displayed on her phone and her heart leapt. "Jack? Hello." Lily sniffled.

"Hi. Um, is your husband home?" he inquired.

"No," she replied, "He's out of town, remember?"

"Just makin' sure. Lily, I need you to come outside."

"Outside? Where? Jack I'm at home getting ready for bed."

"I know. I'm here outside. Now come out, please. I need to talk to you, now."

Here? Outside? "What? You're here, at my house, outside, right now?" Lily looked at herself in the mirror. *Crap! I look like crap.*

"Yes Lily. I am here, at your house, parked on the street. Now, will you please come outside?"

She started shaking. "Okay, I'm coming out, but give me a minute." Lily threw on a pair of sweats and headed out the door. She decided against turning on the porch light and stumbled out to the curb in the dark. Jack was waiting there holding the passenger side door open for her. She looked at him questioningly but climbed up into the truck anyway.

They drove around for a while and ended up at the park. "Want to go for a walk?" Jack asked her.

"Okay. Let's walk. It's only two in the morning," Lily said. Jack's lips curled into a smile and Lily's heart melted. He ran around to her side of the truck and opened the door for her. He held out his hand and she reached for him. When their fingers touched, a jolt ran through her warming her entire insides, and from the way he looked at her she knew he felt it too. As they walked hand in hand through the grass already damp with morning dew, awkwardness transitioned to intimacy and they became increasingly aware of their strong connection. Taking their time, they ambled over to a bench by the monkey bars and sat down. "Jack, what are we doing here?"

Facing her now, finally alone, Jack didn't know where to start. He wasn't good with words, and he was so nervous he couldn't stop shaking, but holding Lily's hand comforted him, and it gave him the strength to try. He looked deep into her questioning eyes. "Lily, something's going on between us, isn't there?"

Lily looked at Jack somberly and held onto both of his hands. "Yes, Jack, there is something between us." He held her gaze, unable to break the trance that their connection created then touched her face gently. Electricity surged through him. She pulled away. "There are two somethings between us, actually. Damien and Hailey."

The trance broke, along with his heart. Knowing there was no solution, Jack stood up and turned away. "I'm sorry, Lily. We...we'd better go." Choking on his own confused emotions, he couldn't say what he so desperately wanted her to hear. He walked back to the truck, glancing over his shoulder to make sure Lily followed.

Chapter Seven

The one who commits adultery… Wounds and disgrace he will find.
Prov. 6:32-33

Jack didn't say a word on the drive back to Lily's house. Neither did she. What could she say, really? She was married. Jack stopped his truck in front of the house, letting the engine run. She looked over at him, but he was already out of the truck coming around to open her door. Always the gentleman, she thought. He reached for her hand to help her as she stepped down onto the curb. She looked up into his eyes with regret, and surprising the both of them, flailed herself into his arms.

He held her tight for a few short moments, taking in her warmth, burning this feeling into his memory, and then he kissed the top of her head, her hair smelling of roses. "'Night Lily." He released her mournfully. She walked slowly to the house, turning to look his way one last time before crossing the threshold. He walked back around to his side of the truck and slowly climbed in, her heat still clinging to his clothes, Lily still clinging to his heart.

Lily lay awake the rest of the night thinking about Jack, wishing they had kissed, knowing they shouldn't, and knowing she'd ruined the one chance she'd had to tell him just how she felt. The next evening was the Galveston catering, which was at least a two-hour drive from the banquet hall. She was still completely shaken from the memory of the night before, the realization that Jack had feelings for her, the realization that her husband was cheating on her, and the realization that she would eventually have to face them both. She did not get a good night's sleep.

The Charlotte House was hired to cater a wedding at a beautiful three-story mansion overlooking Galveston Bay. A middle-aged couple seeking second chances was tying the knot. Sparks of autumn romance filled the air with blue skies and 60 degrees. Red roses and white bows overlooking the rolling waves of the sea transformed the backyard into a Garden of Eden. The scene made her think of her own wedding to Damien not so long ago. It had been only a few short years since she had committed her life to a man who obviously had lesser intentions. An unfaithful man who didn't want to have children. To make things worse, Jack had been avoiding Lily all night. *So, we are back to that, I guess.* Lily's world began to cave in all around her. Her marriage was falling apart, and Jack was closing himself off to her.

Lily gazed at the sea from the kitchen window. She should not have come to work today. She knew her life was messed up, but she didn't know what to do about it. Anna rounded the corner suddenly, catching her in her sullen disposition.

"Lily? Is it all that bad?" Anna put her arm around Lily and attempted to comfort her. She just couldn't tell Anna the horrid truth about Damien. It was just too humiliating. But Anna didn't ask for details. Instead, she looked over her shoulder. They were alone. Anna handed Lily a glass of champagne. "Here. Have one." Then she walked out.

Lily stared at the bubbles speeding upwards from the bottom of the glass. She briefly wondered why they were in such a race to get to the top. Oh well, what the heck. Bottoms up! She held her glass up in the air in salute to the world.

A few minutes later, Anna walked back in and took one long look at Lily. "Oh no."

"Oh yes," Lily giggled.

Jack could tell that Anna had been trying to cover for Lily, but by the end of the night, it was just too obvious that Lily was not herself, especially when she dropped one of the trays during clean up. Jack didn't want to deal with it, but it was his job to handle such situations. Unfortunately, it was Lily who was in the middle of said situation. He knew she'd been upset when she arrived at work earlier that day, and he'd wanted to go to her, but he didn't trust himself. He had to stay away from her. She was married and he was with Hailey. End of story. But he was her boss, and ignoring the situation only seemed to make it worse, so it was high time he dealt with it.

Jack found Lily on the kitchen floor, slumped over a giant mess, attempting to clean it up. He walked over to her, grabbed her hand, and pulled her up. He then led her out the kitchen door to the far corner of the driveway. He opened the door of the catering van, lifted her up, and deposited her into the passenger seat with her feet hanging out like a child, commanding her to stay there. Then he turned to walk away.

"Jack!" she yelled after him. "Don't leave me here, please???" Jack stopped, sighed, and hesitantly turned around toward the van. He shook his head, regret following him with each step he took back toward Lily.

"How did I get myself into this?" he mumbled to himself. He stopped in front of Lily's dangling feet and looked up at her. "Lily, I need to get things cleaned up in there. I have to go back!" he said, exasperated.

"Why are you so mad at me?" Lily asked with those big round blue eyes.

"Why do you think? You're drunk. On the clock! At a catering!" he barked at her.

"I knowwwwwww. I'm sorry, but I mean, why have you been avoiding me? What did I do?" Her arresting eyes filled with tears. His resolve, destroyed. Jack wasn't mad at Lily. He was starting to love her. He couldn't have her, and he couldn't quit wanting her. As much as he tried, he couldn't stop his feelings for her.

Jack placed his hands on top of Lily's feet, still dangling out of the doorway of the van. He leaned in slightly, her feet pressing into his chest, and gazed up into her eyes. "I'm not mad at you Lily. Can't you see? It's just the opposite." He stopped before he could say something he wouldn't be able to take back. "Look, I'll stay with you for a few minutes, then I have to go check on the others." Lily's tears dried up as she broke into a smile and nodded her head. Jack walked around to the other side of the van and climbed up into the driver's seat.

"Can we turn on the radio?" Lily asked.

Jack sighed, "I guess." He turned the key halfway and country music filled the air.

A few minutes passed, and Lily quieted. That feeling filled her heart once again, sobering her. She stared at Jack. His eyes locked onto hers.

"What are we doing?" Jack spoke so softly she almost didn't hear. In answer to his question, she slowly reached up, placed her hand on the back of his neck, and pulled his body to hers. Yearning for his embrace, she wrapped her arms around him, pressing her tear-stained cheek into his broad chest, and held him closely.

Jack wrapped his arms around her, returning her embrace, and nuzzled his face into the side of her neck. It felt good. It felt right. Too right. Then slowly, gently, as if waiting for surrender, hers or his—she wasn't sure, he brushed her forehead with his lips.

Lily closed her eyes as she felt his breath on her face. His lips were so soft. A rousing current moved through her body as he gently kissed the thin soft skin of her eyelid, then gingerly touched his lips to hers. *I can't actually kiss him!* Lily told herself, but he was patient. His fingers tangled in her hair as he carried on with chaste kisses, to the side of her nose, her temple, between her eyes, then to her wanton mouth once more. He gently kissed her unyielding lips again and again as he knocked on the door, pleading to be let in. She eased her mouth open slightly, feeling the distant presence of guilt, but her longing for him was powerful. He seemed to sense her hesitation, and he stopped. But she could deny him no longer. Her tongue searched for his. They touched. Just barely. But that was their undoing. The bounds of her body, her wants and needs, had finally burst. He kissed her at last with fiery abandon as if he had waited a lifetime to surrender himself to her, holding back no longer. An eternity of newly discovered love surged between them. They made out like randy teenagers as they intimately consumed one another, while the words of a country song floated between them, the same words Lily had sung to Jack on Halloween— "Don't Forget to Remember Me."

    Jack stopped and pulled out of her embrace. Breathing heavily, he reached for the door handle. He hastily got out of the van as Lily stared after him, dazed. He walked around to the other side where Lily sat. Pulling her down from the seat, he grabbed her legs and wrapped them around his waist. Thankful that the van was parked in a dark corner of the driveway where no eyes could see this inappropriate display of his affection, he gently but urgently pushed her up against the side of the van, placing his hands strategically to hold her up. He could feel the bones of her hips pressing into his. Heatedly, he kissed her. Every inch of him wanted every inch of her.

    She pulled him even closer. The electricity that surged between them was unbearable. She wanted him badly, he could tell, and he wanted her, but at the end of the song, he froze. With shame, struggle, and regret, he looked into her eyes. Gently, he put her feet to the ground and put his hand to her face. He leaned into her until his forehead joined hers. He took a breath, etching this moment in his memory. Then he pulled back and walked away. The silence was consuming during the ride home that night.

REMEMBER ME

Late the next morning, the bright sun streamed through the bedroom window waking Lily. Her head felt like someone had yielded an ax against it, repeatedly. However, she also woke up with a beaming smile on her face and determination in her step. She finally knew what she had to do. It was time to confront Damien, and the intimate moments she shared with Jack the night before provided just the momentum she needed. Damien, however, still hadn't returned home. She stumbled to the coffee pot, poured herself a large cup and took two aspirin. She picked up Baxter as he meowed defiantly, but she hugged him anyway. "Well Baxter, I guess it's gonna be just you and me from now on." The future was so uncertain. Lily's heart broke at her husband's infidelity and her feelings for Jack confused her. She had never seen herself getting divorced, but she had always wanted children more than anything, and she could never remain married to an unfaithful husband.

Lily went to the closet and started packing. She sorted through her clothes and shoes making two piles: one to pack and one to donate. Going through drawers proved more difficult. There were so many memories, pictures, letters, and mementos of her life with Damien. This was her life, good and bad. She packed the bittersweet memories into a box to keep in storage. Her mom had a large attic for just such things. Lily called her mom and briefly explained the situation, leaving out the part about Jack. "Come home for a while, Lily," her worried mom beckoned.

Since Lily's mom was a widow and Lily was an only child, there was plenty of room at her mom's house at the ranch. She only wished her dad were still here. She missed him so much. Knowing him, he would have taken care of Damien himself. Mom had not really dated much since his death. Dad was just one of those men who could never be replaced. He was loving, honorable, and God-fearing. Nothing like Damien.

Since Lily had the day off, she made the most of it and packed everything that belonged to her and left everything she could live without. She moved her stuff to her mom's house, but against her mother's wishes, decided to go back and wait for Damien to come home. It felt strange walking into their home with no Baxter to greet her. *Oh well, he will be at Mom's waiting for me.* The house looked bare, loveless. Though the furniture still occupied the house, the curtains still hung on the windows, and even the pictures on the wall still held their place, the house had a noticeable air of abandonment. *Was* Lily abandoning Damien? Even the bible allowed for divorce on grounds of adultery, but Lily knew God still didn't like it. *I can see why*, she thought. It caused too much pain. Lily pushed her confusion aside and passed the time by making sure she didn't forget anything important. After a while, she heard the key in the door. Well, it's now or never.

Damien turned the corner into the living room and found Lily staring at him. "What?" he barked.

Lily tried to be calm, but she was shaking. "Damien, sit down. We need to talk."

"Oh great! Here we go. What? What the hell did I do now?"

Lily looked at him, tears filling her eyes.

"Dammit, Babe! Answer me!"

"Oh, don't call me Babe! Is that what you call her?" Lily spewed out the words. Damien suddenly turned pale. Lily stared at him, her fortitude strengthening.

He sat down on the edge of the sofa, then, as if just now noticing, he looked around the room and realized that some stuff was missing, lots of stuff. The bookshelves seemed bare and all the clutter was gone. Not that there ever was much clutter. Lily hated clutter. But still, the small piles of life's accumulations that had once been scattered here and there were now gone. "Oh no," he muttered. He looked down at the floor and took a deep breath. "Okay. Let's talk," he said but wouldn't meet her eye.

"You mean, let's talk about her?" Damien's head popped up, and for a brief second she thought he might feign innocence. "Don't try to deny it, Damien! I don't have the energy for it. I actually know for sure that you're cheating, and there is no way on God's green earth that you can convince me otherwise!"

Damien looked back down at the floor and his shoulders slumped. "How did you find out?"

"Does it matter?" It seemed that proof would not be necessary. He was confessing. Lily sat down on the opposite couch exhaling all the adrenaline, anxiety, and pain that had energized her fury only moments before. "Why?" It was all she could manage to utter.

"I'm a jerk," he conceded. "Lily," he said as he looked up at her, "*you* are great. It's just that we've been married for three years, and that's a long time to…"

"A long time? A long time to *what*, Damien?" She raised her voice.

"Look, a guy like me has a hard time being faithful, that's all. It's not you—it's me. I love you, I just…" he stammered. "Please, just don't leave."

"Don't leave. That's all you have to say? Don't leave? How can you say you love me then turn around and cheat on me? Do you love her too?" Lily glared at him with building fury. "Well, do you? What's her name, anyway?"

"Candace…and…yes," he said quietly.

"Yes? Yes what?"

"Yes…I do love her." It was almost a whisper.

"You LOVE her?" She jumped up and threw her hands in the air. "You just said you love me?" She shook her head, wishing she could wake from this nightmare. "How could you?"

"I love both of you, okay? That's why I haven't broken it off with her."

"You love both of us," she repeated his words. "That's why you haven't broken it off with her." Lily began pacing the floor. "Okay, I need a minute to process all this." She turned to face him. "Do you even know what love is, Damien? How on earth could you love me and love someone else at the same time?" Irony struck her heart as judgment hung in the air between them. She hastily pushed her guilt aside. "We made vows, Damien: a promise to be faithful, a commitment. Why do you think marriage is such a commitment? Because it takes commitment to fight temptation, and temptation will always show up eventually, won't it?" Again, the irony of her words convicted her. Guilt pushed at her conscience. Was she being fair to him? She sighed but continued on. "It's what we decide to do when it does show up that the commitment part kicks in."

"I know, you're right, and I'm sorry. I really am."

Resuming her pacing, she said, "Well, it doesn't matter now. Apparently, I can't be faithful either." Damien's eyes shot up at her. He stood up, chest bowed, and moved toward her. She stopped and put her hands out in front of her, palms facing him. "Whoa, I didn't sleep with anybody, so get that out of your head, okay?"

His face turned red with anger. "Then why did you say that?"

"Hey!" She pointed at him. "You don't get to be mad at me! I'm not the one having an affair!"

His demeanor capitulated. "Okay, then what did you mean?" he asked calmly. She felt relieved that he was trying to keep his temper in check.

Lily sat back down across the room at a safe distance, and let out a long sigh. "Because I did kiss someone, but that was after I found out you were cheating on me."

His anger let loose again. "Well, when did you find out? WHEN did you kiss someone? WHY didn't you say something?" He slapped his forehead and spun around, his back to her. He looked at the wall displaying their wedding photo. Lily in her long white dress standing next to him, his arms around her, joy written all over her face, and the sun shining on them like a blessing from God Himself. But now...he had screwed it all up, now he'd lost her.

Damien leaned against their wedding portrait, pressing his forehead against it. All of a sudden, as if possessed, he reared his arm back and punched his fist through it, through them, through the wall. Lily froze. What had she done?

Damien panted heavy breaths like an animal intent on his prey. Moments passed and finally silence filled the room and remained there until Damien finally spoke.

"Who is he?" He uttered.

"It doesn't matter," Lily answered quietly.

"Who is he, Lily?" His voice grew louder.

"I'm not telling you."

"Well, I'll find out on my own then." He stood up and grabbed his keys heading for the door.

Lily went after him. "Damien, you don't get to do this." He turned around to face her.

"Do what? Find out who my wife is—?"

Lily raised her hand and slapped him hard across the face, abruptly cutting off his words, shocking them both into silence and regret. He froze, anger, remorse, and shock on his face. Lily took a step back. "I'm...I'm sorry." She nearly choked on the words. "I shouldn't have done that." He stared at her coldly. "But I told you, I only kissed him." Damien didn't respond. "Besides, you are the one out there having extracurricular sex, not me." Her voice shook and she turned on her heel and walked back across the room, arms folded in protection.

Damien shook his head. "I can't do this." Tears filled his eyes and streaked down his face. He covered them with his hands. "So, you *are* leaving, then?" he asked without looking at her, seeking verification.

Lily took a deep breath and said quietly, "Yes. I'm going to Mom's house." Lily couldn't face his tears. Anything but tears. "Damien, I'm sorry. I don't know where we went wrong. I don't know *when* we went wrong." After a few long and silent moments, Lily went to him, and carefully gauging his reaction, slowly put her arms around him. She knew he was angry and hurt. So was she. This was her husband and her marriage from which she was walking away. He allowed her embrace and held her tight while he released the floodgates and sobbed. She could feel the small convulsions racking through his body. Then he took a deep breath and took control of his emotions. He put his hands on Lily's shoulders and looked into her eyes. "I'm sorry, Lily. You deserve better. I hope that one day you can forgive me." Then Damien turned from her and walked out the door.

In a daze, she stood and watched her husband walk out of her life. "What am I doing?" Lily asked herself. "How did it come to this?" She was now more confused than ever.

Chapter Eight

**Do not fear, for I am with you;
Do not anxiously look about you,
for I am your God. I will strengthen
you, surely I will help you,
Surely I will uphold you
with My righteous right hand.
Isa. 41:10**

The next morning, Lily woke up at the ranch to the sound of Harry the rooster greeting a brand new day. *Cockadoodledooooooo.* She rolled out of her childhood Prudent Mallard, hand-carved bed and walked over to the antique dresser with its matching signature egg. She looked in the mirror and leaned in to study her reflection. Dark circles underlining her eyes and a puffy face stared back at her. She had cried herself to sleep last night, waking muddleheaded over her marriage and Jack. "God, what do I do?" she prayed earnestly. She turned away from the mirror, opened the window and leaned out, breathing in the fresh air. The sun burst into the morning, rising above green pastures as far as the eye could see. She loved this place, but she often felt like a teenager around her mom. She would need to find a place of her own eventually, but that could wait. She hadn't been able to see or even talk to Jack since the night of the catering. Was that really only two nights ago? If her mother found out about him, she would blow a gasket. Her Christian upbringing would never allow her to understand how Lily could get involved with another man before she had even filed divorce papers. Not that her mom was crazy about divorce either, but she never really did like Damien, so maybe she wouldn't be too condemning about the mess her daughter had made of her life.

Lily looked at her cell phone. Three missed calls: one from Anna, one from Charlotte, and one from Bob. That's odd. Do they need me to come in to work early? She was supposed to work the late shift tonight. Lily went into the bathroom and put her phone on speaker as she listened to her messages and brushed her teeth.

"Lily, this is Anna. Call me as soon as you get this message. It's important."

"Uh, Lily. This is Charlotte calling. Something has happened and I need you to call me right away."

"Lily, it's Bob. Call me. It's about Jack."

Lily nearly jammed her toothbrush down her throat when she heard Jack's name in the last message. She grabbed her cell phone and called Bob. He didn't answer so she then called Charlotte. She answered on the first ring. "Charlotte?"

"Oh Lily, thank God you called. I need you to sit down, Honey."

Chills went up Lily's spine. She plunked down on the side of her tub, her heart racing. "I'm sitting. What's wrong?"

"Jack was in an accident last night."

A wave of nausea hit Lily like a tsunami. "What? Is he okay?" Panic rose inside her at Charlotte's delayed response. "Charlotte, is he d—?"

"No, Honey. He's not, but he's been badly hurt." Lily breathed a momentary and quickly fleeting sigh of relief. "They have him under sedation and he's on a breathing tube."

Lily gasped and choked down a cry, finding no breath to form words.

"Lily? You still there?"

"Yep," was all she could manage to spit out, her throat thick with sorrow.

"He was on his way home when a deer ran out in front of his truck. He swerved to miss it and flipped several times before landing in a ditch. It was a miracle that someone found him when they did that time of night." Lily didn't respond. "A teenage boy found him on his way home from a party. Jack has a head injury, Lily." Lily quietly sobbed. "Honey, you gonna be okay? You want me to come get you?"

Lily cleared her throat and wiped away the flood of tears that were spilling over. "No. Um, I'll be there as soon as I can. Which hospital?"

"We are at the new trauma center at St. Joseph's in Bryan waiting for the doctor. We will be here waiting for you. Lily, don't drive too fast. In fact, you should ask your mom to come with you, and be careful. Oh, wait! Lily, do you know how to reach Jack's parents or his girlfriend? What's her name?"

Lily cringed at the thought of Jack's girlfriend. "Hailey, but no I don't. Have you checked the numbers in his phone?"

"No. Apparently his phone was lost in the accident, and someone said his parents are out of the country on a church mission trip."

"That's right. I think I remember him mentioning that." Lily couldn't imagine being so far away from Jack. In fact, she was chomping at the bit to get to him now.

"Well, I'll keep asking around. Maybe I can find them on social media. What a terrible way to get bad news though. I'll let you go so you can get on the road. Be careful."

"Okay. Charlotte?"

"Yeah, Sweetie?"

"How do you know it was a deer?" Lily inquired as an afterthought.

"The deer didn't make it," she replied quietly.

"Oh." Lily swallowed. "Charlotte? Pray for him?"

"Without ceasing, Honey. Without ceasing."

Lily hung up her phone, took a deep breath, and immediately threw a change of clothes into a backpack. She ran through the house calling out to her mom, but only silence greeted her, so she left her a note explaining that a friend needed her and that she wouldn't be home tonight. Well, that was the truth. Besides, she didn't want her mother to worry any more than she already was, and her mom might misjudge the situation, or see right through Lily and judge it correctly. That was something she just couldn't face right now.

Lily drove for nearly an hour over the bumpy country roads before reaching the hospital in Bryan. In the single lane road on the way, she got stuck behind a smelly truck spewing exhaust fumes out of its tail pipe. It turned her stomach. She peered around the truck to try to pass it and an 18-wheeler whizzed by her. Her heart jumped. Lily tried to drive carefully, but she was in a hurry. They had done some roadwork since the last time Lily had been to Bryan, and in her confusion, she took the exit into Snook and couldn't figure out how to get back on the right road. She finally came across a store and ran in looking frazzled. "Please help me," she asked the teenage boy behind the counter. "I have to get to the hospital and I got confused on the road. Which way is it?" She blurted out the words in a shaky panic. In her rush to get out of the house, she hadn't eaten any breakfast, making her even more anxious. Her life was in a state of upended turmoil, but she couldn't think about all that just now. Just now, her only focus was Jack. She found her way back to the right road and tuned the radio to a Christian station. The uplifting songs spoke to her soul, calming her. Yep, she'd made a mess of things, but God had not abandoned her, and she would trust Him.

Charlotte was waiting for Lily by the hospital entrance with two cups of coffee in hand. She hugged Lily then handed her one of them. "There's a café on the first floor," she explained. The elevator door opened, and Bob and Anna ran out to Lily, throwing their arms around her.

"Tell me, how is he?"

"He's alive," declared Bob. "But he hit his head in the crash, and he's in a coma."

"Coma? Have you seen him?" she asked, dying for any little bit of information.

"We've each been in, but he hasn't responded to any of us." Anna replied. "You wanna go in?"

Lily took a deep breath. "Yes. Right now if they'll let me." They all took the elevator back up to the second floor, walked through the quiet waiting area and up to the closed double doors of the ICU.

"Wait," Charlotte stopped her. "You need to prepare yourself." She looked at Lily intently. "He doesn't look like Jack right now. There's a lot of bruising and swelling." Lily nodded her head in understanding as tears built up like a dam ready to burst. She pressed the large button that would open the doors to Jack and a future that was unknown.

Lily signed her name in the visitor's log at the front desk. Heeding Charlotte's words, she took a deep breath and released it slowly. This was no time to be weak. She put on her metaphorical armor and headed down the long hallway looking for the correct room number. His door was open. Lily's preacher was standing next to Jack's bed with his eyes closed and his hand on Jack's arm, praying over him. A nurse sat in front of a computer just outside his room. She stood up and spoke to Lily, providing words of comfort. Lily stood in the doorway of Jack's room processing the vision in front of her. She walked in gingerly. Before her was someone she did not recognize, he was so unlike himself. The overwhelming sight of scratches, bruises, and swelling immediately burst the stronghold of Lily's dam. Jack was hooked up to a respirator, I.V.s, and a catheter. Tubes were protruding from his head, nose, mouth, and other parts of his body. He was unrecognizable. Quiet tears flowed incessantly down her face. She closed her eyes and prayed silently, pleading with God to heal this man, this man whom she loved, this man who was not her husband. Would God answer her prayers when she had no business loving him in the first place?

She sat on the edge of a chair in the corner of the room, folded her hands and bowed her head.

> *Dear God,*
> *I know I've sinned and I'm so sorry. I know I left my husband and fell for this man. I know I have no right to ask for your help, but please forgive me. Please have mercy on us, on Jack. Please...PLEASE save him, Lord.*

Lily looked up. Their preacher stood in front of her. She wiped at her tears and walked straight into his open arms. Brother Tim comforted her but did not ask any questions then they prayed together before he left. Once he was gone, Lily scooted her chair closer to Jack's bed. She carefully placed her hand on top of his. She picked up each finger, studying them all. His hand was uninjured, perfect, beautiful with the thick calluses of a working man.

"I love you," she whispered to him, "I'm here and I'm not going anywhere." She laid her head on his bed, touching the tips of his fingers with her own, and prayed again, all the while marveling at how life can change so much, so fast.

The day passed. Nurses came in and out of the room, checking this and that all day, and all day Lily had been there with Jack, holding his hand, singing softly to him, and praying over him. She couldn't bring herself to leave his side. When the nurse came in to ask her to leave for quiet hours, Lily stood up too quickly and a wave of dizziness hit her.

"Are you okay, Miss?" Lisa, the ICU nurse asked her. Lily grabbed the railing on the bed to steady herself and the dizziness subsided.

"Yes. I think so. I just realized that I haven't eaten today."

"Look, I know this man is very special to you. I'm just gonna tell you that you will do him no good if you don't take care of yourself. He's going to need you more than ever when he wakes up, and you will need all the strength you can muster for that. Trust me. Now, you have to leave for quiet hours. That should give you enough time to get something to eat and get out of this room for a while. The chapel is on the first floor." The nurse eyed her speculatively. "Are you a praying woman?"

"Oh yes. That's all I've been doing today." Tears filled her eyes again, reluctant as she was to leave him.

"Well, it must be working, because he's holding steady." Lisa squeezed Lily's shoulder and gave her a smile. "Don't worry. I'm keeping a close eye on him. Now, go take care of yourself for a while. He'll be here when you get back."

Lily nodded and headed out to the waiting room where it was filling up with Jack's friends. Lily saw Bob, Charlotte, and Anna and headed toward them. They stood when they saw her and tripped over each other's words as they begged for a report on Jack's condition. "He's holding steady, still unconscious."

"But don't they have him sedated so that he stays unconscious?" Anna asked.

"Yes. They want him sedated until some of the pressure in his brain is relieved," Bob explained. "The doctor told me that the coma reduces brain activity, which will protect the tissue, or something like that. I can't remember exactly what he said."

Lily didn't understand any of this, nor did she want to. She just wanted Jack to be okay. She sat down on the chair, put her face in her hands and tried not to cry. Charlotte sat next to her and rubbed her back waving the others away. Lily was so tired and so worried. She leaned into Charlotte's embrace and wept. Once her tears subsided she sat up, feeling a little embarrassed.

"Why don't you go write down a prayer for Jack and hang it on the prayer tree over there." Charlotte pointed to the corner of the waiting room.

Lily nodded her head, got up, and walked over to the tree. There were notes hanging all over like Christmas ornaments. Each note held its own plea to God. Lily went over to the desk and picked up the pen lying next to an open bible. She placed her hand face down on the bible drawing from its strength then scribbled out her prayer in earnest. Lily walked back over to the group. "Sorry guys, didn't mean to lose it earlier. Charlotte, what about my shift at the restaurant? I'm supposed to be at work right now."

"Don't worry about that. I called in reinforcements. I'll look at the schedule tomorrow and take your name off this week."

"I don't mind pickin' up some extra shifts, Lily," Anna offered.

"Thanks y'all. I appreciate it."

"Not a problem," Charlotte said. "By the way, Bob found Jack's parents on some social media site and sent them an urgent message. Apparently, they're in Africa on an extended trip. Anyway, he'll let them know what's going on when they contact him. Still haven't gotten Hailey's number though. If we knew her last name that would be helpful," she looked questioningly at Lily who shrugged her shoulders and shook her head, "but no one really knows much about her."

"I met her once. Not my cuppa tea," Anna quipped. That made Lily smile.

"Does anybody know where she works?" Charlotte looked at them.

"I think she works for a lawyer or accountant or something," Bob added.

"Well, Lord knows there's enough of them in our town." Temporarily giving up the search for Jack's girlfriend, Charlotte suggested that they all go downstairs to the café to get something to eat. Bob declined, deciding to stay in the waiting room, just in case. Then he planned to see Jack again before heading back to work. So Charlotte, Anna, and Lily headed to the small café on the first floor. Anna ate quickly and gave Lily a hug goodbye. She needed to get to work too. Lily tried to eat but her mouth was so dry the hamburger tasted like sawdust and she just couldn't stomach it. Knowing Charlotte was watching her, she took a bite of the soggy part of the bun and drank her tea. That was just all she could manage. Then they went to find the chapel.

Peace enveloped Lily immediately as she walked in. The red carpet and wooden pews, the stained-glass window and Jesus overhead on the cross gave Lily a sense that God was indeed right here in the little room. She went to the front and kneeled at the cross to pray, but her throat thickened. She tried so hard to keep it together, but in the presence of the Lord, her resolve crumbled and came tumbling down. Tears welled in her eyes once again, and she sobbed convulsively. *Please God, help him, please. I'll do anything you ask, just please heal him.* As she was making earnest promises to God, Damien's face popped into her head. What was God trying to tell her? She knew divorce was wrong, but she loved Jack. Was God punishing her? Was God going to take Jack from her? Panic set in. No. That couldn't be. Lily was just confused. *Things will get clearer when Jack gets better,* Lily told herself. She crossed her arms over her chest and folded over in pain. She felt Charlotte's hand on her shoulder, rubbing circles on her back, as a mother would to her child.

"Let it out, honey. Let it out. I'm here for you. Jack knows we're here. He knows *you* are here." Lily looked up suddenly at Charlotte's telling words.

"Charlotte, Jack and I…"

"I already know, Honey. It's obvious to everybody how y'all feel about each other."

"But—"

"Don't worry about that now. Right now, Jack needs our prayers, and that's all that matters, right?"

"Right." Lily nodded her head, sniffling. "Charlotte?"

"Yeah, Sweetie?"

"Thanks for being here."

REMEMBER ME

Tears filled Charlotte's eyes. "Where else could I be, honey? Where else could I possibly be?" She wrapped her arms around Lily under the open arms of Jesus looking over them from the cross, and together they wept.

Chapter Nine

**Therefore, confess your sins to one another, and pray for one another,
so that you may be healed.
The effective prayer of a righteous man can accomplish much.
James 5:16**

As soon as quiet hours ended, Bob went in to see Jack before heading off to work. Everyone else had gone except for Charlotte and Lily. They were allowed to go in together, but Charlotte only stayed a few minutes, leaving Lily alone with Jack to once again sit by his side. She tried to hold his hand, but the nurse scolded her and told her not to do anything that would alert him. Apparently, even though he was still unconscious, Jack had been somewhat active in the last couple of hours, and they wanted to keep him from waking and pulling out his breathing tube. So, Lily rested her forehead on the edge of his bed, arms folded in her lap, and quickly fell asleep. The nurse came in and out all night working around Lily who had eventually moved to a chair in the corner of the room. She was asleep the next morning when the doctor came in to check on Jack. He put his hand on her shoulder and woke her.

"Are you Lily?"

"Yes." Lily rubbed her eyes to clear away the sleepiness and cleared her throat and stood.

"I'm Dr. Sturgis, head of the ICU. I just wanted to explain a little bit about what's going on with Jack and what we're doing for him." Lily nodded her head in understanding. "He's had severe trauma to his brain. We ran a CT scan on him shortly after he arrived to the E.R. It showed a fracture to his skull and some bleeding which is causing pressure to build up in his brain." Lily sat down on the edge of the chair, hopelessness feeding its way into her subconscious. "We put him in a medically-induced coma to keep the stimulation low so his brain can rest and recover. We hope that this will minimize the swelling. Unfortunately, he will need surgery to remove pieces of his skull." She gaped at the doctor, trying desperately to keep it together. "Do you have any questions for me?" he asked.

"Um, when will he have surgery?"

"I'm not sure yet. We'd like to schedule it for tomorrow or the next day. We need to confirm with the surgeon." Lily nodded her head. "The nurse will let you know."

"Okay. Thanks Dr. Sturgis—for everything you're doing for Jack." Dr. Sturgis left the room and Lily went to Jack's side. "I'm still here Jack. The doctors are gonna fix you right up. Don't worry about anything. Everybody's praying for you."

Lily grabbed her phone and sent a mass text out to Jack's friends.

Pray for Jack. Scheduling surgery for tomorrow or next day to remove pieces of skull. Please forward to everyone you know.

Immediately, text messages full of questions, prayers, and well wishes bombarded Lily's phone. Charlotte had already arrived at the hospital and was headed her way into Jack's room. She went straight to Lily and hugged her. They held each other up and cried.

Jack's surgery was scheduled for the next morning. Lily had spent another night in ICU sitting by his side talking to him, praying for him, and reading the bible to him, all the while careful not to touch him. Each time he started to wake, he flailed in distress, so it was important to keep him as calm as possible.

Around 6:00 a.m. the nurse came in to get him ready. Lily said one more prayer for Jack and headed to the waiting room. When she walked through the door she was shocked to see so many of Jack's friends filling up the room, all except for Hailey and his parents. She was a mess and looked it. She hadn't been home in days but didn't care how she looked. Her only concern was for Jack. Everyone surrounded her with questions and she answered them all as best she could. Charlotte finally rescued her and took her to the café for coffee.

"Every church in town and the surrounding areas are praying for Jack and even some in Houston too. It's amazing how the chain of God's people can move so swiftly. He will get help from God." Charlotte put her hand on top of Lily's. Lily was happy that Jack had the prayers of so many, and she knew that his strength stemmed from that power. It filled her soul with hope and peace. She decided to go home and shower and eat and check in with her worried mom. She knew that all these people were here for Jack. They've got this. God's got this.

The surgery was successful but Jack was not out of the woods yet. They were still worried about pressure on the brain. Lily spent the next couple of days at Jack's side. The doctors were still keeping him sedated, so he still had no idea what had happened. One morning, Lily walked into Jack's room to find that he was tied to the bed. She immediately went to the nurse in the hallway to find out why.

"Well, since we changed his sedative, he's a little more alert than before. He woke up earlier and tried to pull the tube out of his mouth."

"What happens if he does that?"

"Well, he could die. He's not getting enough oxygen on his own yet."

"But I thought he was doing better."

"Well, he was, but now he's developed pneumonia. His fever spiked during the night. Keep praying Lily. This isn't over yet."

Lily dropped down in the chair next to Jack's bed feeling utterly defeated. A head injury, and they don't yet know the repercussions of that, now pneumonia! She refused to give herself over to hopelessness, however, and began to pray again. She'd developed a strategy the first night in the hospital. Every time worry crept into her heart, she'd stop and pray. Worry would get her nowhere, but prayer had power.

Lily had only been there a few minutes when Jack woke up. At first she was elated to finally see light shining in his eyes again, but elation soon turned to horror as he started to struggle. The hurt, confused look he had on his face was directed at Lily, as if she were the one who'd caused him such pain, as if he were asking, "How could you let them do this to me?" He looked at her pleadingly, trying to pull his hands from their restraints, then with the strength of a buffalo, he sat up in the hospital bed and leaned forward until his face was close to his bound hand, just inches away from pulling out his tube, the tube that provided life. She hopped up to stop him, putting her hands on his chest, but her strength was no match for his determination. Her desire to touch him had been overwhelming, but now she understood the nurse's warning. She and Jack both were now flailing together in a sea of distress. She felt so bad for him, so helpless, so scared that not only would he not recover, but that he might actually unintentionally kill himself. She cried out for help, and the nurse came running, three more male nurses at her heels, helping her to finally get him settled back down. It took all of them to subdue Jack. The nurse spoke to him calmly explaining his situation. She told him where he was, why he was there, and why he was tied down. Then she pointed to Lily and asked, "Do you know who this is?" Jack looked at Lily but showed no sign of recognition. Lily's heart was breaking. *Does he have amnesia? Has he forgotten me?*

As if the nurse had read her mind, she left Jack to the care of the others and led Lily out to the hallway. "It's normal for him to have memory issues right now. He's been on heavy sedatives. He's just confused." Lily nodded. "It's not time to worry about amnesia yet. Once we can take out the tube and allow him to completely wake up, then we will know if his memory has been affected." Lily was grateful for the nurse's words. Nonetheless, fear wound itself around Lily's heart, and as a result, prayer once again found its way to her lips.

After the surgery, she was once again afraid to leave his side, but the nurses forced her to go home each night. Even though the nurse was right next to his room in the hallway, Lily still worried that he might find a way to pull out his breathing tube. She had not been to work since the accident, and by now, all of their co-workers had figured out just how much Jack meant to Lily. She knew it didn't look right, especially since they didn't know that Lily had left her husband, but gossip at work was the least of her concerns. Her mom had probably figured it out too, but to her relief, so far had not questioned her. Jack had developed pneumonia and was fighting for his life once again. That was Lily's only focus. She was starting to wonder if God was punishing them. Nevertheless, she drove to the hospital every day and stayed by Jack's side, praying for God's forgiveness and praying for Jack to be healed.

Chapter Ten

**See now that I, I am He,
And there is no god besides Me;
It is I who put to death and give life.
I have wounded, and it is I who heal;
And there is no one who can deliver from My hand.
Deut. 32:39**

Lily drove to the hospital with the sun in her eyes as a new day dawned. Each morning on the way to the hospital, she listened to KSBJ. They were throwing out the gauntlet for their thirty-day challenge in which listeners would listen to their station every day for thirty days, believing that their lives would be better for it. Lily had been desperate and would have done anything to get through this trying time, so she took that challenge and listened to the singers of God's Word on the way to the hospital and on the way home each day. Between the songs and the prayers, she'd felt as if she were in a bubble of peace, which helped her in each moment of this difficult journey.

Lily parked her car in the hospital parking lot and then checked her phone. Damien had tried to call her several times. *I just can't deal with him right now,* Lily thought. When she arrived at the hospital, she was surprised to find that she wasn't allowed to go in to see Jack since he already had two visitors in with him.

"Lily, I'm so sorry. Jack's mom and a young woman are both in there, and I don't think they are coming out anytime soon." Jennifer, one of the nurses who had taken care of Jack when he first arrived told her. "His mom was finally able to get back into the country. I heard her say she came straight from the airport. They both arrived early this morning."

It must be Hailey. Who else could it be? Lily was relieved that Jack's mom was here, but unhappy about the fact that she wasn't allowed in. Lily took a deep breath. "Well, how is his mom holding up?"

"Lots of tears, of course, but she's hanging in there. The other woman was crying pretty loud, however. The doctor told her she had to get herself together or go out to the waiting room."

The other woman? No, that was Lily's title. Guilt crept into her heart. Lily could only imagine how Hailey must feel. No one had known how to reach her to tell her about Jack's accident. She must have been worried sick about him all week, wondering where he was.

Lily went downstairs to get a cup of coffee and headed back up to the waiting room, unsure if she should even be there now that Jack's girlfriend and mom had shown up. She looked around at the somber looking people who were waiting to see their loved ones. It was sad. Every face in the room had a heart-breaking story to tell. Lily walked over to the prayer tree and read over the simple but desperate prayer requests on the slips of paper hanging from the branches. She came across the one she had written for Jack that first day he was in the hospital. "God, please save Jack. I love him." Lily's short prayer brought back the unbearably painful memory of that first day. She glanced over at the desk and noticed the open King James Bible and sat down to read it. Her eyes immediately landed on Psalm 34:17 "The righteous cry, and the LORD heareth, and delivereth them out of all their troubles." *Righteous. I'm a married woman in love with another man. Not exactly righteous, am I?* Lily continued reading for some time until she came to Psalm 84:11 "For the LORD God is a sun and shield: the LORD will give grace and glory: No good thing will he withhold from them that walk uprightly."

Lily had been thinking about the meaning of the verse and all that it implied when she felt someone standing next to her. She glanced up into the kind handsome face of Jack's father.

"Excuse me, are you Lily?"

"Yes, I am."

"I'm John Walker, Jack's dad." He held out his hand. Lily stood and placed hers into it.

"Yes sir. I recognize you from church."

"Really? Well, now that you mention it, you do look familiar, but we are gone most of the time on mission trips."

"Yes. I know. That must be pretty exciting."

"Well, yes. I guess. I just wanted to thank you for being here for my son."

"Of course." Lily could see the gentleness in his eyes that so resembled Jack's.

"I see that you're reading the Bible. Is your faith strong?"

"Oh yes! Very."

"Then you will continue to pray for Jack," he declared.

"I will." Lily smiled tentatively.

"Well, maybe the next time we see each other, it will be under happier circumstances." He gave her a warm smile and walked down the hallway toward the elevator leaving Lily feeling like she'd just encountered an angel.

Lily sat back down and checked her phone, scrolling through all the messages and inquiries from Jack's friends. After a while the double doors opened and a well-dressed woman walked out. Jack's mom. She looked at Lily and walked over to her. Lily stood up with the intension of introducing herself and held out her hand, but she didn't take it.

"Are you Lily?" she asked.

"Yes." Lily dropped her hand.

"I'm Patricia Walker, Jack's mother."

"I'm so pleased to finally meet—" her words were cut short.

"May I sit down? I think we should talk."

"Of course." Lily attempted a smile, but it was not returned.

"I understand that you have been by my son's side every day since his accident?"

"Well, yes. I guess I have." Lily looked at her sheepishly.

"Of course I appreciate it immensely. And I know that it has helped him a great deal. Apparently you two are close?"

"Well…" Lily stammered.

"Well, I understand he cares for you, but aren't you married?" she quipped.

It was hard to believe that this woman was married to Jack's dad, the kind man she had just met. Lily looked down at her toes. Her first thought was how badly she needed a pedicure. These thoughts were interrupted, however, with Patricia's next words.

"Hailey is here now. She will take over. We won't be needing you here anymore."

Lily looked up with eyebrows raised. *Not see Jack anymore? Not sit by his side?* The thought broke her in two.

"I truly do appreciate you, Lily, but it's highly inappropriate. What would your husband think?" She paused then looked at her pointedly. Taking Lily's hand in hers, she asked her quietly, "Are you and my son having an affair?"

Lily's mouth gaped open. She had no clue how to answer that question. "I'm… I don't…I'm not sure. I don't think it's gotten that far." Technically, it hadn't, or had it?

"Lily, I'm not trying to be harsh, but I don't want to lose my son, and I don't want him to be out of the good graces of God. Does that make sense to you?"

Actually, that's just what Lily had been thinking herself.

"I will always appreciate what you've done for my son. You may even be the reason he's held on to this life, but he cannot possibly find true happiness with a married woman. I hope you understand."

Patricia stood and turned away from Lily then walked back through the double doors that led to Jack, doors that Lily could never walk through again. Though she felt like she'd just been run over by a truck, she could understand where Jack's mom was coming from. She would probably feel the same way in her shoes.

Lily's phone rang, startling her. She answered it quickly before its ringing made too much noise in the quiet, somber waiting room, then gathered her things and headed for the long hallway leading to the elevator.

"Hello."

"Lily, it's Mom. Damien's been trying to reach you."

"I know, Mom. I just can't deal with him right now. Everything with Jack and—"

"Honey," her mom cut her off, "you need to call him. Now."

Lily was taken aback. Something must be wrong. What now? As she was walking out, Lily glanced back at the double doors leading into the

ICU. She went back to the table to grab her forgotten coffee and looked down at the bible. "O LORD of hosts, blessed is the man that trusteth in thee." Psalm 84:12. *I have to trust in the Lord to take care of you, Jack. Please understand.* Lily walked out of the hospital, having no clue what was ahead, but having little hope that life would end up the way she wanted it.

When Lily walked out the front doors of the hospital, the heat of the day assaulted her, replacing the cold chill of the building. *Indian Summer*: a normal occurrence here. The heat was so stifling she could barely breathe. She sat on the bench next to the flowerbed that struggled to bring healing and hope and some beauty to this place, this place of sickness, death, and heartache. She gathered her strength, took a deep breath, and called Damien's number. "Damien, hi. It's me." A few minutes later she hung up the phone. She thought back to everything that had happened in her life the last few weeks. She thought about Jack, kissing him for the first time, sitting next to him while he fought for his life, being utterly dismissed by his mother, the phone call with Damien. Now she knew, as much as she loved Jack, she could never be with him. She would have a breakdown if she only had the time, but she was needed, so she decided to do what any strong woman would do, take a deep breath and call her mom.

"Mom, I'm on my way. No, I won't be staying. It's time for me to go home."

When Lily got into town, she drove straight to the church. She didn't have an appointment but she knew that Brother Tim would see her. She opened up the wounds of her heart to him, leaving out some of the more torrid details with Jack. She knew what he would say. She knew what God would want. She could not leave her husband in his time of need, even if he deserved it, and she wasn't quite sure that anyone deserved that. If Damien would promise to change then it was her duty to stand by him, especially now. Brother Tim told her to read her bible, talk to God, and as she suspected, open her heart back up to her husband.

Lily drove home, contemplating all that she must do. She'd received God's answer, and His answer wasn't Jack, only confirming to her that God is not Santa Claus, and He is not here to fulfill our wishes. Only He sees the broader picture, and His plan is not to harm but to give hope and a future. So Lily decided not to lean on her own understanding, but instead trust God's will for her life. Faith could be a hard pill to swallow sometimes, but Lily's faith was strong, and she would put her trust in God.

Lily pulled into the driveway next to Damien's green Camaro. In the house she found him sitting on the couch staring at the T.V. She plopped down beside him and put her hand on his knee. He turned to her and hugged her to him tightly, weeping. After a time, his sobs abated and Lily went into the kitchen to make them some hot tea.

"What did the doctor say?" She sat down across from him and held out a cup.

Damien took the tea from her then took a deep breath. "I have colon cancer."

Lily's heart sank. She looked at him, but he would not meet her eye. "How did they find that out?"

"I was having some pains. I've been ignoring them for a while but they kept coming back so I finally went to the doctor."

He seemed so stoic Lily wondered if he had already given up. "How long has this been going on?" she asked gently.

"A long time, Lily."

She sat back in disbelief. How could she not know? "Why didn't you ever say anything?"

"I don't know. I'm a man. I ignore stuff." He put his tea down on the coffee table and picked the remote back up, still staring at the T.V. "Anyway, since colon cancer runs in my family, they decided to do a colonoscopy, and I have colon cancer, and I have to have surgery and then treatments." He scrolled through the channels.

"I'm so sorry Dame, I'll come back home and help you through this. Don't worry." She patted his knee.

He finally looked at her. "But will you stay, Lily? I mean, once I'm better?"

Lily knew she couldn't make any promises, but she was here now. "We'll see how it goes, okay?"

He nodded his head and turned from her again. "Lily, that's not all. The doctor said…" Damien looked down at the floor as if searching for the right words. "I don't know how to tell you this."

"Tell me what?"

"How can I say it? How can I say the words?" Tears pooled in his dark eyes.

Lily's frustration grew by the second. "Damien, just say it."

He turned to her. "I can't give you children, Lily."

"I know. You already told me you don't want children. We can worry about that later. We still have plenty of time. You'll change your mind."

"No, Lily. You don't understand. I CAN'T give you children." His eyes bored into hers.

Lily's world crashed around her. All her hopes and dreams shattered in an instant. She fought desperately to hold her composure, but tears escaped, betraying her. Lily shut her eyes. She took in a deep breath and stood up and turned away. She couldn't look at him right now. "Because of the cancer?" she asked, focusing on the hole in the wall his anger had left behind.

"No. It's not that. I didn't know Lily. I swear. I'm sterile. I've probably always been sterile. I would have never been able to give you children." He stood up and walked over to the wall, placing his hand over the hole. "I'm so sorry, Lily. I've let you down. I've been a terrible husband. Now I'm going to be a burden, and I can't give you the only thing you ever asked of me." He squatted down right there on the floor as if he couldn't bear his own weight and cried. "I wouldn't blame you if you ran away and never looked back!"

She knelt on the floor, level with him, and hugged him, hiding her face so that he wouldn't see the true destruction of his words. In a daze, she looked up at the calendar hanging by the door and noticed that today's date was circled with a big red heart. Today was their third wedding anniversary.

Chapter Eleven

**Just as a father has compassion
on his children,
So the Lord has compassion
on those who fear Him.
Ps. 103:13**

A couple of months later, Christmas had passed, and a new year began. Lily stared down at the dark green carpet, wondering how Jack was doing, as she sat with her husband in the waiting room of Dr. Jenkins office. It was time to start treatment. Damien's surgery had been successful, but according to the doctors, the cancer would likely come back without the prescribed radiation. They had been waiting a while when Lily stood up to stretch her legs. She wandered over to the "borrow a book" shelf and took down a book about racing. She brought it back over and handed it to Damien, knowing his love for cars. He thanked her and reached for her hand. It was shaking. "You nervous?" she asked him as she squeezed his hand.

"Would I sound like a coward if I said *yes*?" Damien gave her a weak smile.

REMEMBER ME

"No. You aren't a coward. Would I ever marry a coward?" Lily sat down next to him. He was still clinging to her hand.

Damien had so much to say to Lily, but words didn't come easily for him, especially honest ones. He'd been secretly meeting with Lily's preacher since his surgery. Finding out he had colon cancer, the same disease that had taken his mother when he was only five, broke something inside him. His carefree youthful selfish days and ways were over. Death had a way of staring a person in the face and revealing all of his faults. He'd been a terrible husband to Lily. He'd been a terrible person. He realized he was standing in the hallway between two doors: one leading to Christ, the other leading to a place he did not want as his final destination. God sure had a way of convicting a person, and Damien had definitely felt convicted. He loved Lily and he knew he'd come too close to losing her. Now he wanted to change and he wanted his marriage to work. The preacher explained to him about their marriage needing to be Christ-centered and that they had been unequally yoked all these years together. He didn't enjoy Brother Tim's harsh words, but he understood that it was his job to share the truth. Damien still struggled with his sins and failures, and he could not fathom a God who could love him. He knew he didn't deserve it.

"Lily," Damien looked at her, searching for the right words. "Thanks for coming back." He reached for her hand. "I know I don't deserve you, and I just want you to know how sorry I am, and—you know this is not easy for me—but I appreciate—"

Lily cut him off. "Damien, through sickness and health, right? We're in this together." She touched his face gently. "Trust in God." Lily looked down. "I know you aren't spiritual, but—"

"Lily, I want to be." He touched her chin and turned her to face him, fervently looking in her eyes but keeping his voice low, "but after what I've done, how I've treated you. You're my wife. I cheated on you," he whispered. Lily flinched at his words. He saw the pain in her eyes and felt like he'd just been punched in the gut. He shook his head and leaned back in his chair. "God wouldn't want me. I have no right to ask anything of him." Damien put his head down, hiding the shame on his face.

"Everyone who asks, receives," Lily spoke so quietly he barely heard the words. He looked up at her. "It's in the bible." Her eyes pierced right through him. "Damien, we've all sinned. That's why we need Jesus. Your sins can be forgiven. Just ask."

She made it sound so easy. "But I don't deserve it. I feel like a hypocrite."

"Huh! Don't we all?" Lily shook her head. "None of us deserve forgiveness. That's why it's a gift, the gift of grace. It can't be earned because we will never be good enough to earn it."

"Then how can anyone ever get to Heaven? I mean, all those commandments…it seems like you have to be perfect." Brother Tim had indeed explained the mechanics of salvation to Damien, but he just wasn't sure he was buying into it, or that he could ever measure up.

"Damien?" The nurse called out.

Damien wiped his sweaty palms on his knees, stood up and reached for Lily's hand, and they walked in together. "Can we talk more about this later?"

"Absolutely."

In the car on the way home, Damien and Lily picked up right where they had left off. Lily took a deep breath as she clutched the steering wheel. She'd waited years to have this conversation with her husband. She prayed a quick prayer for the right words. "Well, the bible says that God loves us. We are his children." Though she wished she could look into his eyes instead of having to focus on the road, Lily was grateful for the opportunity to finally be able to share the good news of Jesus with her husband. "Damien, if we had children, if we had a son, and he broke a window or wrecked your car, would you stop loving him?"

"No. Of course not, but what does that have to do with—"

"Well, it's the same way with God. We mess up, but when we're sorry, He forgives us." She glanced over at him, meeting his gaze. "But Damien, you have to ask."

"Right." He looked away, staring out of the window as the trees passed by. "I don't know Lily. It sounds too easy. What about all the sins I committed? Don't sinners go to hell?"

"Jesus took the punishment for our sins—on the cross."

"Jesus did that? That's why he let those assholes beat him, torture him?"

"Well, yeah. I mean, He could have stopped them, but He didn't. If He hadn't chosen to pay the price for our sins, we would have to. We would be lost with no way to get into Heaven."

"Oh man! Why would he do that?"

"Because He loves us."

Damien looked pensive, "Lily, I don't deserve it."

"Well, are you truly sorry for the things you've done?"

"You have no idea." He shook his head from side to side as if he could shake away the memory of all the bad things he'd ever done.

"Are you gonna keep doing them?" She looked over at him, wanting to know for herself as well.

"No! No. I'm done with all that." Damien put his hand on Lily's knee and asked her to pull the car over. She complied, turning on her hazard lights and carefully pulling onto the shoulder of the road. Damien turned to face her, took both of her hands into both of his and looked into her eyes. "Lily, I swear I will absolutely never, ever, dishonor you, or myself, or Jesus again. Losing you almost killed me. If you hadn't come back to me, I would've just let the cancer take me."

"Damien, don't say that."

"It's true! I love you, Lily." He softly brushed back her hair from her face.

"Damien, I have to ask you something," she looked down, and he waited patiently while she gathered her courage, "this is not easy for me to ask, but you once told me you also loved her. Do you still?" She waited anxiously for his answer.

"Who…No! No, Lily. No! It wasn't love. I didn't know real love till I lost you." He lifted her chin, gently forcing her to look at him. "Do you think that one day you might be able to forgive me and love me again?"

"Damien, I already have, and I already do." Lily knew at that moment that her words were true.

He leaned over and softly kissed her. His kiss was warm and sweet. "Now that I know *you've* forgiven me, tell me how to get God to forgive me too."

"That's easy. Just ask Him for forgiveness, and then ask Jesus to come into your heart. He will help you to be a better person. Even though you'll never be perfect—none of us will—He will continue to forgive you and love you. Your job is to do your best to follow Him. Damien," she squeezed his hand, "just open your heart to Him."

Tears fell down Damien's face as he tried to grasp the concept of being forgiven for all the horrible things he'd ever done. Relief flooded over him at the thought of starting over with a clean slate. He closed his eyes and prayed a silent prayer. Then, he felt lighter somehow. Like he'd been given a second chance. A second chance with Lily, a second chance at life, a second chance with God.

"Lily, I want to be baptized. If Jesus can take that kind of abuse for me, then I can do this for him. I can live my life for Him."

Lily broke into the biggest smile he'd ever seen. "Ya know, God really does answer prayers, even though it sometimes takes years."

Chapter Twelve

**Many a man proclaims
his own loyalty,
But who can find
a trustworthy man?
Proverbs 20:6**

Jack waited as his mom poured them both a cup of coffee. She handed him a mug that said, "World's Greatest Dad." His lips curled into a smile as he remembered giving it to his dad one Father's Day when he was a kid. Life sure was simpler then. He pulled up a stool and sat down at the kitchen island and stared at the mesmerizing steam floating upward from his cup, remembering. This was his favorite room in the house. When he was a kid, he'd loved to sit in this very spot and hassle his mom as she cooked and baked things that always smelled so good, like home. Now he was an adult and living on his own, and his house never smelled like this, even when Hailey was there. She didn't like to cook. If he married her, either he would be the cook in the family or they would have to order out. *I bet Lily's a good cook.* He pushed the thought away. He looked behind him through the open kitchen into the living room. "Is Dad around?" he asked his mom.

"No, he went fishing early this morning. He should be back around lunch time though." She sipped her coffee and looked at her son assessing him. "Anything I can help with?"

"No. I was just hoping to catch him before he left the house."

Not one to be deterred, Patricia asked her son, "Jack, is something on your mind?"

"I don't know. Guess I'm just tired."

"Are you feeling well? Your next doctor's appointment isn't until next week. Do you think you need to go sooner?"

"No, Mom. That's just a checkup, and it's nothing like that anyway. Don't worry so much."

"Don't worry so much? You nearly die, and you tell me not to worry so much? Just wait until you have kids. Huh!" She shook her head and took a sip of her coffee.

"You're right. Sorry, Mom."

"So then, what's going on in that head of yours?"

"It's just...I can't explain it. I can't remember anything that happened when I was in the hospital, and..."

"Well, Honey, they had you on so many drugs. Of course you can't remember."

"But I remember bits and pieces, or maybe it's just more like feelings that I remember. I don't know. It sounds crazy, but I remember someone...Oh never mind." Jack shook his head. "It's stupid."

Patricia leaned over and touched her son's hand reassuringly. "It's not stupid. Tell me. You remember someone what?"

"Well," Jack cleared his throat and worked at pulling his thoughts together. "It sort of felt like...like someone was with me. I knew it. I could feel it," he blurted out, feeling relieved to have finally said it.

"You mean God?"

"No, I mean, yes, God too. I could definitely feel Him, but I'm talking about a person. I know Hailey was there," Patricia flinched, "but I don't think it was her that I'm remembering." Jack looked at his mom expectantly. "Do you think it was an angel?"

Patricia knew exactly who had been there for him, sitting at his bedside all day, every day, and it hadn't been his girlfriend, but she just couldn't tell him. It wasn't right. Lily was married, and he was with Hailey. "I don't know, Honey. Maybe it *was* an angel. The Bible does say we have angels guarding over us." Patricia walked over to the sink and busied herself with the breakfast dishes, silently reminding herself that ignoring things doesn't make them go away.

"Yeah, maybe." Jack looked back down at his coffee. "I just wish I could remember."

As Jack was getting ready to go to therapy the next morning, it dawned on him that if he wanted information, Anna was the one to ask. He decided to swing by the restaurant after his session. He walked in the door around 10:30 that morning while the staff was setting up for lunch. Bob was restocking the bar, but he didn't see Anna or Lily. *That's strange*, he thought.

"Hey Bud!" Bob gave Jack a high five and a hug, patting his back. "So good to see you back. What are you doing here, though? Thought you were gonna be out for another month at least."

"I am. Just goin' a little stir crazy at home with two women hovering over me all the time."

"Yeah, what a problem!" Bob raised his eyebrows and laughed.

"It's not as much fun as you think. Actually, I was hoping to catch Anna before the lunch rush starts. Is she comin' in today?" Just then, Anna rushed in hurriedly.

"Yes, I am. Sorry I'm late…again." Anna said apologetically. "I guess I need my boss back to keep me in line." She smiled coyly.

"Well, that will happen soon enough." Jack grinned. "Anna, can I talk to you for a second?"

"Sure, if you don't mind following me around while I set up my tables."

Jack shadowed Anna from table to table helping her with her preparations and finally got around to asking her about his stay in the hospital. "It seems like someone was there," he said as he filled a salt shaker, spilling some on the table. "I know Hailey and my mom were." Jack wiped the excess salt into his hand. "But I don't mean them. It was someone else, and I wish I could remember, but all I remember is a feel…"

"It was Lily," Anna said, cutting him off.

Jack looked up abruptly. "Lily?"

"Yeah. Charlotte called her after your accident. She drove straight to the hospital and never left your side for like, a week." Jack followed Anna to the next table. "Then your mom and Hailey finally showed up." Anna handed him several rolls of silverware. "Your mom had been out of the country, as you know, but none of us knew how to reach Hailey." Jack methodically set them in their proper place on the table. "I guess your mom must have contacted her when she got back in the country."

"Wait wait wait, hold up, so you're telling me that Hailey wasn't there until my mom came back?"

"Pretty sure she wasn't. No one around here told her."

"But that was a week after my accident."

Anna looked up toward the ceiling as if doing the math in her head. "Yeah, I guess it was. Lily was there every day. She would know."

"Lily was there every day?"

"Yeahhhhh. That's what I just said."

"So you're saying that Lily came to the hospital every day, but Hailey didn't?"

"Well…" Anna stopped what she was doing, and looked as if she were reaching down into her memory. "At first Lily stayed the night in your room, but after a while they wouldn't let her, but after that, yes, she drove there each day. She didn't wanna leave you. She didn't come in to work at all, and we were so busy, but Charlotte said to leave her alone and—"

"Anna, focus."

"Right…and Hailey, well, we didn't have her phone number, so how could she know?"

"But my mom never said…Hailey must have wondered where I was. Why did she let me think she'd sat next to me on my deathbed every single day?" Jack muttered to himself. "Why didn't my mom tell me? Hailey must have wondered why she hadn't heard from me all week." Jack was trying to make sense of it all. He directed his attention back to Anna. "She never called work looking for me?"

"I don't think so. Not that I know of. Did you ever ask her about it?" Anna straightened the chairs around the table.

"No." So Hailey lied. His mom lied. Not only that, *Hailey never even wondered where I was that whole week. It doesn't make sense.* He had in fact suspected all along that it hadn't been Hailey who had sat by his side as she'd claimed. "But Lily wasn't there after I woke up. Why didn't she come back?" Jack asked Anna.

"Well, I think it had something to do with Hailey. Also, your mom had words with Lily. Maybe I shouldn't have told you that, but it's true."

"What do you mean my mom had words with her?"

"How do I get myself into these things?" Anna mumbled. Just then, she knocked over the pepper shaker with the tips of her fingers and it went flying, pepper spilling all over the table and the floor. "Crap! I soooo don't have time for this!" She slapped her hand to her forehead, exasperated.

"Anna? Please."

She sighed. "Okay, okay! Keep your shirt on! Your mom told Lily not to come back to the hospital—that she and Hailey were quote…" Anna mimicked the quotation signs with her fingers. "…taking over. Unquote."

"She never told me that!" Jack erupted in sudden indignation.

"Well, it's true." Anna reached down to retrieve the pepper shaker. "Lily was pretty upset about it too. She made Charlotte promise to call her everyday with updates about you."

Jack shook his head trying to wrap his mind around what Anna was telling him. He had to talk to Lily. "Where's Lily now? Is she coming in today?"

Anna headed to the next table. "No. She's been taking some time off, but today I think she's at the doctor with Damien."

"At the doctor? With Damien? Is she…?" he asked incredulously.

Anna stopped and turned to look at Jack. "You really need to get the story from Lily, Jack. It's not mine to tell."

Anna was right. Jack said his good-byes and walked quickly out of the restaurant. *Lily and Damien at a doctor's appointment. Why would she be taking time off? Why would she see a doctor with Damien, unless?*

Jack started to drive home, but which home? His house, where he would find no answers? Home to his mom? But neither was where he wanted to go. *I have to talk to Lily. I have to know.* Jack turned toward Lily's house, but as he approached the white house with the red shutters, he saw Lily and Damien getting out of the car. They were walking into the house hand in hand. Jack's heart fell at the sight of them together. *I've lost her.* Jack drove passed Lily unnoticed and straight over to Hailey's apartment. He pulled into the parking lot and saw that her black BMW was sitting in its place. He parked his pick-up truck next to it. *Opposites do attract apparently*, he thought to himself. But he was angry and he flew up the steps two at a time to her second story apartment. He banged on the door for several minutes and had almost turned to go when she finally opened the door. Her hair was messy, which was unusual for her this time of day, and she didn't invite him in.

"Jack, what are you doing here? I thought you had therapy."

"I did, early this morning." He barged in.

"I'm sorry I'm such a mess, I wasn't expecting you." She stole a quick glance at her closed bedroom door as she folded her robe around her and tied the sash.

"Why did you let me think you were at the hospital with me every day?"

"Wh...what do you mean? I was." Hailey turned her back to him and walked into the kitchen.

"Well, who told you I was in the hospital?"

"Why, your mother, of course." She opened the cabinet and grabbed a glass, filling it with water.

"When?"

"When? When you were in the hospital. What's going on? Why are you giving me the third degree?" Hailey opened a bottle of aspirin sitting on the counter. "I went there as soon as I heard." She swallowed two and drank a long sip of water. "Your mom saw me there. She can tell you. She called me and I met her up there."

"So, you came the same day my mom did."

Jack knew Hailey realized her mistake. "What I mean is…"

"What you mean is that I was in the hospital for a week before you knew, right?"

"Well, yes. No one called me, except your mom. That's not my fault!"

"No, it isn't, but you let me believe that… I was there a whole week before my mom came! Didn't you wonder where I was?"

"Well, yes, but I told you I was going out of town. Don't you remember?" He didn't.

"That may be true, or not, I don't remember, but even so, I wouldn't have gone a whole week without calling you. Didn't you try to call me?"

"Um, yes. I tried to call your cell, but you didn't answer. Then I called you at work, but you weren't there."

"Really? Okay. Guess I have to give you the benefit of the doubt." But Jack remembered what Anna had said and knew that if Hailey had called him at work, they would have told her he was in the hospital. He stood up and started for the door.

"Where are you going?"

"My mom's." He left Hailey's apartment completely disenchanted with her, which only made him long for Lily all the more. Now he had to face his mom and accuse her of misleading him. He sure wasn't looking forward to that! Jack left and slammed the door in a rage.

"You can come out now," Hailey said to the closed bedroom door, "He's gone."

Lily and Damien returned home from his doctor's appointment. His treatments seemed to be going well, even though he was tired and nauseous. She couldn't wait to get back to a more normal life. Lily knew she'd made the right choice between Damien and Jack, *or should I say decision? My choice was Jack, but my decision was my marriage.* However, she still thought about him all the time. *Dear God, please help me get over Jack.*

Chapter Thirteen

If you love Me, you will keep My commandments.
John 14:15

Weeks later, Damien's treatments had ended, and Lily went back to work. He seemed to be doing fine now, and he didn't need her there all the time. It was good to get back to a routine, to a job she liked, and friends that she was lucky enough to get to work with. But Anna's confession brought Jack to mind when she told her about his visit weeks before.

"I didn't tell him about Damien, but it slipped that y'all were at the doctor. I'm sorry, Lily. Me and my big mouth."

"Anna, don't worry about it. It's not a secret. Everyone knows that Damien is sick."

"How is he, by the way?" asked Bob, popping up from behind the bar.

"Well, he's finished with his treatments. We just have to wait and see." Lily quickly got busy setting up her tables for the rush hour. Bob and Anna looked at each other and shrugged.

"Well, he's lucky to have her," Anna said.

"Yeah, but is she lucky to have him?"

"Well, maybe now that life has slapped him in the face, I hope he'll realize how lucky he is and fly right."

"Yeah, maybe. I hope so."

Lily, overhearing their conversation, hoped so too.

Lily had only been back for a short time when Jack was finally scheduled to return to work. It would be a light schedule for him at first, Lily was relieved to hear. He would only work a couple of shifts per week for a while. She didn't want him to overdo it too soon, but she also knew the less they saw of each other, the better. She had to admit though, she had butterflies in her stomach at the thought of seeing him again. It had been so long. *I wonder how he looks, if he's okay, if he's still with Hailey.*

Jack had scheduled a staff meeting that morning so he could talk to everyone before the shift started. Anna brought doughnuts and Charlotte made coffee. Everyone was excited about Jack coming back to work. Lily seated herself next to Anna in the back of the meeting room. The door opened and Jack walked in. His eyes scanned the room and immediately locked on hers. Lily's heart started beating in overdrive. Anna looked from Lily to Jack. She sighed loudly, breaking the trance. Jack quickly gathered his wits and relayed his happiness at being back then went over a few items of importance. The meeting was short, sweet, and to the point. Everyone either hugged Jack or shook his hand as they walked out of the meeting room. Lily was the last out, and Jack stopped her.

"Lily, can you stay for just a minute?" Anna looked back at her and rolled her eyes.

Lily stopped and turned back, trying not to react to Anna. "Uh, yeah. Sure."

Jack closed the door softly. Lily started to walk to one of the chairs to sit back down, but seeing him again threw all her resolve out the window. She turned to face him. All these months reconciling with Damien, all this time praying to forget Jack, all the effort of pushing her feelings away, all came crashing down, gone in an instant. There was so much in her heart she wanted to say, and even though she knew she didn't have the right, she didn't think she could stop herself. She felt such longing, and it hit her like a ton of bricks. She loved him. Trying so hard to forget him these past few months, trying so hard to be a good loyal wife, trying so hard to do what God wanted her to do, what did it get her? Did she get over Jack? No! Instead, she fell in love with him. She knew that now. She'd failed. She'd failed God. She'd failed Damien. She'd failed herself by denying her own heart. It wasn't right. *She* had no right. But how on earth could she stop herself from fessing up when all she wanted to do was fly into his arms? Regardless, she knew she had to rein in her emotions, so she took a deep breath attempting to slow her beating heart.

"How have you been, Jack?"

"Better than I was a few months ago." He stepped toward her. "When you sat by my side…"

Another step closer. "At the hospital…" Another. "And held my hand." He stood right in front of her now, only inches away. He picked up her hand and held it to his heart, all the while gazing into her eyes. "And sang to me, and read the bible to me, and prayed over me."

She froze. A current of relived emotions flowed through her as memories came rushing back. Jack continued to look into her eyes. Then he inched even closer and waited. Silent moments stood between them. She held his gaze, but made no other move. Her heart beat faster and faster with each moment, but his phone rang, breaking their connection. Lily took a step back, dropping her hand from his grasp, then turned away and walked across the room, maintaining a safe distance. She looked back at him. "How…how did you know? Do you remember?"

"No." Jack shook his head, turning off the ringer on his phone. "But I remember feeling it." He met her eyes once again. "And Anna confirmed it. I talked to Charlotte and Bob about it too. They filled in the details. Lily…"

Jack couldn't let this moment go. Seeing her again, knowing how much she really cared about him flooded his heart, threatening to spill over. He wasn't strong enough. He couldn't help it. It was now or never. He stormed across the room, breaking through the distance between them. He opened his arms and wrapped them around her tightly. Returning his embrace, Lily pressed into him with her entire being. He held her so close he couldn't tell where he ended and she began. They held on for what seemed like a wonderful, glorious eternity, but guilt struck him. Jack pulled back, just enough to look into Lily's telling eyes, and he knew. She could never be his. He touched a tear running down her face and felt her shiver. He held her gaze and slowly, gently kissed her. He touched his forehead to hers and looked down into her yearning eyes.

"I wish this…wouldn't have to end," he said.

"I love you, Jack," she whispered.

"God help me, I love you too." Guilt be damned. He wanted her. He needed her. He pulled her to him and kissed her with all the love he felt inside, but just as quickly, a thought struck him and he let her go, his next words pouring ice onto a fire. "Lily, I have to know something…are you pregnant?"

She stumbled back, breathless, and looked at him, dumbfounded. "What? What on earth would ever give you that idea?"

"You and Damien?" he stammered, "um, didn't you go see a doctor?"

"Yes. We…Ohhhhh, I see. Yes, we did."

"Well? So, are you?"

"No Jack." She hugged herself defensively and turned away. "I'm not, nor will I ever be. Damien has cancer." Lily looked down at the floor.

Jack took a step back. He needed a moment to think. He sat down and put his head in his hands. "That's why you stayed with him," he said, more to himself than to Lily. Silence filled the space between them. Lily didn't answer. She turned to go.

He just watched as Lily walked to the door. What else could he do? She looked at him once again. His eyes pleaded with her to stay. *I can't,* she seemed to say. Then she walked out. Shaken, Jack repeated to himself, feeling utterly powerless, "That's why you stayed." He walked out of the meeting room and down the long hallway to his office and closed the door.

The next day, Jack went into work still confused, but he was at least cleared up about Lily's situation. Lily had stayed with Damien because he had cancer. He had some difficulty feeling bad for the guy after the way he'd treated Lily, and he also resented him for keeping Lily from him. *Would she ever leave him now? Life just isn't fair.* Jack knew he had to get himself together before the restaurant crew came in. But his heart was breaking, and he didn't know if he would ever be able to smile again. He'd been reading his bible the night before to try to gain some perspective into the situation. While he was searching the scriptures, the phrase "Deny self" seemed to jump right out at him. He knew the right thing would be to let Lily go, to let her work on her marriage, but how could he ever get over her if he had to see her every day? Immediately, his question was answered when he looked down and saw her letter on his desk. There were two letters. One, an official resignation letter, and another, a personal letter addressed to him. The resignation letter was short, effective immediately, a gut punch. He slowly unfolded the second letter addressed to him.

> *Dear Jack,*
>
> *I have thought an awful lot about everything: us, my job, my marriage, Damien's cancer, what's right, what's wrong, God. I've come to the conclusion that I cannot follow my heart. It is breaking right now as I write these words to you. I took vows. God would not want me to abandon my marriage, especially now that Damien is trying so hard to find redemption. He's really not a monster, Jack, just somewhat misguided, a sinner, like us. His illness has made him think about what's important. He's even been baptized. Even so, none of this changes the fact that I fell in love with you. I can't change how I feel. I can only choose to follow the right course and deny my own heart. You are a man of God (That's one of the reasons I fell in love with you.), so I know you must surely understand why I have chosen my marriage. Unfortunately, I can't trust myself around you. I'm weak. So, I have no other choice than to resign. I*

just can't work with you every day. It wouldn't be fair, not to me, you, Damien, or even Hailey. I wish you a wonderful life, full of love, a family. I only wish it could have been with me. Please forgive me if I've caused you any pain. I never meant to lead you on. There was a time I truly had every intention of leaving Damien and starting a new life (I'd been hoping with you). I see now that this is not in God's plan. Though we are not meant to be together, I fear you will always remain in my heart. I love you, always, so please don't forget to remember me.

Love, Lily

Jack folded the letter and put it in the back of his desk drawer. *Lily loves me. Lily resigned.* He couldn't believe it. What was Charlotte gonna think? She was crazy about Lily. Everybody was crazy about Lily, and it was his fault she had to quit. *If I just hadn't kissed her!* So, now he could add a new guilt to his broken heart.

After work, Jack headed over to his parents' house. His mom had apologized for misleading him about Hailey and Lily and the hospital, and he had forgiven her, but he was still a little irked about it. Nevertheless, he gave her a kiss on the cheek and greeted her warmly when he arrived at the house to see his father. After all, maybe he really couldn't blame her. What mother would want her son pining away for a married woman?

John Walker looked up from his desk when he heard a light knock on the door to his study. The door opened slowly. His grown son peeked in looking completely downtrodden.

"Dad, you busy?"

John removed his reading glasses and gently placed them on the corner of the large mahogany desk, passed down from his grandfather to his father to him knowing it would eventually be passed on to his own son one day. He stood up and walked around the desk to greet Jack, his one and only child.

"Never too busy for you, Son. Come on in." They shook hands and lightly embraced then sat down facing each other in the leather covered arm chairs, each one bordering the small stone fireplace that was only used once or twice a year.

"So, what can I do for you?"

Jack leaned back in his chair, looked up at the ceiling, and sighed.

"Ahhh, woman troubles," Jack's father stated with certainty.

Jack looked at his father and laughed. "That obvious, huh?"

"I'm a man. I recognize the signs. So what's going on with you and Hailey?"

Jack shifted in his seat. "Uh, it's not Hailey, Dad. It's Lily."

"Lily." John scratched his forehead and cradled his chin with thumb and forefinger, peering over at his son. "Ah. I see."

"I'm in love with her, Dad." Jack took a deep breath and released it loudly, exhaling the enormous weight of his feelings.

"So your mother was right." He paused. "Huh. Well, I'll be." John leaned back into the overstuffed cushions and prepared for a lengthy visit.

"Mother? Right about what? What do you mean?" Jack stammered.

"Your mother tried to tell me that something was going on with you and that young lady from church who'd stayed with you at the hospital, but I told her there was no way on God's green earth you would have an affair with a married woman." He shook his head in disbelief. "Son, was I wrong?"

"No Dad!" Jack exclaimed. "Well, yes, maybe a little." Jack conceded, hanging his head in shame knowing he had disappointed his father. Shame struck him twice knowing he'd disappointed his heavenly Father also.

"Well Son, which is it? Are you having an affair with her or not?" John was kind and gentle with his words but not one to beat around the bush.

"Dad, there's been no affair, but we came close…too close. Things weren't going well in her marriage and…I didn't mean to, but I fell in love with her. She's just this amazing person with a huge heart, and Dad, she's a Christian and…"

"Son, I have no doubt about that, none whatsoever," John cut him off, "but you have to understand that the devil strikes in our weakest moments. He struck her with her marital problems, and you, you fell right into his trap with your desire to help her, like a knight in shining armor."

"Actually, I think she was my knight in shining armor." Jack's level of shame went up a notch. "Anyway, I thought she might leave him, but she didn't."

"Son, as long as she's married, she's off limits to you." John stated simply. "You must not interfere in her marriage. You must walk away from her or you will never find peace."

"Well, it doesn't really matter now. I've already lost her." Jack took a deep breath and fought back his pain. "Dad, I think my heart's broke."

John reached over to grab his bible off his desk. He handed it to his son. "Jack, follow God's Word, not your heart. Our hearts can deceive us. Someday, you will have a family of your own, and you will be happy."

Jack took the bible from his father's hand. "But what about Lily? Her husband doesn't treat her right. She's not happy."

"But she chose him. The Lord can change people, Jack. You need to pray for Lily and for her husband. If you love her as you say you do, you will pray that God blesses her marriage so that she can find happiness with him. That is the truest of love."

Jack sat quietly for a few minutes taking in all that his father said. He was right and he knew it. An honorable man would never tell him to follow his heart and break up a marriage, and his father was the most honorable man he knew.

"Let's pray about it, and don't feel guilty for loving someone. We can't help who we love. We can only control our actions, and we can't even control those without God's help."

"So, it's okay with God that I love her?" Jack looked at his dad expectantly. "But it's not okay that I have her."

"That's just about the stink of it, Son."

"Man, life's hard."

"Yes it is."

Jack clutched his father's bible to his chest as his father prayed for him, then they embraced, and Jack knew in his heart that it would all be okay eventually. Peace was already beginning to take hold of him, and what a good feeling that was. He knew that no matter how much it hurt he had to let Lily go and move on with his life. There was just no other option.

Chapter Fourteen

**For I consider that the sufferings of this present time
are not worthy to be compared with the glory
that is to be revealed to us.
Rom. 8:18**

Time carried on. Leaves changed color and fell to the ground then winter found spring. Flowers bloomed their brilliant colors then wilted in the hot summer sun, and the leaves changed once again. Whether living life to the fullest, whether happy, sad, or indifferent, the years had a way of marching on. And as years passed, Jack carried on at work without Lily there to brighten his day, and Lily focused on her marriage with Damien, trying to make it work.

"Damien, I'm goin' to the store. If you think of anything you need, just call me." Lily called out to her husband as she started to walk out the door.

"Can you get some aspirin?" Damien quietly rounded the corner looking pale and tired.

Lily looked at her husband, concerned. She felt his forehead for fever. "Are you okay, Dame? You look like you're coming down with something."

"I just have this damn headache. It won't go away. It's making me nauseous."

"Okay, I'll get you something at the store. Why don't you just take it easy today? It's your day off, so lay down and binge watch something on TV."

"Yeah, I think maybe I will." He kissed her on the cheek. "Thanks for taking such good care of me."

Lily touched his face. "For better, for worse, right?" She winked at him. "I'll be home in about an hour or two."

Lily impatiently drove through the heavy traffic to get to the store. She didn't care for the grocery store in this town. It was always so crowded. If she didn't get there early enough, she had to fight the masses just to get her cart through the aisles. It was enough to bring on a panic attack.

Lily and Damien had moved to Bryan/College Station three years earlier after Lily quit her job at Charlotte's. She now worked as a teacher's aide at the local elementary school. It was a good job with good hours, and unlike waitressing, she had off nights, weekends, and holidays. She loved being around the inquisitive little children, and although it was a tough job, it was very rewarding and began to fill the large hole in her heart left empty by the children she would never have.

Bryan wasn't quite the quiet life of living in a tiny country town, but it was so much more convenient to be close to Damien's doctors than to travel back and forth, and the move had helped them to make a fresh start, putting their mistakes behind them. Since they didn't have children, just Baxter their beloved cat, they bought a small house in a subdivision near the hospital. They avoided the College Station area due to the thousands of crazy college kids living there. The only time they ventured out in that direction was to go out to eat. Lily didn't get to see her mom as much, but she tried to drive out to the ranch at least once a month for a weekend sabbatical. Damien usually didn't go with her. Preferring the busyness of city life, ranching was not exactly his thing. Lily, however, missed the peace and quiet of the country.

Lily's love of nature had come from her dad, and she missed him terribly. She'd always felt closer to him at the ranch where she was surrounded by wildflowers, horses, and fresh-cut hay, all the things he loved. Just as Lily was squeezing her cart around a family of six, her phone rang, breaking into her thoughts. The phone continued to ring as Lily struggled to find it in her purse.

"Hey Mom. What's up?"

"Well, I wanted to invite you and Damien to lunch next Sunday after church. Can you make it?"

"I think so. Damien isn't feeling very well today, so I'm not sure, but I can let you know Saturday."

"What's wrong with him? Do I need to worry?"

Lily sighed. Her mom was such a worry wart. "No Mom, he just has a headache. No fever."

"Okay, glad he doesn't have a fever. Just let me know, Honey. Tell Damien I'm fixin' King Ranch Casserole, his favorite."

"Yum. Okay, I'll let you know." Lily hung up and finished her shopping, trying to get out of the crowded store as quickly as possible.

She finally arrived home and retrieved her mail. There was a card, so she opened that first. The envelope held a wedding invitation. A former co-worker from Charlotte's was getting married. She wasn't sure if she wanted to go, but it might be fun to see the old gang again. Butterflies and regret filled her stomach at the thought that Jack just might be on the guest list too. The wedding was set for December 10th. Lily decided it was time for a new dress.

Weeks passed, and the day of the wedding arrived, and despite herself, Lily got very excited at the prospect of seeing Jack again. The department store was having their Christmas sale, and she had bought several dresses on her recent shopping spree. After all, it had been a long time since she'd had a reason to dress up. The day of the wedding, she spent hours picking out the right outfit and doing her hair. Damien had decided to stay home. He wasn't feeling up to socializing. Lily was disappointed that he wasn't going. She didn't really want to go to a wedding alone, and she'd thought that maybe they could have had some fun together. Free beer, free barbeque, dancing. It could have worked wonders for their marriage, but Lily learned long ago not to pressure her husband into going somewhere when he didn't want to. It did no good.

She had thought about staying home. After all, it was raining, and he wasn't feeling so good. She could stay and keep him company, but she really wanted to see the old gang again. Lily looked in the mirror and blotted off her excess lipstick.

On the hour drive to Chappell Hill, Lily went over it in her head a thousand times. Would Jack be invited? Of course he would be invited. If she had been invited, then he would be invited. Would he show up? Would he show up to see her? Would he stay away because of her? Would he have Hailey with him, or would he be alone? If he were alone...?

After all these questions bounced around in her mind, Lily came to the conclusion that she would probably see Jack tonight, which made her feel excited and nervous and guilty. And as the rainy drive brought her closer and closer to her past, the cloud of guilt grew bigger and bigger, so she tamped down her excitement and told herself to get over it. She had to. She was a married woman, and a Godly one at that.

Just outside of town on an old dirt road stood the old white church perched on a hill, its tall steeple casting long shadows over the steps adorning the front entryway. It was a setting for a fairytale wedding. She signed the wedding book by the door and moved into the nave. Dark walnut pews gleamed in the dim glow of candlelight. White bows ornamented each pew. As she walked down the aisle she spotted Charlotte and Bob and scooted in to sit beside them. It was a beautiful ceremony, and listening to the wedding vows brought back memories of her own wedding with Damien, and guilt over coming so close to breaking those vows. She loved Damien. He had hurt her deeply earlier in their marriage, but his illness had changed him, and they were able to get their marriage back on track. They really were happy together again, and she really did love him. So, why then was she still looking around the church for Jack?

Lily arranged to meet Charlotte and Bob at the reception. The rain poured down as Lily ran out to her car. Too bad she didn't have four-wheel drive. She'd had to park in the grass by the little country church, and the grass was quickly turning to mud. Lily arrived at the reception unscathed however, and immediately found the open bar. She was sipping on her drink and looking for Charlotte's table when she ran into Anna.

She carefully reached out to hug Anna with one arm, in hopes of trying not to spill, but Anna had other ideas.

"Lily!" Anna screeched, tackling her, sloshing her drink all over the floor.

"Anna! How are you?" They stood for a while catching up on their time apart. "I'm going to sit with Charlotte and Bob," Lily told her, "Do you want to get a beer and sit down?"

"No, I can't. I'm fixin' to go to the other wedding."

"Really? Someone else getting married today?" Lily asked as she looked around the banquet hall for any other familiar people. "Anyone I know?"

"Yeah. Jack and Hailey." Anna looked at her speculatively. "I thought you knew."

Lily stopped cold. She was dumbfounded.

"Lily, I thought you knew. I'm sorry," Anna replied softly.

Lily's throat swelled as she fought back long-buried feelings. She cleared her throat. "Um, I didn't even know they were engaged," she tried to reply light-heartedly.

"So, you never got an invitation?"

"No."

"I'm sorry, Lily."

Lily held her head high mustering up as much dignity as she could find and said, "Would you tell him that I'm happy for him?"

"Yeah, I'll tell him."

They hugged their good-byes, then Lily threw her drink into the trashcan and left. The rain still poured outside, but somehow Lily managed to get her car out of the muddy gravel parking lot. She looked up and thanked God for aiding her in a quick escape.

The storm had not let up, and it was difficult to see through the windshield. The large raindrops pelted down so hard it sounded as if God were dumping truckloads of marbles on the roof of her car. She pulled out onto the dark road with her windshield wipers at full speed. The rain harmonized with the tears she could no longer hold back. Finally, she cried, and cried, and cried.

The once tight lid holding in years' worth of heartbreak, self-pity, and guilt all finally burst.

I'm such a hypocrite, Lord! Why am I crying over him? I'm married to a man I love. Now he's married too. I wanted him to be happy. So, why am I hurting so much? Please forgive me, God. I can't help how I feel. Driving down the road towards home, a home where she felt safe, wanted, and needed, but where she was also half empty and unfulfilled, Lily cried so grievously that between her tears and the dark and the rain, her vision was completely veiled. She began to slow down, but it was too late. When she rounded the curve in the dark road, a big truck pulled out in front of her. The last thing she remembered was a loud screeching sound and glass shattering.

Lily struggled as she slowly opened her eyes to the sound of beeping noises. Her vision blurred and her body felt heavy and tied down. She turned her throbbing head to the side and saw her mother asleep in an armchair. She looked around the room and saw Charlotte sitting to her other side. She was asleep too. Lily was so out of it that she didn't question her surroundings and closed her eyes again, but sometime later she woke to Jack's voice arguing with someone nearby.

"I need to see her," he pleaded.

"Jack, it's not a good idea. It would only upset her. Besides, Damien wouldn't like it."

Jack looked around, "Is he here?"

"He will be...once I get in touch with him." Lily's mom defensively folded her arms across her chest.

"You mean he doesn't know yet?" Jack asked.

Margaret looked down at the floor. "No, I haven't been able to reach him yet."

"Unbelievable!" Jack threw his hands up in the air and paced back and forth. He stopped in front of Lily's mom and took a deep breath. He knew he needed to calm down or she would never let him in that room. "I'm sorry. I'm just worried. Tell me, what do the doctors say?"

"She looks worse than she is. She only has a mild concussion, and nothing is broken. So, you don't need to worry, and you can go back to...your wedding."

Jack peered into Lily's room.

"Jaaaack," Lily managed to squeak out.

"Shhhhhhh, hush now. Save your strength," Charlotte told her.

"I wanna see Jack." Lily whispered in a weak voice. Charlotte got out of her chair and walked out to the hallway.

Charlotte and Jack made eye contact as she walked out of Lily's room. "I have to see her, Charlotte! She's asking for me!" Jack said.

"Let him go in, Margaret. She wants to see him," Charlotte said to Lily's mom.

"No," she countered. "Absolutely not!"

"She's awake now, and she knows he's here, so you might as well let him in, otherwise she'll get upset. You don't want that, do you?" Jack stood by helplessly waiting for Lily's mom to change her mind.

Margaret looked into the room then pointed at Jack. "But isn't he the reason she's in this mess?"

"No, Margaret. Lily just had an accident. It happens," she said as she gently placed her hands on Margaret's shoulders, trying to steer her away from blocking the door to Lily's hospital room. Margaret sighed but didn't stand in Jack's way any longer. "Let's leave them alone for a few minutes. Come on, I'll buy you a cup of coffee," Charlotte said. Margaret capitulated and went down to the cafeteria with her, leaving Jack alone with Lily.

Still donning his tuxedo, Jack eagerly stepped toward Lily's bed but stopped short at what he saw, wondering if she had felt the same way the day she'd walked into his hospital room all those years ago. The irony did not escape him, and he hated that he could not sit by her side the way she had so faithfully sat by his. She looked up at him, her blue eyes sparkling. Bandages wrapped her head, she was connected to an I.V., and she was as pale as a ghost except for the red scratches and dark bruises emerging on her face, neck, and arms. He swallowed the lump forming in his throat and sat down next to her, carefully reaching for her hand. It had been so long since he'd seen her, since they'd touched, but nothing had changed. The feelings flooded back to him. He may have hidden her deep in his heart, but seeing her again opened that door and brought all those old feelings back out. Oh God, how he wished she were his.

Lily looked at Jack sweetly and lightly squeezed his hand as he laced his fingers through hers. As she tried to talk, she started to cough, so Jack carefully helped her sit up and held her cup while she took a sip of water. Finally, the coughing subsided.

"Jack, why am I here?" she asked in a soft raspy voice. "Did we wreck the catering van?"

Jack stared at her incredulously. *Catering van? Oh no.* "Lily," he began slowly, "You were in an accident…but you're going to be okay…just some bumps and bruises."

A confused look came over Lily.

"Lily, what's the last thing you remember?"

"Um…being in the van with you—kissing me," she whispered. She reached over and touched his arm with her other hand. "I love you. I'm leaving Damien. We can be together now." Then her eyes closed and she fell back into unconsciousness. He fought back tears, but realizing he was alone, he finally just let them flow. A short time later, Jack heard Margaret and Charlotte in the hallway. He knew it was time to go. He leaned over and kissed Lily's forehead gently and whispered, "I love you too, Lily. Always." As he got up to leave he turned back and said, "Remember me." Then he walked out of her room, and out of her life.

Lily's amnesia was short-lived, but she didn't remember Jack coming to see her in the hospital, and Margaret and Charlotte thought it best not to tell her, so they swore each other to secrecy. Jack needed a chance to start his marriage off the right way, and Lily needed to get over him. Besides, it would hurt Damien who had stayed by her side ever since Lily's mom had finally reached him that next morning.

  A couple of days later, Lily was discharged from the hospital. She spent her recovery time watching Christmas movies, alone with her thoughts that would not leave her in peace. Lily wasn't sure what bothered her the most: the fact that Jack got married, or that he didn't care enough about her to invite her. It was a little embarrassing that Anna had received an invitation when she hadn't. After all, she and Jack had been so close at one time, in fact, a little too close. It felt just like being in junior high P.E. class when she was always picked last by the team captain. At any rate, she could not lose this feeling of heartache that consumed her. She wondered how she could possibly love two people so deeply at the same time. *The heart is a funny thing, and God has a funny sense of humor.* She was so tired of this unrelenting depression that had such a tight hold on her. It was getting late, and Damien was already asleep beside her. She turned off the TV and then turned to God who knew her thoughts, knew her heart, knew her sins, and loved her anyway.

> *God, I always thought that if you really loved someone then it would be impossible to love another. I was wrong. Why does this have to hurt so*

much? I want Jack to be happy. I've prayed for his happiness. I know that I can't be the one to make him happy. I want him to be able to have kids, a family, and I know I can't give that to him. And yet, my heart aches over it, that we aren't the ones getting married. I love my husband, and it would kill me to lose him, but right now Jack is the one I've lost, and it's killing me.

Though Lily's prayers helped, she was still sad, but she also felt in her heart that this is the way it was meant to be.

The next few days didn't bring Lily any more peace, however. She still carried a certain heaviness inside her heart. Unable to let it go, she kept trying to rationalize the reason she wasn't invited to Jack's wedding. She came up with three possible conclusions: Number one: Jack still loved her. Number two: Hailey knew about her. Number three: Her invitation got lost in the mail. But then there was one more conclusion that Lily just couldn't face: Jack just didn't care about her anymore.

A few days before Christmas, Lily decided to get out of the house to do some Christmas shopping. She thought that maybe that would brighten her mood. She shopped all day fighting the crowds and looking for just the right gifts for her family. By suppertime she was exhausted and headed home. Damien was lying on the couch when Lily walked into the house, and Baxter greeted her with rapid meows. His hungry voice. It was obvious no one had fed him yet today. Lily hung up her keys and put her purse on the table. She looked over at Damien who barely raised his head in greeting. Maybe it was time to go see the doctor. She put her packages in the closet and called the doctor's office. Luckily, they'd had a cancellation and would be able to squeeze him in that next morning. After examining Damien, they wasted no time in sending him over to the hospital for an MRI.

Christmas came around but no one was in good spirits. Even the end of *It's a Wonderful Life* couldn't bring Lily or Damien out of their doldrums. The doctor called and confirmed what Lily had suspected—Damien's cancer had come back. It was brain cancer this time. His surgery was scheduled for the first of the year. Then, radiation would follow. They had been down this road before, but could not fathom the immense difficulties it would bring this time around.

Chapter Fifteen

**The LORD will give strength to His people; the LORD will bless His people with peace.
Ps. 29:11**

Lily, her mom, and Damien's father waited for Damien to get out of surgery—brain surgery. His tumor, about the size of a quarter, took residence on the left side of his brain, the side controlling language-related brain activity. The plan was for Dr. Dyson to remove it along with some surrounding tissue.

Damien's father, Angelo, stood tall, broad-shouldered, a tower of physical strength. He gazed out of the window as birds flew from the roof of one building to another. Down below, people walked quickly to and fro while a young woman casually pushed a stroller down the sidewalk. The busyness of life going about its day made him realize that the world had not stopped just because his world had. Arms folded across his chest, he reached down into the depths of his memory back to a little boy sitting at the kitchen table eating canned spaghetti. He'd done the best he could for his only son, but when he'd lost his wife, he became lost himself. He'd worked most of the time and had left Damien to practically raise himself. They weren't close nevertheless, Damien was his only son, his only family, and he loved him. They'd had their fights, their struggles, and their distance. He knew he needed to change that.

"When was the last time you saw Damien's father?" Lily's mom asked as she glanced at him from across the quiet waiting room.

"Not since the wedding." Lily looked over at her solemn-looking father-in-law. She'd only met him the one time, the day of her wedding. His and Damien's relationship seemed strangled. Though Damien saw him once or twice a year, he never took Lily with him. Lily walked over to the window and stood by her father-in-law, putting her hand on his arm to comfort him. He placed his large calloused hand over hers. A tear trickled down his face as he stared straight ahead, avoiding her eyes. "He'll be okay. God will see him through this," Lily said. Angelo took a deep breath and let it out.

"I know, Lily." He patted her hand. "It's just that I watched his mother…I can't believe this is happening again." He squeezed her hand. "Damien's mother died of cancer…he was just a little boy."

"He told me," she answered quietly.

"His childhood wasn't the greatest. I had to work two jobs. He was in charge of his own meals. I…" Angelo moved over to a chair close to the window. He sat down hard and covered his face with his hands. He broke down. "Why can't God do this to me instead of him? It's not fair." He looked up at Lily. "I'm sorry. I should be encouraging you, comforting you. I don't mean to make things worse. I'm not helping much, am I?"

"Angelo, Dad…may I call you Dad?"

He smiled. "Yes. I would like that very much."

Lily sat down in the chair beside him. "Dad, God has a plan and a reason for everything."

"So you think God caused my son's cancer?" he asked quietly.

Lily paused before answering. "No. I don't believe God causes bad things to happen, but when they do happen, He uses them for good."

"But God could stop it. He could stop all the bad things from happening in the world, but He doesn't." He looked back toward the window.

"No, I guess He doesn't, but He could, and someday He will. You remember Adam and Eve?"

"Of course. I'm Catholic, remember?"

Lily bit back a smile. "By disobeying God, Adam and Eve invited sin into the world: sin, pain, and death. These things didn't exist until they did the one thing God warned them not to do."

"Eat the forbidden fruit." Angelo finished. "So why do you think they did it? Why didn't God stop them?" He looked back at Lily.

"Because God gave people free will. The will to choose Him or reject Him, the choice to sin or to be faithful to His word."

"Do you think God is punishing my son, Lily?"

Lily took a deep breath. She put her hand on Angelo's back and looked at him. "No. I think we just live in a flawed world full of sin, disease, and evil, and this world affects all of us, whether we're Christians or not."

"So the same rain falls on sinners and saints. Is that it then?"

"Yes, I guess so. In a nutshell."

"Then what good is any of it?"

"Angelo...Dad, God helps his children. Imagine all that He's protected us from that we don't even know about, and God did heal Damien before. Remember? And when bad things do happen to us, He gives us the strength to endure. I know He's given me strength."

Angelo looked over at his wise daughter-in-law. "Lily, you are one smart lady. My son is one lucky man. If he doesn't treat you right, you just let me know."

"There was a time, but not anymore. Damien is a Godly man. The Lord is pleased with him, and so am I."

A few hours had passed when Dr. Dyson finally emerged from surgery. They flocked over to him hungry for news. "Well, everything went well. We got the tumor and the surrounding tissue. I'm very pleased. He'll be in ICU tonight then I'll evaluate him in the morning. After that, we may move him to a regular room."

"That's great!" They all exclaimed at once.

"Lily," Dr. Dyson's tone of voice changed. "I want you to understand something. This surgery was to extend Damien's life."

"Right. Of course. We knew he would die without it."

Dr. Dyson drew a thoughtful breath. "Lily, the chance of recurrence is high."

Lily's eyes went wide. "What are you saying?"

"I'm saying that with treatment the cancer may still come back. In a few months or maybe a year, but without treatment it would be a matter of weeks."

"If he has treatment, the cancer will still come back? And in a few months?"

"I'm sorry, but yes, it's likely, but without treatment he may only have weeks."

"Weeks? For the cancer to come back?"

"Weeks to live, Lily." Lily couldn't believe what she was hearing. Her world came crashing down, again.

"So, it's not like before when he had colon cancer, treat it and then have a normal life."

"I'm afraid not. This is most likely a metastatic tumor caused by the colon cancer. Eventually, it will come back."

"Wha...what's the best-case scenario?" Angelo asked.

"I really can't answer that."

"Well, in your experience, what's the longest...the best we can hope for?"

Dr. Dyson shifted his weight. He looked uncomfortable. "Three years." He cleared his throat.

"So you're telling me that my son only has three years to live, tops?"

"I'm afraid so, but most likely not even that long. I'm so sorry. I thought the oncologist explained all this to you."

"Well, I guess he thought he did," Lily said. "He used the exact words you used earlier, that the surgery was to 'extend his life'. Unfortunately, he didn't elaborate." Lily crossed her arms over her chest, anger building inside her.

"Again, I'm so sorry. I know this is difficult, but Damien is here now, and he will be for a while longer. It's a blessing to have more time with him, isn't it? If the tumor hadn't been detected, Lily, he would've been gone within the month."

Lily was shocked. She just couldn't believe it. "Dr. Dyson, Damien doesn't know all this."

"I'll explain it to him in a few days, when he's able to really understand. Until then, you probably shouldn't say anything to him about it. He needs time to heal first." Lily nodded, thanked the doctor, then turned away and sat in a nearby chair, turning her back to the world. Angelo walked over and sat down next to her. She could hear her mother talking with the doctor, but she tuned them out. Her brain couldn't handle any more information just now. Angelo put his arm around her, and she leaned into him and cried. Her whole world was about to change and she was terrified.

A few days later, Damien was released from the hospital, and Lily and Angelo took him home to get him settled. Lily made sure he was comfortable on the couch and all of his needs were met before she left to go to the pharmacy for his prescriptions. Angelo stayed with his son to keep him company.

"You don't have to stay, Dad. I'll be fine."

"I'm not here for you, boy. I'm here for that sweet wife of yours. That young lady is worn out." Angelo sat in Damien's recliner and reached for the T.V. remote.

"Yeah, she looks pretty tired." Damien fluffed his pillow and tried to get comfortable.

"She loves you, ya know?" Angelo said, scrolling through the channels.

"I know. I'm lucky. Dad?"

"Yeah, Son." Angelo stared at the T.V.

"Did you know, she left me once."

Angelo's eyes went wide as he looked at his son. "Son, you never told me that!"

"Well, it was only for a week or so. Longest week of my life though. I was a real ass. I deserved it. Can't believe I treated her that way." He grabbed the glass of water Lily had left by his side and drank. He put the glass down on the end table with a thunk. He looked up at his dad, "But I've changed, and I've tried my best to be a good husband to her, but now I'm sick again and…"

"Son," Angelo leaned over and put his hand on Damien's shoulder, "that's not your doing. Lily is a good woman. She'll stand by you no matter what. You know, she reminds me of your mom."

"She does? I wish I'd had more time with her."

"Me too. Oh how I miss that woman. She was an angel."

"I miss her too sometimes. Wish I could remember more about her."

"Well, she sure did love you. The one regret she had about leavin' this world was leavin' you. She was so worried about you growing up without a mother." Angelo crossed his arms over his chest and stared back at the T.V. "She was right to worry. I couldn't do what a mother can do. I could barely be a father."

"Dad, I know you did the best you could."

"No, Son. I was lost without her. I was so focused on my own pain and misery. It consumed me. Your mom, she used to take you to Sunday school. She was a God-fearin' woman. I lacked faith back then. I should have taught you more about God."

"How's your faith now, Dad?"

Angelo smiled. "Well, I've grown a lot in the Lord. He's softened my heart, and I hope that you can forgive me and allow me to be a part of your life. A bigger part."

Warmth filled Damien's heart. He knew right then that he could forgive his father, for God had softened his heart too. "Dad, why is it that we figure out the secret of life just when it's starting to end?"

"Son, God used a bad situation for good. It's what He does. Besides, this isn't the end yet. But when it is, your eternity is safe, and someday, you'll be with your mom again."

"I know," Damien said, picturing his gentle mom in his memories. "That's the good part about all this. I can't wait to see her, but I hate leaving Lily…and you. This may not be the end yet, but I know it's the beginning of it." Damien looked across the room at the portrait of him and Lily hanging on the wall. "Dad, Lily doesn't deserve this. We should be happy and healthy with kids running around the house. We're young. Now, she's just become a care-giver for her dying husband, a husband who wasn't able to give her the children she always wanted."

"I feel bad for her too, Son, but one thing I've learned is that God takes care of his children, and Lily is special. He will reward her someday."

"I hope you're right, Dad. I hope you're right. I'm a little jealous, but I hope God gives her a good husband and a house full of kids…someday." Damien fell asleep a few minutes later, guilt and compassion for Lily in his heart, and prayers for her future on his lips. He asked God to take care of her and to someday give her the family that she'd always wanted, knowing that God listens intently to the prayers of His children, he fell into a peaceful sleep having unburdened his heart.

Chapter Sixteen

**But we do not want you to be uninformed, brethren, about those who are asleep, that you may not grieve,
as do the rest who have no hope.
1 Thess. 4:13**

After a few weeks, Damien's strength slowly came back, and Lily went back to work at the elementary school. He was glad she liked her job so much—he knew she didn't really like living here. It was nice enough, but Lily liked the small-town life, and compared to Chappell Hill, Bryan was not that. It weighed on him heavily that he hadn't been able to give her the kind of life she deserved. He'd been selfish back when he was healthy. Now that he wanted to focus on Lily's needs, he was unable. "God, please forgive me for letting her down, and please give me the strength to make her happy for just a little while," he prayed.

Lily walked into the house around 4:00 pm and dropped her school bag and purse on the table near the entryway. Her mouth immediately began to water from the aroma of roast luring her to the kitchen. "Dame, you cooked! Ahhhh…it smells wonderful! Thank you!" She reached up to kiss him on the cheek.

"Well, I was feeling pretty good this morning so I went to the store and bought a roast and some potatoes. I've been craving it lately."

"I didn't realize you knew how to cook a roast."

"I looked it up."

Lily walked over to the slow cooker and looked through the glass lid. "How long before it's ready?"

"Probably another hour. Go on and get comfortable and I'll pour you a glass of wine."

"Thanks, Dame—the kids were a little wiry today." Damien's increase in energy filled her with hope. Doctors didn't know everything. Maybe God would give them a miracle. The next few weeks gave Damien an energy he had not had in a very long time. He knew, however, that this time was fleeting, even if Lily didn't want to face it. He decided to make the most of it with one goal in mind: to make this time happy for Lily, to give her special memories of their marriage together, to hopefully make her forget all the bad ones. He walked up behind her and put his arms around her.

"Let's go to the ranch this weekend," he said.

"Really? You can't stand the country. Are you sure you're up to it?"

"Yes. I'm sure. I'm feeling good these days. Besides, I think I should give this country thing another chance. I wanna see what you see in it."

Lily was thrilled and they made plans to stay at her family's ranch that weekend. Saturday morning, they woke up early and went outside to watch the sun rise. They swung on the porch swing while her mom's cats cozied up on the porch pillows and watched them.

"It's beautiful here, Lily. How come you never bring me out here?"

"Uh!" Lily gently slapped him on the arm. "I've been trying for years!"

Damien laughed then put his arms around her. "I love you, you know that, right?" She nodded. The swing rocked them back and forth as he kissed her and held her hand, just enjoying being together. The next few weeks, they came out to the ranch several more times. Lily's mom was thrilled that Damien was making her daughter happy. Unfortunately, Damien's next doctor's appointment would result in the beginning of the end of his good days.

After his surgery, he'd had the recommended whole-brain radiation. Unfortunately, no one had explained to them that this brought its own death sentence, and this was only the beginning. He'd been taking a steroid since his surgery, which helped to increase his strength, but the doctor's appointment had resulted in the tapering off of that medication, which ultimately led to weakness and debilitation. Steroids were not something that could be taken long term, especially for someone with brain issues. The long-term side effects included seizures, stroke, and violent outbursts, and the list went on and on. The risk of continued use was just too high. As a result, Damien lost his strength as the dose decreased. With his strength in decline, he would not be able to work, and within the year, Lily had to quit her job to care for him.

   Lily and Damien had naively believed that surgery and radiation would heal him, at least for a short time, even though they were warned the cancer would come back. However, they were not prepared for the progressing side effects of the radiation, which were beginning to emerge now that he was getting off the steroids. From here on, the negative effects would only increase. Necrosis and atrophy of the brain diminished Damien's abilities one by one. Lily stood helpless as she watched her husband's strength waste away. As his cognitive function slowly declined he would lose the ability to complete tasks such as balancing his checkbook or fixing things around the house. By the second year, the doctors were surprised that his cancer had not come back, but he had difficulty using the T.V.'s remote control, and after several falls, he had no choice but to use a walker to get around. His short-term memory was affected, but his long-term memory was still sharp—a small consolation. He still knew everyone and understood what was going on around him. It was a relief to Lily that though his abilities had declined, her husband was still her husband. He had not developed Alzheimer's disease, but his brain was losing the ability to tell his body what to do. It was as if he was rapidly aging right before her very eyes.

Lily spent as much time with Damien as possible. They lived on disability payments and help from their parents. She became his full-time caregiver, and she dreaded the day when she would not be enough. She feared having to move him to a nursing home, but as fate would have it, that fear never came to pass.

One morning, Lily woke to the sound of the alarm clock beeping. She hit the button to quiet it, sat up, and slipped into her house shoes. She looked over at Damien noticing the white hair that had grown back in place of his beautiful dark shiny locks. He had his back to her, still asleep. She shuffled into the kitchen to perform her morning tasks then poured herself a cup of coffee and headed back into the bedroom to retrieve her bible.

Walking into the bedroom, with the morning light shining through the window, she could see that something was horribly wrong. Damien seemed to be asleep, but his eyes were wide open. "Oh God." Her hand flew up to her heart. Her coffee spilled all over the floor. "God, please, no!" She ran to his side. He was still breathing, but she couldn't wake him. She ran to the phone and dialed 9-1-1 and then kneeled by the bed to pray. The first responders showed up within minutes, followed by EMS. Lily continued to pray as they loaded her unresponsive husband into the ambulance and took off toward St. Joseph's hospital right around the corner from their subdivision. At the hospital, Lily was forced to wait in the waiting room alone in complete despair. She dialed her mom's number. "Mo-m?" She could barely choke out the word.

"Lily?"

"Mom," Lily began to cry.

"Lily! What is it? Are you okay?"

"Mom...I need you." Lily could barely breathe; she could not keep the sobs at bay. "We're at St. Joe's...it's Damien."

"I'm on my way! Hang on Lily. Just pray."

"I am." Lily hung up and sank to the floor and cried. Her heart was breaking, shattering into a thousand pieces. She began to pray in earnest. Her mom arrived within the hour and told her Angelo was on his way. According to the doctor, Damien had had a stroke sometime in the night. It was severe. He would not bounce back from this. God had given them more time, but all of a sudden, now their time had run out.

They all knew the end was near. Damien was put under Hospice Care. He could have remained in the hospital, but they decided to bring him home. He clung to life for nearly three more weeks with Lily by his side. Angelo stayed with her, relieving her so that she could sleep. Her mom stayed also. The Hospice nurse would come daily to check on him and to administer pain medication. There they sat, taking turns, day by day, night by night, never once leaving his side. Lily thought she was prepared to let him go. He was, after all, living with one foot in this world and the other in the next.

    But when Damien took his last breath, and neglected to take another, Lily, still holding his hand, broke down and wept. Her husband, her partner in life, her best friend was gone. Still, she had hope because she knew she would one day see him again.

Chapter Seventeen

**After you have suffered for a little while, the God of all grace, who called you to His eternal glory in Christ,
will Himself perfect, confirm, strengthen and establish you.
1 Pet. 5:10**

Weeks passed and this year's flowers were in bloom—nature's call for a new beginning. Still, Lily didn't feel the usual carefree feelings of spring but instead was weighed down by the cold bitterness of an unrelenting winter. Nevertheless, it seemed the world was telling her it was time for her to move on, to make a new start, and to create a new beginning.

Lily lay on her swing in the backyard gazing up at the clouds. When she and Damien had first started dating, that was one of the things they enjoyed together. Happy in their newfound love, like little children they would lie on their backs in the grass, holding hands, staring up at the clouds, imagining shapes that weren't really there.

WALKER LANE

Damien had been gone for almost a month now. The funeral had been somber and sad—not a celebration of life, but a goodbye to a difficult life, and a life cut way too short. Angelo had stayed for a while to help with the funeral arrangements and to fix some things around the house, but now he was gone too. The house was too quiet so Lily liked to sit outside and listen to the birds sing. They always had a song, no matter what was going on down here below. Oh to have wings, to be able to just pick up and fly away...

Baxter hopped up on the swing and curled up next to her, seeking his own comfort. He missed Damien too. Lily gently stroked his fur as she let relaxation take hold of her. She had not been able to sleep at night without her husband's warm body next to her, and in her exhaustion, the back-and-forth creaking motion of the swing lulled her into a deep sleep. Sometime later she awoke to *him*, a ghost from her past saying her name. Was she dreaming? Then she felt his gentle touch on her face. Somewhere between the fantastical world of sleep and consciousness she thought, *What a sweet dream*.

Jack hung up the phone with Anna and typed the address she'd given him into the GPS. After the hour-long drive to Bryan, Jack arrived at Lily's little brown brick house wondering if he should be here at all. He noticed the difference between this house and the one in which she had lived in

Chappell Hill. No red shutters. Very plain. He released a long swoosh of air. *Would she even want to see me?* But how could he not see her? How could he stay away from her at a time like this? He'd been out of town and hadn't found out about Damien's death until after the funeral, and the thought of Lily facing such a thing alone tore him up inside. He pulled in behind Lily's car in the driveway. He rang the doorbell, but no one answered. Feeling like a peeping Tom, he peered into the living room window and could see her purse lying on the chair. *That's strange. Where could she be? Maybe she's asleep...or...* A slight panic started to set in. *Or maybe something's wrong.*

    Jack decided to take a chance and walk around to the back door and knock. He peeked into the kitchen window. The light was on and there was a half empty glass of wine sitting on the counter. Just then he caught a swift movement out of the corner of his eye, startling him. He breathed a sigh of relief when he realized it was just Lily's cat jumping down from the swing. There she was, lying there like Sleeping Beauty. Oh how he wished he could be her prince. He quietly walked over to her and softly said her name. She made a small noise and turned a bit, but remained in slumber. She must be exhausted. He hesitated to wake her. Looking so peaceful, so beautiful, he couldn't resist watching her. Temptation winning out, he just had to touch her. He reached out and gently swept aside the wisps of hair that had fallen over her eyes. She began to stir again, and he pulled back quickly. He really didn't think he should wake her, so he went over to the chair and sat down, feeling a little like a stalker, but knowing he could not leave without speaking to her.

After a little while, Lily began to stir again. She cried out something unintelligible in her sleep and tossed around so much the swing began to flip, but then she felt someone's hands steady it. He called out her name, telling her it was okay, that it was just a dream. She opened her eyes and saw Jack, of all people, which made her believe she was still dreaming. In fact, she *had* been dreaming about him. In her dream, he'd been walking away from her with Damien at his side. She'd lost them both. But here he was, right in front of her, his yearning eyes staring into her own. He had his hand behind her head, his fingers tangled in her hair, and he was on his knees holding onto the swing. Her watery eyes looked up at him, then without preamble, she buried her face into his warm neck and sobbed. The smell of him brought memories flooding back to her, memories of being in his arms, warm and protected.

Desperate to ease her pain, Jack wrapped his arms around Lily in a cocoon of protection. He held her there for a brief eternity, feeling as though this was where he was meant to be, but powerless to remain. After a while her sobs quieted. He helped her sit up and sat next to her on the swing. They needed no words at this moment even though it had been years since they'd last parted. She leaned down and put her head in his lap and he laced his fingers through her hair gently. His foot motioned the swing back and forth slowly as he shushed her tears with empty promises that everything would be all right. They remained that way for some time wrapped in peace, comfort, and a sublime feeling of rightness. Jack's heart was torn. He didn't want to hurt Lily. He didn't come here to add to her pain, he just wanted to see her. Hearing of Damien's death, knowing she was alone and hurting, wild horses couldn't have kept him from her. Not even the one to whom he was married.

As they swung together in that gentle rhythm, he gently stroked her hair. She eventually sat up and looked at him questioningly. His arm fell around her, holding her loosely. He looped his thumb through her back belt loop as if it were the most natural thing in the world, as if she belonged to him, and she would have had fate not been so cruel. They looked into each other's eyes, their lips only inches apart, and like a moth to a flame, she leaned in and kissed him, gentle and searching, but then the heat of their bodies betrayed them. He returned her kiss with fervor, wrapping his arms around her in a tight embrace as if to never let her go. Together they stood from the swing in perfect harmony holding on as if parting would mean sure death. He placed his hand on her lower back, her heat nearly searing him, and pulled her into his realm, an existence created for only the two of them. He could feel her heart beating against his, her hips pressing into him, her soul binding to his soul. He picked her up and she wrapped her legs around him. Holding her tight he began to walk toward the back door, but stopped, knowing he could not take her in Damien's house. His body would not be so easily appeased, however, so he walked her over to a soft grassy spot in the yard and gently laid her down. Hovering over her, he sensed her body responding to every inch of his. They kissed with a passion that neither of them had felt since they were last in each other's arms, feeling they would die if they ever had to part. But they would have to part. The news that Jack came to tell her would see to that. But oh, she was impossible to resist. The hunger in her kisses devoured him and any self-control he might've once contained. His hips moved into rhythm with hers, and they kissed unrelentingly. He ran his hand down the length of her and back up to the button at her waist. Tempted as he was to continue, it would be the one move that would make or break him, the one move that would change his life and leave him in a pit of unforgiving, relentless guilt. No, he could not, would not, do that to Lily. He wasn't able to give her what he so desperately wanted. He was not free. Jack was 100 percent man, but he was still a Godly man, and God had a funny way of showing up to remind him. So Jack rolled over, leaving the heat and headiness of Lily's body—that body and soul that he'd wanted to possess for so long. He wanted her as his, to belong to him only, forever, but he'd messed up, and now he wasn't free to give himself to her.

"Jack, I'm sorry, I shouldn't have started this," he heard Lily say, breaking up his thoughts. They both sat up reluctantly and then faced each other.

"Lily, *I'm* sorry." He looked deep into her forgiving eyes and held both of her hands in his. "Lily, I have to say this before I lose my chance to ever be able to say it again… I love you." His fingers lightly touched her cheek. He gazed intently into her eyes. "I love you with my whole heart, my entire being. You and I were meant to be together, but we've…"

"We've always had the worst timing, right?" She smiled a little and squeezed his hand. "Jack, I've loved you for a long time. Ever since that night you protected me at the restaurant when that jerk grabbed me. You were my hero then, and you are my hero now. Showing up at exactly the moment I needed you most." She took a deep breath and looked down at the grass, breaking off the smooth green strands piece by piece, seeming to have gone back in time to another world. "I stayed with Damien because I made a commitment to him, and he needed me. It's what God wanted me to do. So, I did it." She threw each strand into a small pile, then paused and looked up at the sky. Jack kept silent sensing she had more to say.

"He changed a lot, and our marriage improved. He treated me well after I took him back, and I found that I still loved him. But you, dreams of you…plagued me for years." She shook her head as if to dispel the memories and looked at him intently. "May God forgive me, you were never out of my heart, not for a second, and you were never far from my thoughts. I know I let you down when I went back to Damien, but I had to go."

"I know Lily. You were right to go back to him. I never blamed you for that. In fact, your loyalty and commitment only made me love you more because it just shows what a good person you are."

"Good person? Look what I'm doing. What we're doing. You're married! I was married. I don't feel like a good person."

He had no words for her sudden outburst of self-indignation. In the eyes of the Lord, neither of them was good. "If only I hadn't married Hailey." He looked down at her tiny little piles of green grass. "It's not that I don't love her, but it's not the same. Does that make sense?" Lily nodded her head. "But now, now I'm not available to you, especially when you need me most."

"Look at me, Jack," she said with determination in her eyes, "I'm going to be okay. God will help me get through this. The house is quiet, and yes, I'm lonely, but I know God will carry me through."

Jack nodded his head and guiltily remembered the news he'd come to tell her. Regret already filled his heart for the words he had yet to even say. "Lily, I have to tell you something, but I don't want to hurt you," he said, realizing the cruelty of his impending words, knowing he was just stacking blocks of pain upon pain. "I don't want to make everything worse for you or add to your suffering, but I need you to hear this from me."

"What is it? I can handle it. I think." She smiled reassuringly.

"Lily..." he paused.

"What? Spit it out."

He steadied himself, for he knew this would not be easy for her to hear. "Hailey is gonna have a baby. I'm gonna be a dad." He was so happy and proud at becoming a dad, but telling her was killing him, especially when he saw the look on her face as his words sank in.

At this moment, Jack's news was too much for Lily to bear. All that she employed to hold herself together collapsed. She felt punctured and drained. She and Damien could not have children, and now with no husband, having a child was out of the question, and that's what stabbed Lily in the heart all over again. She'd always wanted to be a mom, and now it seemed she probably would never get the chance. Losing Damien was hard, losing Jack over and over again was devastating each time it happened, but losing the children she would never have left an empty hole in Lily's heart that could never be filled by any man. Nevertheless, if this was what God chose for her, she would not question it.

Tears filled her eyes, betraying her. Jack wrapped his arms around her tightly, rocking her gently back and forth. He stayed as long as time would allow, but he knew he had to go. He knew he had to let *her* go. They walked to his truck hand in hand, not wanting this last moment together to end, not wanting to let each other go, but knowing they must. She stood up on her tiptoes to reach his lips and gently kissed him and said, "No matter what, you will always be in my heart, and maybe, just maybe, God will find a way for us to be together someday."

    Jack nodded, hoping that could be true. "I love you, Lily, always… always. Please don't ever forget that." Jack's heart shattered as he climbed into his truck and drove away. He watched Lily wave to him through his rear-view mirror. Though the words were never spoken, his heart called out to hers, *Remember me.*

Chapter Eighteen

But the Lord stood with me, and strengthened me.
2 Tim. 4:17

Kabooooooom! Thunder shook the house. Lily bolted straight up in bed, jolted out of a deep sleep. Her heart pounded. Gasping for breath, she grabbed her chest and forced herself to breathe slowly and deeply to calm her racing heart. The next minute her alarm clock signaled it was time to wake up. She was still trembling from the loud noises of the storm, plus she'd been having nightmares. And now, Lily realized, there was no one to offer comfort when she woke up screaming. A huge sense of loss engulfed her. *I'm alone. I have no one to take care of. No one to take care of me.* For the first time in a long time, Lily didn't know her purpose. She was lost on a sea of calm waters.

Baxter appeared at the side of her bed and looked up at Lily, meowing with concern. He missed him too. He hopped up onto the bed and stepped into Lily's lap. She hugged him tightly feeling so grateful for his presence. The house was quiet —too quiet. Her usual routine was staunched with the reality that she now had very few clothes to wash and no one to cook for. It had been difficult learning how to cook for only two people, but one? What was the point? She didn't even have a job to ready herself for, no means of escape, nothing to distract her from her loneliness. Due to Damien's generous life insurance policy, she wouldn't have to go back to work for a long time. However, she needed something to do, she needed to be productive. She couldn't sit around the house all day feeling sorry for herself or she'd go crazy.

Lily made coffee, took a shower, and got dressed. She knew she should fix breakfast but didn't feel like eating. Her heart hurt, and a big rock took residence in her stomach. She took a sip of her coffee. The warm liquid ran down her throat, warming her. She looked around at the house she'd shared with Damien. The old Formica countertops cast a yellowed hue on the wall where her and Damien's engagement portrait hung. Who were those people? They looked so young and healthy, full of hope. It hadn't been that many years ago. Lily wondered if everyone's life moved so fast, had so much tragedy as hers. She knew she was heading towards a pity party, and she needed to snap out of it. But being in this house wasn't helping matters. They'd moved here to be closer to Damien's doctors. It had been a necessity. If she'd ever liked this house, the years here had ruined it, years filled with grief, illness, and hopelessness. They'd never had much of a chance to be happy here.

The phone rang breaking into Lily's dismal thoughts. It was her long-time friend Allison, and once upon a time roommate, who lived in Florida. They chatted for nearly an hour catching up on life. It was good to hear from her. After they ended their phone conversation with promises to keep in touch, Lily stared out of the window at the gray rainy day. *I wish the sun would come out.* At that moment, Lily made a snap decision. It was time for a drastic change. She picked up the phone book scanning through the yellow pages then landed on the number she was looking for. With shaking hands and a strong resolve she dialed the number. A feeling that she hadn't had in years filled her— excitement.

Lily had just finished painting the last wall in the house when her phone rang. It was the realtor. "Yes. Great! Thank you. I appreciate all your help. I'll be out by the end of next week, and then you can start showing the house. Yes, you will be able to reach me on my cell phone, but I'll be moving out of state. Okay. Thanks. Talk to you soon."

Lily walked outside to the water hose and washed out the paint supplies. Baxter ran up to the water to get a drink. "Well, Baxter, are you ready for a new adventure?" She waited for a response, but he was too interested in the colorful splashing water droplets landing on her feet. For the first time in a long time, Lily felt excited about life. It was time to start over, and what better place than sunny Florida. People always said you could never go back, but that was a ridiculous notion. She was going back all right, back to Florida, back to the same apartment complex where she'd lived before her dad's unexpected death, and most likely back to the same line of work—waitressing. Sure it wasn't glamorous, but it would get her out of the house and pay the bills, so she wouldn't really need to spend any more of Damien's life insurance money. She would find a job when she got there, after she got settled. It wouldn't be difficult to find a restaurant job. It never was.

Lily spent the next week sorting through her things, donating most of her stuff to charity, and packing up the few belongings she wanted to take with her. Minimal stuff, minimal memories. Finally on Friday, she loaded up the small moving trailer and loaded Baxter into his cat carrier, placing it in the bed of her new pickup truck. He would be happier riding back there. He hated riding inside. As long as it didn't rain, he would be fine. She was so thankful for Baxter. As long as he was with her, she would never really be alone.

Lily hopped in her truck, said a quick prayer, and with a smile in her heart took off down the road that would lead her towards a new life. A few hours later, with a weary heart, Lily waved goodbye to her home state and crossed the long bridge in Louisiana. She loved Texas, but right now, she needed a big change. The immense size of the Lone Star State could not compare to the enormity of her guilt and sorrow, and as long as she was there, she would never find escape. So, she traded in her boots for a pair of flip-flops and drove on to a new adventure.

REMEMBER ME

The two days on the interstate heading east were uneventful. Lily's worrying mom would be relieved. She hadn't wanted Lily to make the drive alone, but what choice did she have? She *was* alone. After nearly twenty hours on the road and a stay at a roadside hotel, tall palm trees and a warm salty breeze greeted Lily upon her arrival. The Palm Beach Gardens apartment complex office was closed, so Lily drove on to Jupiter to see if there was a room available at the resort where she'd once worked so many years ago.

Lily pulled into the parking lot of the Jupiter Resort and parked in front of the pink oleanders adorning the curb. Unexpectedly, a harsh memory hit her, and she froze behind the wheel. The last time she had set foot in this place was the day her father died.

The sun was shining as Lily sang with her windows down and the radio up on her way to work at the Jupiter Resort. She was scheduled to work at the pool bar today and had to get there at 10:00 a.m. to set up. She was in an especially good mood this morning, singing along with the words of a Don Henley song. She pulled into the parking lot where bright pink blooms greeted her all around. She quickly clocked in and got to work setting up her tables for the busy lunch shift ahead. Just after she'd gotten started, one of the other servers came up to her and told her that she had a phone call inside. Lily was curious as she walked to the office. Her manager, Diane, was very quiet as she handed her the phone.

"Hello."

"Lily, I tried to call you on your cell phone but you didn't answer."

"Allison? I'm at work. What's up?"

"You have to come home."

"Come home? I can't. I'm at work. They aren't just gonna let me leave for no reason. What's wrong?"

"Just come home."

Diane took the phone from Lily. After a few words, she hung up and turned to her. "Go home, Lily. I'll get your shift covered."

"Diane? What's wrong?" Lily could feel panic taking over.

"Just go home. Allison will explain when you get there."

"You aren't gonna tell me?" Diane just looked at her. "Please, don't leave me wondering, thinking the worst. What is it?" Diane placed her hand on Lily's and shook her head. Lily didn't wait for an answer. She grabbed her purse and hurried out to her car. All kinds of horrible thoughts went through her head, so she began to pray, "Lord, I don't know what's going on, but please don't let it be anything too bad." She arrived home and walked into the apartment that she shared with her best friend Allison. She held the phone out to Lily. Lily looked at her questioningly, and took the receiver.

"Hello."

"Lily."

"Mom? Hey, what's goin' on? Everything okay? You sound upset."

"Lily, it's your dad."

"Wha…"

"They think… he had a heart attack."

Lily took a deep breath. This was bad. But heart attacks are treatable, right? "Okay, what hospital is he in?"

"Lily…"

"What? Where is he?" Silence was the only response. Lily's arms went numb. "Mom? Mom? Where is he? Tell me, please tell me!" She yelled into the phone.

"Lily, there was nothing they could do." Her mom began to sob.

Lily could feel the blood draining from her face. A wave of nausea struck her and she felt faint. She couldn't believe what her mom was saying.

"Honey," her mom said between sobs, "the new ranch-hand found him in front of the house. He did CPR but it was already too late."

"Too late? He's…? He's dead? Mom! Please, please don't tell me he's dead! He can't be! He can't be!"

"Lily, I'm so sorry."

Lily's legs gave way and she crumpled to the floor. Allison ran to her and put her arms around her. She took the phone and spoke to Lily's mom and hung up. Then she did the only thing she could, hold onto Lily while she wept.

An hour later, they were in the car headed to the airport. Allison drove while Lily stared out of the window trying to make sense of her world that had just turned completely upside down. What would they do without him? He was their rock. Lily remembered the last time she saw her father, the day she moved to Florida. They all went to church together then out to lunch at her dad's favorite steakhouse one last time. She tried to pretend that everything was okay, but Lily was breaking up inside at the thought of leaving her parents. She excused herself from the table and went into the rest room and cried. She knew she was being silly so she told herself she could come back for a visit the next month. She wished she had kept that promise, but life had gotten in the way, and she'd been too busy to make the trip. As the three of them walked out to the parking lot, she hugged her teary-eyed mother, then her father. He stepped back to look at her one last time with unbidden emotion. He pointed his finger at her and as his deep voice cracked, said, "Call your mother every week!"

Lily hugged him and laughed then saluted him and said, "Yes sir." Pulling out of the parking lot, she looked into her rearview mirror at her father ambling to his truck, dressed in his Sunday suit. Oh, her heart. As she turned the corner and lost sight of her dad, Lily finally released her tears and sobbed.

Through her rearview mirror… that was the last time she ever laid eyes on her father. Lily looked through her rearview mirror again at her reflection. She wiped the tears that had unexpectedly spilled down her face. After all these years, grief still had a way of coming out of nowhere to hit you. But today was a happy day, a day in which she was starting her brand new life. No more death, no more disease. A life of fair weather and simplicity. This was not a day to be remembering sad things, so Lily took her unwelcome memory and placed it in a tiny box deep in her heart.

She grabbed her overnight bag and her cat carrier and headed for the front desk. She was in luck. They had one room available. It was pricey, but it had an ocean view, so she and Baxter checked in. When she walked into the room, moonlight, sparkling like diamonds off the ocean waters, beckoned her through the glass. "Oh Baxter! Isn't it amazing!" She put her things down on the bed and opened the sliding glass door leading to the balcony. A strong ocean breeze lifted her hair and wrapped around her in a warm embrace. She stepped out onto the balcony, inhaling the salty sea air and realized that finally, she could breathe again.

Chapter Nineteen

**God is in the midst of her,
she will not be moved;
God will help her
when morning dawns.
Ps. 46:5**

Lily took full advantage of her weekend stay at the beautiful resort where she had once worked. Diane was no longer employed there, nor did she recognize any of the other servers, but it had been years since she'd run these floors, so she was not surprised. She attended a church service on the beach on Sunday morning, visited her friend Allison, who was very excited that her long lost friend had returned, then spent the rest of the day reading and napping by the water. It had been a wonderful day, and she realized that today she hadn't cried. That today was the first day she had not felt her heart breaking, that today really was the first day of the rest of her life. This choice had been the right one.

She felt like she was on vacation, and she hated to leave, but Monday she checked out of her ocean front room and drove to the apartment complex to pick up her key to her new home, a one-bedroom apartment on the second floor. It wasn't fancy, but it had a balcony overlooking a pond and beautifully manicured grounds. It also had a swimming pool and exercise room, there was a shopping center close by, and she was only a five-minute drive to Juno beach. Other than the resident alligator napping by the pond, this place was perfect.

Loose strands of hair wisped across Lily's face. Hands on hips, and a determined glare, she stared into the back of the trailer realizing that she did not have the muscles to get her furniture up the stairs. Bob and Charlotte had helped her load it from her house into the moving trailer, but she had not thought about the fact that her new apartment was on the second floor and she had no muscle-bound friends here. She looked over at a little girl drawing chalky pictures on the sidewalk in the doorway of the apartment directly below hers. The little girl stared at her, but smiled. Lily smiled back.

Dropping her chalk, she walked over to Lily, eying her. "I'm Julie. I'm seven. Are you new?"

"Yes. I am. I'm supposed to move up there." She pointed to her open door at the top of the stairs. "But I don't know how on earth I'm gonna get this furniture up there by myself." Just then Baxter appeared in Lily's doorway and meowed.

"Ohhhhhhh, you have a kitty! What's its name?"

"His name is Baxter, and he just rode all the way from Texas to be your neighbor." Lily smiled at the little girl.

"Texas? Wow! Texas is so big! Do you know any cowboys?" Julie asked with wide eyes, but without waiting for an answer exclaimed, "I love kitties! Can I pet him?"

"Well, why don't we ask your mom first?"

"Okay, but she's at work. Can I ask my uncle?"

"Uh, sure."

The little girl ran back into her apartment. A few minutes later she came out dragging a reluctant, but handsome, twenty-something-year-old of the male persuasion behind her. Sun-streaked hair and ocean-blue eyes, he towered above Lily at around six feet tall. His tan skin looked as if he spent plenty of time at the beach. Lily was staring at him when he looked up at her. Their eyes locked in a moment of instant mutual attraction. "Oh boy," Lily said under her breath as she looked away quickly.

"Uncle Jayme, this is our new neighbor and she has a cat Baxter and I wanna pet him is it okay?" The little girl toppled out her plea.

"Um, let's not be rude, Julie. Just a minute, okay?" Jayme walked over to Lily and held out his hand to shake hers. "Hi. I'm Jayme."

Lily reached for his hand and shook it. It was warm. "Uh...Lily. It's nice to meet you. I'm moving in upstairs." She released his hand and unnecessarily pointed upwards, shifting her weight from side to side.

Jayme looked up the stairs, looked at Lily, and then looked at the furniture in the back of the trailer. "Is uh, your husband helping you with all the heavy lifting?"

Lily stuck her thumbs in her back pockets and rocked back on her heels. She was starting to sweat. "Um, no. It's just me."

The corner of his mouth ticked upward. "Well, tell you what…how about if I help you with some of this stuff while Julie pets your cat? Would that be okay?"

Lily smiled and nodded her head. "Yes. I would love some help. Thank you."

Lily, Jayme, and Julie spent the next hour emptying out her moving trailer and arranging her furniture. Baxter and Julie got along famously. So did Lily and Jayme. During the course of all the heavy lifting, going up and down the stairs, and many water breaks, Lily discovered that Uncle Jayme actually lived about twenty miles down the road in Hobe Sound, and Julie lived downstairs with her widowed mom who works at an ocean-front bar and grill called Uncle Nick's. The last three boxes out of the truck were labeled BOOKS. Jayme carried them up the stairs for her while she watched from the open doorway.

"Are all these boxes really full of books?" He struggled as he carried the last one up the stairs.

"Yep. I love to read. You?"

"Me? Read? Uh, no. Not my thing. It's too…um…" He dropped the heavy box to the floor, wiped his brow with his sleeve, and sat down on the top step where a nice breeze was blowing.

"Calming?" Lily raised an eyebrow.

"Uh, sure. Yeah that. Only, *calm* is boring." He looked at her with a twinkle in his eye and ran his fingers through his thick hair.

"Well, sometimes *boring* fits the bill." Lily went to the fridge and came back out, handing Jayme a cold beer. "Beer?" she asked.

"Thanks," he said, taking it from her. "I suppose, sometimes. What's your genre?"

"Ya know, romance, Christian novels."

"Christian novels? That's a thing?"

"Oh yeah! Actually, some can be quite the thriller." She sat down next to him on the steps to watch Julie play with Baxter.

"Thriller? Really? How's that?"

"The novels relating to end times events can definitely keep you up at night. Pretty scary stuff."

"You mean like the end of the world, apocalypse, that sort of thing?"

"Yeah. You should read one sometime. You can borrow one of mine."

"Uh, no thanks. I don't believe in that stuff."

"Oh, okay." Lily looked down at her toes while awkwardness grew between them.

"Don't get me wrong. I believe in God, but all that other stuff just sounds like science fiction to me."

"And you don't like science fiction?"

"I like *Star Wars*." He grinned, and then nudging her with his arm, briefly leaned into her.

"*Star Wars*, huh? I can work with that." She turned before he could notice the blush creeping up her face.

So far, this move was going well. Lily already had new friends.

That night, Lily called her mom to check in and then unpacked and organized while Baxter investigated his new surroundings. She hung her shower curtain, put her towels and toiletries away, and had a pizza delivered. *The ballad of starting over.* That was the one good thing about not living in the country, pizza delivery. No one delivered anything out in the country except the mailman. Later after supper, Lily was unpacking her books when she came across Damien's bible. She held it to her chest for a moment then opened it to the book of Isaiah. In verse 41:10 she read, "Fear thou not; for I am with thee..." then an envelope fell out onto her lap. It had her name on the front in Damien's shaky handwriting. A sharp breath escaped her. Inside was a letter. She opened it slowly and began to read.

> *Lily,*
> *I left this letter for you in my bible because I didn't want you to find it until after I'm gone, to give us one last good-bye. We have had some tough years, you and I. They were mostly tough for you, and it was mostly because of me. I'm sorry. I'm sorry for the way I treated you before*

I got sick. I was selfish. I was self-serving. I know you forgave me, but I never quite forgave myself. You stood by me through it all, through my cheating, my illness, and my dying on you. I'm so sorry. For me, dying is the easy part. Going to Heaven will be awesome. However, leaving you is the hard part. I don't want to be away from you, and I don't deserve to be happy in Heaven while you are here on earth suffering with whatever else life throws at you. I have so many regrets. I regret wasting precious time that I could have spent making you happy. I regret being unable to give you children and that it was my fault that you didn't get to be a mom. Trust me when I say I never meant to ruin your life. I love you, and because of you, I found God again. Without you, I was destined for a bad place. Because of you, my soul was saved. You brought me to God. Thank you. Don't cry for me. I'm the lucky one. I got to be loved by you, and now I get to go hang out with Jesus. Thank you for all that you did for me. Thank you for loving me. Now, go find happiness. I will always be with you, watching over you.

Always my love,

REMEMBER ME

Damien

Tears streamed down Lily's face as she rolled onto her side and cried. She missed Damien, and her whole body felt it. After a while, she carefully folded the letter and put it back in its place in his bible, then placed his bible on the bookshelf. She prayed to God for strength, then went to bed and cried into her pillow until she fell asleep.

Chapter Twenty

**Do not call to mind the former things, Or ponder things of the past. Behold, I will do something new,
Now it will spring forth;
Will you not be aware of it?
I will even make a roadway in the wilderness, Rivers in the desert.
Isa. 43:18-19**

A few days later, unpacked and completely settled in, Lily decided to hit the gym and then head to the pool. She was basking in the sun and reading a romance novel that she had picked up at a nearby grocery store when she heard laughing and splashing. Lily looked up to see Julie, her young neighbor sitting on the steps of the pool splashing her mom who was sitting on the edge. Nancy, Julie's mom, waved to Lily and then turned back to watch Julie's antics.

"Miss Lily's here, Julie," Nancy said to her daughter.

Julie turned around and yelled, "Miss Lily, come get in the pool!"

"Okay, be there in a minute." Lily folded down the corner of her page then put her book in her bag. She ran and yelled, "Cannonball!" before splashing into the deep end. Julie was giggling up a storm when Lily swam over to her and Nancy whom Lily had met the night she moved into her new apartment when Jayme introduced them. They hit it off right away.

"So, are you unpacked and all moved in?" Nancy asked Lily.

"Yep. Finally. Now I need to start looking for a job." Lily pulled herself up out of the water and sat on the edge of the pool next to Nancy.

"Well, what kind of job are you looking for?" Nancy asked.

"Maybe work as an aide at a school or probably waitressing. That's pretty much what I've always done." Lily put on her strongest Texas twang, "Unless thare's ranchin' 'round here." Lily laughed.

"Ranching? Really? I mean, I knew you were from Texas, but I didn't want to assume you had a ranch. Wow!" Nancy kicked her feet in the water. She looked back at Lily. "Wait, did you?"

"Actually, I grew up on a ranch. It was great! We had horses, and chickens of course."

"Wow! That sounds incredible. Julie would love that. Does your family still live there?"

"Well, my mom does. My dad passed."

"Oh, I'm sorry."

"It's okay. It was a long time ago.

"Well, there are a couple of ranches around here. In fact, one of them was owned by Burt Reynolds. Probably not too easy to get a job there though."

Lily smiled. "Probably not."

"Maybe President Trump would hire you." She grinned.

"Mar a Lago isn't a ranch, is it?"

"No, but it's HUGE." They both laughed. "Uncle Nick's is hiring. It's a nice place. Not fancy, but nice people come in there. A lot of locals, not too many tourists. I could talk to my boss if you're interested."

"Oh definitely! Thanks. I'm gonna go stir crazy if I have to sit around all day keeping myself company."

Nancy's expression took on a pensive look. "I understand. If it weren't for Julie, I don't know what I would have done after my husband died." Silence seeped into the conversation.

"I lost my husband too." Lily said quietly. "Recently, in fact. The days are deafening sometimes. I have Baxter to keep me company though."

"I'm so sorry. I didn't know. Jake, he never made it back from Afghanistan." Nancy looked down. "My brother lived here, so he invited us to stay with him for a while, and then we decided to make a fresh start. So, here we are. Transplants from Louisiana."

"Louisiana huh? Well, that's practically Texan." Lily laughed.

"Yep. Guess so. Good neighbors, anyway. If you don't mind me asking, what happened to your husband?"

"Cancer."

"Oh man! That must have been devastating."

"It was a long arduous journey, that's for sure."

"Any kids?"

"No. It wasn't in the cards."

The sad conversation ended abruptly when out of nowhere they heard, "Geronimooooooo!" Jayme yelled as he jumped into the water. A big splash of water hit them in the face. All three girls laughed and squealed with delight. He swam over to Julie and put her on his shoulders. "What are you lovely ladies doing sitting over here on the side of the pool?"

"Oh, just talking about fresh starts," Nancy said as she splashed her brother. Jayme wiped the water out of his eyes then grinned at Lily.

"Well, here's to fresh starts." He winked at her.

"What do *you* know about fresh starts? You're young. You haven't had your first start yet?" Nancy teased.

Jayme blushed. "I'm not that young! I'm not that much younger than you, and you're an old lady." He splashed her back then took off across the pool with Julie in tow.

"Old lady. I'll show him old lady." Nancy murmured under her breath as she tried to splash him, but he'd quickly moved out of her reach.

"I'm the old lady around here. Not you." Lily quipped.

"Really? How old are you, anyway?"

"Let's just say, somewhere between twenty and forty." Lily laughed.

"Yeah, me too. Sometimes I feel closer to forty than twenty though." Her new friend smiled.

Jayme played Marco Polo with Julie across the pool. Lily couldn't help but watch. "How old is Jayme?" Lily knew he was younger, but she was extremely curious as to how much younger.

"Jayme is twenty-three, but he acts like a five-year-old."

"Don't they all?"

"Yes, I guess they do, don't they?"

"Maybe we should start acting like five-year-olds too."

"Maybe so. Race ya?"

"You're on." Nancy and Lily dove into the water and raced to the other side.

They all stayed in the pool for another hour enjoying each other's company then made plans to go to dinner that night. They decided on hamburgers at Uncle Nick's so Nancy could introduce Lily to her boss and so Lily could get a feel for the place. Lily sat between Julie and Jayme who kept scooting closer to her as the night wore on. She enjoyed his company but wasn't sure she was ready for romance.

"So what did you think?" Nancy asked.

"I like it. It's not fancy, but not a dive either. The customers seem like regular folk."

"They are. Mostly just hard-working, middle-class people...locals. We don't see too many tourists come in here. The customers here aren't the biggest tippers, but they're pretty nice, not too demanding."

"Well, I'll come back tomorrow and fill out an application."

"Good. I'm glad. It will be fun working together."

"Well, I don't have the job yet."

"Sure you do. I already talked to Nick. He's crazy about you." Nancy winked.

"Uh huh. Okay. Well, we'll see what happens tomorrow."

That night, Lily thought about the new friends she'd already made. This new start was already proving to be the right decision. She hadn't felt this free in years. Unfortunately, she also couldn't stop thinking about Jayme. *Twenty-three. That's downright dangerous.*

Nancy was true to her word and helped Lily get a job at Uncle Nick's Bar and Grill. Nick took a liking to her and gave her lots of hours. It helped her to pass the time, keep her mind off of her past life, and pay the bills. Besides all that, she loved the view from the deck. It was right on the water, so she really liked being assigned the patio section. She'd be out there every second of the day if she could. Jayme got into the habit of sitting in her section every time he came in, which was almost every day. He was an endless flirt and truth be told, Lily liked the attention. It made her feel young again.

Lily and Nancy often worked together and became close friends. In a way, she reminded her of Anna, her co-worker at Charlotte's. Only, Nancy was a little less flirty and a little more settled since she had a daughter to take care of. Nick was a good guy and was flexible with Nancy's schedule so that she worked mostly when Julie was at school. Jayme helped out and watched Julie on weekends. He was an expert on sea turtles and worked at the sea turtle rehab and sanctuary. The perfect job for such a free spirit. They had become fast friends and he offered to take Lily snorkeling. In fact, he wouldn't take no for an answer and bugged her relentlessly. She wouldn't admit it to him, but Lily was slightly afraid of the water; however, she finally caved and decided to face her fears and get a little adventurous. They set a date for the next Saturday.

Jayme met Lily at her apartment Saturday morning. They drove to the beach in his little red car with the windows down singing old eighties tunes along the way, wind blowing through their hair. The sun was out and the day seemed perfect, except for Lily's stomachache, which would not go away. She knew it was only nerves, but that knowledge didn't help.

Jayme noticed the pinched look on her face as they pulled up to park close to the beach. "Lily? What's wrong? You feeling okay?"

"Um, yeah. I just have a few butterflies."

"Butterflies? Why? We're just going snorkeling. Don't *tell* me you've never been."

"Um, no. Never been."

He eyed her speculatively, "Well, don't worry. You'll love it."

"Yeah, okay. Um, Jayme…" She clenched the door handle. "Do you ever see sharks in the water?"

"Ohhhhh…that's it…Okay, how many times have you seen *Jaws*?"

"I lost count about twenty years ago." It dawned on her that twenty years ago he was only three. She quickly shook that thought away. "…but I've also read the book, and it doesn't really end so well for most of the characters." She looked at him sheepishly.

"Lily. Stop worrying. I've got you. I won't let any sharks come near you."

That statement did absolutely nothing to calm her nerves, and she noticed that he never did answer her question, but Lily didn't want to chicken out, so she got out of the car and let him lead her by the hand to the waves. It took her a few minutes to adjust to breathing through the snorkel, but she finally started to relax and enjoy the scenery. The underwater world was breathtaking and so far, no sharks. After a few minutes, Lily noticed that Jayme was no longer by her side, and she was no longer swimming in the shallows. Though she was fascinated by her underwater view, her nerves got the best of her and she turned and headed back to the beach.

She was a little discouraged that her fears were interfering with her chance to enjoy this time with Jayme. She liked him, but she could see some differences between them. He was a free spirit, adventurous, young, and energetic. She was older and still carried the weight of responsibility and loss. *Well, they do say that opposites attract.* Lily looked out at the water. *They never say for how long though.* She watched the waves rolling in and rolling back out, the repetition of change—the only thing that stays the same.

Her wandering thoughts led her to Damien. She missed him but was glad his pain had finally ended. He hadn't had the easiest life, but now he was with his Heavenly Father, enjoying peace at last. She wondered about Jack, and her thoughts eventually led her to their last visit. Warmth and longing filled her at the memory of his touch. In her heart he belonged to her and she to him, but in this life, he belonged to another, and he would have children with her, not Lily. Lily pushed her jealousy aside and said a prayer for him and his new little family. She really wanted the best for him.

Lily twisted the top off her thermos, poured herself some coffee, and looked out on the water. She tried to focus on the moment, the seagulls cawing as they flew through the sky, the sea breeze drying her sticky hair full of sand and salt. The sun shining in her eyes as it greeted a new day. She held her cup and watched the steam floating from her coffee and relished in its strong bitterness easing down her throat, warming her from the inside, calming her. She thoroughly enjoyed the peaceful moment all alone on this wide expanse, thanking God for bringing her to this place, this place of peace and serenity. She had come through. God had helped her after all.

Lily looked out at the water for her snorkeling partner. It had been a while since she'd seen him. Then like Aqua-man in all his gloriousness, Jayme rose up out of the turquoise sea, water reluctantly dripping off his taut muscles. He sauntered over to her, kicking up sand in his wake, and plunked down beside her, dripping all over everything.

"So, what did you think?" he asked.

Lily handed him a beach towel. "I liked it."

"Liar," he teased, nudging her with his elbow.

"No really. I did like it, and now I can mark it off my bucket list."

Jayme eyed her warily. "But you don't really want to do it again?" he asked.

"Mmmmm, not really." Lily leaned back in the sand on her elbows.

He proceeded to dry himself off with the towel. "It's okay. The water isn't for everybody."

"It's not that. I love the water. I just also have a healthy fear of it." She smiled thinly. He smiled back and her heart melted just a little.

"So what about kisses? Do you like kisses, or have a healthy fear of them?" He leaned in close to her lips.

"Fear, definitely fear." Lily blushed but didn't turn away.

Jayme leaned in and kissed her with his wet salty lips warming her through and through.

"Let's go get some lunch. I'm starving!" He hopped up, abruptly ending their first kiss, leaving the lingering touch of his lips behind. "How about Flamingo's? They have great burgers."

Still a little shaken from the intimate connection, Lily replied, "Sounds good," and she reached for his hand, which he held all the way back to the car.

Jayme and Lily sat outside under a big pink umbrella at Flamingo's. It was the perfect place to eat lunch after a morning at the beach.

"So, tell me about yourself. How did you end up in Florida, all the way from the giant state of Texas?" Jayme asked.

"How many weeks do you have? This story could take a while." Lily sipped her iced tea.

"Well, if this day gets any better, I'd say I have all the time in the world—for you."

Lily blushed. He was such a flirt. "Actually, I used to live here a long time ago."

"Like, when you were a kid?"

"No, *like* when I was your age, so yeah, when I was *like*, a kid." Lily teased.

"Hey," Jayme tore off a piece of his bread and threw it at her. She ducked and the bread hit the ground just before a bird swooped down and pounced on it.

"See what I mean?" Lily laughed. "Anyway, my friend Allison moved here with her parents. I came to visit during Spring Break and fell in love with the place. I was staying at the Jupiter Resort and thought it might be a fun place to work, so I applied for a job."

"And they hired you on the spot?"

"Well, they hired me and gave me a month to go home to Texas to get my stuff and get back here."

"So, what happened?"

"Well, I moved in with Allison, and I worked eighty hours a week at the resort. Rough schedule, but fun. The people were really nice and loved my accent."

"I love your accent too. Bet it got you some good tips." Jayme winked. "So how did you end up back in Texas?"

Lily's smiled faded. She looked off into the distance. "My dad died." Lily picked up her iced tea and took a sip, trying to slow her beating heart.

"Damn. That sucks. I'm sorry. How old were you?"

Lily carefully placed her slick glass back down on the table, meditating on the condensation trickling down the glass. "Twenty-one. I'd only been here a few short months."

"So you went back to Texas?"

"Yeah. My mom was devastated." She looked down at her food.

"Nancy told me you grew up on a ranch."

"Yeah, another reason I had to go back. My mom needed help running it, so my Florida adventure ended almost as quickly as it began."

The pretty young waitress came by the table to check on them. She also seemed to be checking out Jayme, but to Lily's relief, he took no notice of her interest.

"So Lily, you ride horses?" he asked with his mouth full.

Lily was glad for the shift in their conversation. "I did when I was younger. We have chickens too."

"Chickens? You are a hillbilly girl, aren't you?"

"Hey!" Lily laughed, throwing a french fry at him across the table. "Okay—maybe I am." She picked up another one and stuffed it in her mouth.

"So, why did you come back to Florida this time?"

"Oh, this isn't really a fun story either. You sure you wanna know?"

"Yes, but only if you want me to know." He reached across the table and squeezed her hand.

"Nancy didn't tell you?" Lily looked up at him.

He shook his head from side to side. "No. Tell me what?" He gazed back at her.

Lily took a deep breath. "I was married…"

Jayme took his hand away from her and leaned back in his chair. "You were married?"

"Yes." Lily looked down and fiddled with the straw in her drink.

"Well, what happened? Did you get a divorce?"

"No…"

"So you're *still* married?" he asked with a raised voice.

Lily shook her head. "No."

"Oh. I'm such a jerk. Sorry. Continue."

"My husband died. Cancer."

"Wow! I really am a jerk! I'm sorry I brought it up."

"It's okay. You needed to know."

Jayme reached for her hand again and held it lightly.

She relished in the intimate gesture.

"Well, can I ask when?" he asked.

"Um, just a few months ago."

"Wow." Jayme shook his head. "Lily, you are a really strong person. I'm impressed."

"No, not me. I'm not the strong one. God is the one who helped me through all of it." Lily looked off into the distance, remembering. "I was weak. If I didn't have God, I'm not so sure I would be sitting here right now."

"Don't sell yourself short, Lily. You deserve some credit."

"No. I was devastated, but God held me up and gave me strength. I don't know how people can survive in this world without Him. Makes no sense. I mean, why would they even try?" His lack of response was noticeable, and they finished their meal in awkward silence.

Jayme took Lily home after lunch and promised to call her soon. *Was it something I said?* Lily wondered. Nevertheless, Jayme did call as promised and they made plans to see each other again. The next day, she called Allison to fill her in on her date.

"Well, how'd it go with the youngster?" Allison teased.

Lily curled up in Damien's recliner. "I don't know. He's cute…and nice."

"And?"

"No ands. He's a little more adventurous than I am."

"A little more, huh? That wouldn't take much. Is he a good guy?" Allison asked.

"Yes. I definitely think so."

"Well, just give him a chance and see what happens. You don't have to marry him, ya know."

"Yeah, you're right. He is fun. I need fun."

"Yes, you definitely do! Sooooo...was there any kissing involved?"

"Of course you'd ask that. He kissed me once." Lily twirled her hair as she thought about that kiss.

Allison squealed with delight. "And? Any sparks?"

"Yes." Lily beamed. "There were sparks. It was just a quick kiss though. Nothing else to report."

"Oh, Girlie, my face is heating up. Good for you."

"Oh stop! It was no big deal."

They made plans for lunch then hung up. It was so good to have a friend here.

Against her better judgment, Lily agreed to try snorkeling again. Jayme was persuasive and didn't give up easily. In exchange though, he agreed to go to church with her once in a while. They went snorkeling several more times and she enjoyed it, but only a little. She was still somewhat afraid of the water, and Jayme seemed disappointed that she hadn't taken to it more. They went to church together only once though, and she was disappointed that he hadn't taken to church more. Nevertheless, they liked each other very much and spent a great deal of time together, quickly falling into a comfortable, companionable relationship. Jayme was young and adventurous, exuberantly energetic, extremely handsome, and tons of fun. He was just what Lily needed after the serious and solemn past decade of her life, and he routinely forced her out of her comfort zone. In spite of their age difference, they seemed to be good for each other, and their relationship progressed into a committed one. It was good to put the past heartaches behind, all of them.

Part Two

Chapter Twenty-one

**Do not be bound together with unbelievers;
for what partnership have righteousness and lawlessness,
or what fellowship has light with darkness?
2 Cor. 6:14**

"I'm just not ready." Lily sipped her iced tea then set it down on the table.

"But why?" Jayme leaned toward her on his elbows. "We've been together five years, Lily." He held his hand in the air and stretched out all five fingers, looking like an angry kindergartener put out that he was forced to explain his age. "How can you not be ready to get married?" He slapped the table and sat back in his chair, crossing his arms over his chest, still resembling same kindergartener. Some of the other patrons looked over at them.

"Do we have to talk about this here? We're in a restaurant." Lily shrank down into her seat.

"Why are we in a restaurant today, Lily? It's our AN-NI-VER-SA-RY! So much for a happy one."

"Let's just go." She grabbed her purse and headed for the door. Jayme looked around at all the staring faces, quickly threw some cash on the table for the meal they'd barely touched, and rushed out behind her. He caught up to her just as she got to the car. "Lily!" He grabbed her arm and spun her around to face him.

Adrenaline shot through her veins. She looked down at his tight grip and pushed him away. He stumbled. Lily braced herself for a face-off, but Jayme put his hands up in the air and said, "You win." He walked around to the driver's side and got in the car. "Are you coming?"

"Depends. Are you gonna calm down?"

Jayme took a deep breath and slowly let it out. "Yes." She looked at him but made no effort to get into the car. "I promise." Lily capitulated and slid into the passenger seat. She put on her seatbelt but refused to meet his gaze. He quietly drove her home then got out of the car.

Lily pushed her door open, hopped out, and glared at him over the roof of the small vehicle. "What are you doing?"

"I'm walking you to your door."

"Not necessary." She turned away but he followed.

"Look, I'm sorry Lily. I got angry. I know I shouldn't have grabbed you like that."

Lily stopped to face him. "Then why did you? You've never done that before."

"I know. I just…I don't want to lose you, and I'm frustrated. Please…just explain to me the reason you don't want to get married."

She stared at him for a moment trying to make up her mind. "Okay. Come on in. We can talk about it—calmly."

They entered her apartment and Baxter immediately wound himself around Lily's legs. She stepped over him to get to the kitchen and headed for the fridge. "You want a beer?"

"No. I'll pass. All I want is for you to talk to me." Lily grabbed two bottles of water and sat down on the couch to face Jayme. She handed one to him noticing the pained look in his eyes. "Lily, don't you love me?" he asked her straight out. No beating around the bush.

"Yes. I do, but…" Lily grabbed the throw pillow and held it close. "This is hard to say."

"Just say it." His eyes pleaded with her.

"Jayme…" She put her hand on his. "I do love you, I just, I don't think it's enough for marriage." There. She said it. It hurt, but she'd said it. She let go of his hand and sat back and stared at the floor.

"How can you say that?"

Oh, how it hurt her to hurt him. Lily sighed. "Jayme, we have differences that have not been dealt with."

"Such as?"

"You and I are not on the same level when it comes to God. You won't even go to church with me."

A look of indignation quickly replaced the pleading in his eyes. "My relationship with God is my own business and it has nothing to do with us." He stood up and walked over to the window.

"I disagree. A marriage can't work without God as its center. At least, not for me." Lily knew where this was headed and it scared her. She put her hands between her knees. They were starting to tremble.

"So that's the reason you don't want to marry me?" He turned back to face her. "Don't you want to have kids?"

"Of course I wanna have kids, but how can I raise my kids with a man who—"

"Who what? A man who won't go to church? A heathen! An atheist! Is that what you think I am, Lily? I mean, that's what you're saying, isn't it?"

"No. That's not what I'm saying." Lily hugged the pillow tight to her chest.

"Is church really that big a deal to you, Lily?"

Lily wondered how on earth she could make him understand. "Yes. It is a big deal and if you don't get that by now then how can we get married?"

"It's not enough that I believe in God?" He entreated.

"No. Not this time," she answered softly.

"This time?" His voice rose. "Oh wait. I get it. Are you comparing me to your husband?"

"Look Jayme, my marriage to Damien was difficult at best. We loved each other, but I wasn't happy with him…we were unequally yoked, and it nearly ruined our marriage."

"But you stayed with him."

"Yes. He got sick, and we'd made vows. I did what I had to do. But I can't go through any of that again. Can't you understand that?"

"No. All I understand is that my girlfriend of five years doesn't love me enough to marry me." Lily didn't deny the truth of his words. "I'm going. Let me know if you change your mind."

He slammed the door as he left. Baxter came out of his hiding place meowing incessantly. He jumped up onto the sofa and curled up in Lily's lap. This time Lily didn't cry. She had no more tears to offer.

Chapter Twenty-two

**Yet if the unbelieving one leaves,
let him leave...
but God has called us to peace.
1 Cor. 7:15**

"I'lllllllll get iiiiiiit!" Little Grace yelled from the other room.

"Grace, no! You don't open the door for strangers," Jack yelled back. They both arrived at the door at the same time. Jack called out "Who is it?" as he picked up Grace, whirled her through the air, and landed her on his hip.

"Sheriff Marshall," the muffled voice replied.

Jack looked through the peephole and opened the door.

"Are you Jack Walker?"

"Yes..." Jack eyed the stranger speculatively, looking at his badge. "I am."

"May I see your driver's license?"

Jack's stomach turned over. "Of course." Jack repositioned Grace on his hip and reached into his back pocket to pull out his wallet. He showed his identification to the sheriff.

"Please sign here."

Jack reached for the pen and signed for the large envelope.

"You've been served. You have thirty days to respond."

Jack nodded quietly then closed the door and put Grace back down on the floor.

"What is it, Daddy? What is it?" Grace hopped up and down like a bunny rabbit. "Did someone send you a pwesent?"

Jack had a bad feeling in the pit of his stomach that he knew exactly what it was, especially since Hailey had moved out the week before.

"Nothing Baby. Just something for work."

Grace's big smile faded into a look of indifference, and she ran back to her room to play.

Jack opened the thick legal sized envelope. Divorce papers. He went to his bedroom and gently closed the door then skimmed through the pages. "Ouch!" A paper cut. *That figures.* Carefully, he went back through them for clarity. He could not believe his eyes! Hailey wanted a divorce and a settlement but only every other weekend with Grace. Jack's knees gave. He dropped to the edge of the bed. He knew that the judge would have likely made Hailey the custodial parent as her mother and that he would be the one getting weekends, but she must have rejected that right. *Unreal.* He reached for the phone and tried to call her but there was no answer.

Several days later, Jack sat at his computer searching the internet for a vacation destination for little Grace and himself. Of course she wanted to go to Disneyworld, but she was only four, so she might be too young for some of the rides, and of course, she was a complete daddy's girl, so he was pretty sure he would say *yes,* regardless. He also wanted to go to the beach. He'd heard the east coast of Florida was incredible. Maybe he'd try surfing. Yeah, a vacation was just what he needed.

Jack hoped that this might be a good distraction for them. He hadn't talked to Hailey since he'd been served divorce papers, and Grace was starting to ask a lot of questions—questions for which he had no answers. Jack knew that he and Hailey hadn't been happy together in a long time. They had tried to make their marriage work, but there seemed to be something hindering them, creating a distance that should not be between man and wife. It was his fault. He knew. He'd tried and tried, but he'd never been able to get Lily completely out of his heart.

Jack thought back to his wedding day—he hadn't been married even a few hours and he'd already lied to his wife. He never told her he'd gone to see Lily at the hospital during their reception. He hadn't been gone that long and he was surprised she had even noticed him missing, but she had, and she wasn't happy about it. He'd been vague about his whereabouts but Hailey suspiciously questioned his story, and they'd started their new marriage on an argument and a lie.

They never quite seemed to get back on track either. They had tried counseling for a while, but a counselor couldn't make two people love each other, especially if maybe they never really did. Even so, he just couldn't understand how she could leave Grace. Grace was the light of his life. It still amazed him just how much of his heart was filled by this tiny little person. Jack was still researching Disneyworld when his phone rang. It was Hailey.

Jack and Hailey had decided to meet at a quiet restaurant downtown. When he arrived, the sun was shining into the room through the large windows of the quaint eatery revealing tiny dust particles floating in the air. It took a minute for his eyes to adjust, but there she was, beautiful yet unfulfilling, sitting at a small table in a dark corner beyond reach of the sunlight pouring in, a table no doubt meant for romance but would instead mark the death of their marriage.

"Hey," he said, pulling out a chair across from Hailey.

"Hey," she replied, looking up at him.

"So, what's good here?" Jack picked up the menu and began to study it.

"I dunno. I'm not eating. Let's just order coffee or something, okay?"

"Sure." Jack released a long sigh and put the menu down.

"Why do you do that?" she asked.

"Do what?"

"Sigh like that. It's irritating."

"Sorry. I didn't mean anything by it. I guess...I'm nervous, and frustrated. You just left. How could you just leave?"

"Stop." Hailey held up her hand, her palm facing him. "I didn't come here to argue with you. Let's keep emotions out of this and see if we can come to some sort of understanding so the lawyers don't eat us alive."

The waitress came over and took their order: two cups of coffee.

Hailey's cold demeanor took him off guard, though he knew it shouldn't have surprised him. "Okay. I can try. So, you want a divorce," he stated rather than asked.

"I do."

Irony struck him at her choice of words—those two little words that had started their marriage would also now end it. "Look, I know we haven't been close lately, but can I ask why you're so eager to give up on our marriage?" The waitress stopped short and placed the steaming cups on the table and quickly made her exit.

"Jack, I don't want to hurt you, but I have to be honest." Hailey stirred artificial sweetener into her coffee.

"Okay. So be honest."

She stopped stirring and looked up at him. "Jack, I'm in love with someone else."

Her brazen answer, an icy tidal wave, deluged his heart. He wanted to reply with a sarcastic *So what! So am I*. After all, he'd been in love with someone else too, but that had never kept him from keeping his commitment to his wife.

"I'm having an affair," she said.

Jack felt another gut punch, and he in turn wanted to punch something...hard, but he knew he had to keep a lid on his anger.

"Look, I don't want to hurt you, but I want to be with him. I can't live a lie anymore."

Jack gritted his teeth. Any hope he'd had of reconciliation abandoned him.

"And Grace?"

"I love Grace, but she's better off with you. I'm not exactly the most nurturing mother and... she's happy with you." She looked down at the table, picked up her coffee and sipped it. The oversized cup covered her face.

Jack could not believe a mother would so easily give up her child, but he knew she was right.

"Has she asked about me?" She looked at him with veiled hope.

"Yes, she has," Jack replied.

"Has she cried for me?"

He looked down. "No."

Her demeanor turned cold once again. "Grace should live with you. I just want a basic visitation schedule."

"What else do you want?" He knew there would be more.

"Well, I thought maybe you wouldn't mind paying off my car and my credit cards, just so I could start off with a clean slate. After all, they are in your name also."

Jack shook his head in disbelief. "Hailey, are you sure this is what you want?" Jack reached for her hand. "We could try counseling again."

"Jack, even if you were willing to forgive me I wouldn't come back."

He pulled away, hurt, but he had to admit he probably wouldn't want her back. He nodded his head in capitulation and they drank their coffee and discussed the details of her requests. He felt sick, sick with failure and defeat and disappointment at being an unfulfilling husband.

Hailey confessed to Jack that she never really did love him. Then she revealed that her affair had been going on for over a year. Jack was overwhelmed by her confession and demands and her willingness to give up Grace so easily, but for him it was a small price to pay for his daughter.

He went home with the promise to think about all that she'd said. He knew that God hated divorce, but he also knew that if he did divorce Hailey, he just might have a chance with Lily, a thought that immediately flooded him with guilt. He was confused, but it didn't look like Hailey was going to give him any choice in the matter. She was leaving him for another man, whether he forgave her or not.

The next day, after speaking with his lawyer, he called Hailey and told her he would agree to her stipulations. Then he went to church and prayed for forgiveness. That night he went home, got on his computer, and continued his search for beach resorts in Florida, knowing that Lily lived and worked somewhere outside of Palm Beach. *Well, it may be a long shot, but why not?* A few months later the divorce was final, and Jack and Grace headed east on their way to Florida with the sun leading the way.

Chapter Twenty-three

**But if any of you lacks wisdom,
let him ask of God...
and it will be given unto him.
James 1:5**

Today was Lily's day off. She'd cleaned her apartment all morning, but no amount of scrubbing could clean up the mess she'd made of her life. Usually, being busy helped keep her mind off her problems, but today she just couldn't rid her thoughts of Jayme's demands. Her brain needed a break, and so did her heart.

Hauling her cooler, her beach bag, and a good old-fashioned romance novel, she hit the beach. The romance novel she was reading made her think of Jack. She still missed him even after all this time, and sometimes it was his kisses she dreamt about at night, not Jayme's. Jack's kisses had been arresting, intense, yet gentle and loving. It had never been like that with Jayme or Damien. Gazing out to the open sea, as the sun glinted off the water, she wondered how Jack was doing, if he was happy being married to Hailey, how he enjoyed being a father. She was happy for him, if not even a little jealous.

Lily was just settling into her novel when she noticed a father and child playing a game of Frisbee way down the beach. Lily desperately wanted that scene in her own life. If she married Jayme, she could probably have that in her near future, but would she be marrying him out of fear that this might be her last chance to have children? As much as she wanted a family, she knew that was not a reason to get married. She was just all mixed up, and after five years together, shouldn't she know by now?

"Earth to Lily," Allison said, breaking up Lily's thoughts.

Lily squinted up at her friend. "Hey woman! 'Bout time you got here."

"Well, my hubby was nagging at me about the credit card bill again. It took me a while to smooth things over. How goes it?" She plopped down next to Lily and opened up a wine cooler.

"It goes." Lily took the drink from her friend. "Thanks."

"You're welcome." Allison shot her a snarky grin and opened another one. "So what are you so intensely thinking about that you didn't even see me walk up?"

"Actually, I was thinking about Jack."

"Jack? Ohhhhhhh. That guy in Texas. The one you worked with?"

"Yeah."

"You still think about him?"

Lily nodded. "Sad, isn't it?"

"Well, I dunno. Sad, or maybe a little romantic."

"You see that man with his daughter way down the beach?" Lily pointed at the Frisbee players.

"Yeah, why?"

"Well, he looks just like him. So weird."

"Really?" Allison leaned around Lily and looked down the beach. "It's hard to tell what he looks like from here. When was the last time you talked to him?"

"Gosh. I don't know. Right after Damien died, I guess. He came to see me."

"He did?"

Lily blushed as the memory came rushing back.

"Okaaayyy, so, it's been a few years." Allison said.

Lily shifted up on her elbows. "Yeah. He's got a kid now."

"So, how was your date?" Allison asked, changing the direction of Lily's thoughts. "You know, with Jayme, of the here and now."

"Oh. Not good. We had a fight."

"Again?"

"Yeah. He brought up marriage and I stormed out of the restaurant."

"Stormed out! On your anniversary?"

"Yes. It was so embarrassing."

"So do tell, do tell. You told him no, I take it."

"I didn't say no exactly. I just didn't say yes. There are just...so many reasons."

"Such as..."

Lily held up a finger. "Well, his age for one."

"Oh please. He's not that much younger." Allison leaned back on her elbows and tilted her chin to the sun.

"Nine years!"

"Yeah, but that's not that bad," she replied with her eyes closed.

"I know, it's just, well, at the beginning, we were just having fun. You know?" Lily looked out at the ocean. "Damien had just died and I was looking for a way to move on, and..."

"And his energy and charm were irresistible?" Allison finished Lily's thoughts.

"Well yeah. He made me feel young again."

"And now?"

"Now five years later, I don't feel so young." Lily grabbed the sun block and squeezed the cream into her hand.

"Okay, what else?" Allison sat up on her beach towel.

"Church."

"Yeah, that one's important."

"I mean, maybe I could accept the fact that he doesn't like to go to church. At least he believes in God. He could change. Damien did. But..."

"I don't know, Lil', you aren't getting any younger. If you want to have kids..."

"I know. I know. I'd better get started soon, right?"

"Well, maybe. So what now?" Allison took the sun block from Lily and applied it to her arms.

"I called him and asked for more time. He agreed, but he won't wait forever."

"And you still haven't decided."

Lily shook her head.

"So, what now?"

"Well, now Jayme is in Louisiana visiting his family and giving me some space to think about our future."

"Do you miss him?"

"Yeeeees. I do."

"So, what's holding you back, Chicky?"

Lily shrugged her shoulders. *So, what is holding me back?*

The sound of her mom's ringtone jarred her out of her thoughts. She dug through her bag and grabbed her phone.

"Hello. Hey Mom. I'm good. He's good too. Okaayy. I am sitting. What's the news?"

Allison looked at her inquisitively.

"That's great! I'm happy for you. Really Mom. What? California? Well, what about the ranch? Okay. Well, I'm just glad you aren't selling it. Aren't you gonna miss it? Okay. I'll call you in a few days. Have a safe flight."

"What on earth?" Allison asked.

"My mom. She's getting married…and moving to California."

"California? Wow! Go Mom!"

"Yeah. Wow," Lily replied with very little enthusiasm.

Allison eyed her friend. "You okay with it?"

"Yeah, I guess. Just a lot of changes. I mean I always thought I could go home if I needed to, but now with Mom not there, it's not home."

"But she's not selling it, right?"

"No, thank goodness."

"So, not that I want you to, but you could still go back then, right?"

"Not if I marry Jayme. He's given me an ultimatum. When he gets back, either marry him, or he's prepared to move on. But if I marry him, I can never go back to Texas."

"Well, you didn't seem so happy when you lived there. That's how you ended up here, remember?"

"I know. My last few years in Texas weren't happy ones. I mean, I loved him, but the years with Damien weren't exactly good, between his cheating...cancer...and Jack." It seemed like a lifetime ago, yet she carried it with her in the depth of her being. No, her last few years there had not been happy, and marriage had been hard. Even so, Texas was still home, and Lily loved and missed it very much. "Marriage was hard. I'm not sure I could survive it twice." Lily said to her friend.

Everything was changing. Her dad was gone, her husband was gone, and now her mom would be gone too. Home would never be home again. She was on her own now, and Jayme might be her last chance to have her own family, but Lily had always harbored hopes that she could someday move back to the family ranch. If she married Jayme, someday wouldn't come.

"Lily? Have you asked God for guidance?" Allison asked.

Lily looked at her friend. "No. I guess I haven't." But she would. She would take this to the Lord in prayer. "Thanks, Al."

Chapter Twenty-four

The LORD Will Provide.
Gen. 22:14

Lily's stomach growled as she wiped down the sticky, crumb-laden bar after the late crowd at Uncle Nick's Bar and Grill. She could smell the salty ocean breeze coming through the open French doors overlooking the Atlantic Ocean. Lily stopped her work and stepped out onto the deck to enjoy the view. The bright moon cast its glow, glistening over the water. Lily breathed deeply, enjoying the peaceful moment. As long as she worked here, she would never tire of the beautiful scenery or the salty smell of the ocean breeze, God's handiwork. This was her escape, the place to which she had run years earlier after Damien's death. Yes, she had run, run away like a hopeless teenager. She had run from the sadness, despair, and empty house that had been choking her. She'd just had to get out and move on with her life, but after her mom's big news, she just couldn't stop thinking about home, and the memories flooded back assaulting her at every turn. It seemed as if her past was catching up to her, and God was telling her to face it before she could move on with Jayme. Jayme—he was waiting for her answer.

It was late when Lily's shift ended. As always, Nick walked Lily out to her truck to make sure she got there safely. "Lily, I forgot to tell you. This guy called earlier, but you were busy, so I asked him to leave a message. He didn't leave a number though."

"Well, who was it?" Lily looked down as she put one foot in front of the other—a habit she'd picked up growing up in the country where she had to constantly be on the lookout for snakes, and she was also focused on keeping pace with Nick's long strides.

"I think he said his name was Joe."

"Joe? Who's Joe?" she asked without looking up.

"No, that's not it. Jack. His name was Jack."

Lily's head snapped to attention—her heart nearly stopped. "Jack? Are you sure he said his name was Jack?"

"Yeah, it was Jack. I'm pretty sure. Why?" He looked at her questioningly. "Who's Jack?"

"Jack," Lily whispered to herself, then got into her truck and closed the door in a daze. Nick stood there looking confused. Lily finally realized he was still standing there and rolled down her window. "Did he say anything else, Nick?"

"He just asked to speak with you. He sounded like he was from Texas. You know, he talked funny like you." Nick wiggled his eyebrows up and down and grinned at her. She rolled her eyes at him. "But no, he didn't leave a number or anything. I told him you were busy and couldn't talk, and he just told me to tell you he called. Who is he?" Nick inquired curiously.

"A ghost from my past." Lily started her engine, slowly turned out of the parking lot, and drove home dumbfounded. *How did he find me?*

Jack sat in his truck flipping through stations trying to find some country music, waiting for Lily to get off work. The door finally opened and there she was. He stared in awe as she walked out to her truck. It had been so long since he'd laid eyes on her. Even though he was parked directly across from her line of sight, Lily didn't see him. She was staring down at her feet as she walked. *Some things never change*, he couldn't help but smile. She was still so beautiful and looked exactly the same with that ponytail bouncing behind her, but she was with a man. Jack tried not to jump to conclusions, but then the man leaned into her window, *to kiss her?* He wondered. His stomach turned over. Anna had told him Lily wasn't married, but he didn't think to ask if she was seeing anyone. He'd been hoping that she wasn't. Of course, a woman as beautiful as Lily wouldn't go unattached for long. He felt so stupid. What was he thinking? After the parking lot cleared out, Jack started his truck. He missed his chance. As creepy as it seemed, for a moment he thought about following her but decided against it. He just couldn't take it if he saw that guy follow her home. Instead, he decided to call Anna in the morning to get more information. Jack looked over the back of the seat at his sleeping daughter. He felt a little foolish bringing her here with him, but he'd had no choice. She was only four, and he wasn't too keen on the idea of leaving her with the hotel babysitter. He smiled warmly as he looked at her sweet face. She filled his heart with such tremendous love. He may have his regrets in life, but she was not one of them. The memory of Lily's confession of never being able to have children suddenly hit him. How sad. She would have been such a great mother. Jack shook his thoughts away and drove back to his hotel room at the Jupiter Resort.

The next morning, Jack and Grace walked out to the beach to watch the sun rise. The sand was still cool from the night before and felt gritty between his toes. He spread out the beach blanket that Grace had picked out in one of the surf shops they had stopped at along the way. It billowed up and down in a cascade of colors as the wind caught it. He spread it out on the sand, organized all of their beach paraphernalia, and finally plunked himself down while Grace sat in the sand building a sand castle. The ocean waves hit the shore with a small roar. *It's so beautiful here. No wonder Lily likes it so much,* he thought to himself as he drank his morning coffee. *It doesn't get much better than this.* He stared out at the water, the waves rolling in and out, taking out to sea the tiny life forms that couldn't dig deep enough into the sand to hold on. Like he hadn't been able to hold onto Lily.

He couldn't believe he was here in Florida, so close to her. His thoughts took him back in time, to the moment that his affection for her had finally revealed itself to him, to the first time he'd kissed her, to the last time he'd kissed her. The blue of the water was the same blue of her eyes. Was he crazy for coming here? People say you can't go back—maybe not, but they'd never had the chance to go forward, and nothing would stop him from finding out now.

"Jesus wuvs me, this I know," Grace's voice jerked him away from his thoughts and back to the moment. She was singing a bible school song. Grace...what would Lily think of her? Would she be able to accept her? After all, they were a package deal. He took a deep breath, realizing he was getting way ahead of himself. First, he just had to go see her, but how? Where? Should he get her address from Anna and show up at her apartment? He didn't think so. Should he go to the restaurant where she works and just plop down at the bar? Jack looked over at Grace. What exactly should he do with Grace? When he did see Lily again, he'd like to be alone with her, with no distractions. She'd never met Grace. It might be too difficult for her. He stared at the water as if the answers would just emerge from the sea. All of a sudden a young woman in a resort t-shirt came up to him and introduced herself as the kids' activity director.

"Good morning." She looked down at him.

"Mornin'." Jack looked up at her, squinting into the sun. "Gracie, can you tell the nice lady 'Good morning'?"

"Hi. Mornin," Grace replied then swiftly resumed her sandy construction project.

"My name is Kayla. I work at the resort. Is it okay if I sit down for a minute?"

"Of course. Jack Walker. Nice to meet you." He leaned over to shake her hand as she plopped down next to Grace. "This is Grace."

"Hi Grace. Whatcha doin?" she asked with a southern drawl.

"I'm making my daddy a castle." Grace replied without looking up.

"Where are you from, may I ask?" Jack inquired.

"Texas. Could you tell?" Kayla giggled. "Grace, can I help?" Grace nodded her head and they continued building the sand castle together. "Sounds like you might be from there yourself."

"Actually I am. Small world, huh?"

"Sure is. But big state. What part?"

"We live near Chappell Hill, just outside of Brenham, where they make Blue Bell ice cream. You know where that is?"

Grace looked up, "Ice cweem, ice cweem! We all scweem for ice cweem!"

Jack and Kayla both laughed.

"Oh yeah, I know where that is. I'm from College Station, actually. Wow. It is a small world."

"Isn't that something?"

"Yeah. I have an aunt who lives close to Brenham. She owns a restaurant in Chappell Hill."

"Really?" This was too much. "What's her name?"

"Aunt Charlotte." She grinned. "Oh sorry, Charlotte Adams."

"This is unbelievable."

"What's unbelievable?" she asked.

"Well, your aunt is my boss."

"What??? Get outta town, no way!"

"Way." Jack grinned.

"Well, that is very cool! It's awesome to meet a fellow Texan, especially one from home. I'll have to call my aunt later and tell her I ran into you, unless of course you're on the lam?" Kayla grinned. "Well, I better get back to work. Grace, wanna come do some arts and crafts with us later? There will be a bunch of kids there." Kayla looked at Jack for permission.

"Can I Daddy, can I?" Grace begged.

"We'll see, Honey."

Kayla handed Jack an activity schedule. "You have a pen? I'll give you my number in case you have any questions." Jack dug a crayon out of Grace's bag and handed it to Kayla. She scribbled her number down on the activity sheet and handed it back to him. "It was really nice to meet you. Such a small world, huh? And don't worry, if you let Grace come to any of the kids' activities, I promise I will watch her myself. Oh yeah, almost forgot, I also babysit for the resort."

"Okay, I'll give it some thought. Thanks." Kayla turned to wave to Grace as she walked up the trail leading back to the resort.

"Bye bye," Grace waved back. Maybe this was an answer to his prayers.

Jack took Grace back up to the hotel room to watch cartoons before lunch. He decided to give Charlotte a call. She confirmed that Kayla was her niece and reassured him that she was great with children. He then called Anna to ask her about Lily's relationship status.

"Well Jack, last I heard, Lily was seeing some younger guy. I think his name is Jayme." Jack's heart sank. "Have you talked to her yet?"

"No. Now I'm kind of afraid to if she's seeing somebody."

"Jack, you are so exasperating! Just go see her already! She's not married! *You* are not married! Just do it. It might be your only chance. Stop your darn pussy-footin' around and go see what happens."

Jack knew she was right. "Okay Anna. We'll just see what happens. But if this doesn't go well I'm taking it out on you!"

"And I will be happy to let you take it out on me." Anna said flirtatiously. He instantly regretted his choice of words. "In all seriousness Jack, I know how you feel about Lily, and I don't think she ever got over you either, so just take a chance. What have you got to lose?"

She was right again. For the first time since Jack had met Lily, they were both unmarried, and at the same time. This may be his only opportunity to find out if he and Lily could ever have a chance. This could be their *last* chance. If God was giving him this opportunity, who was he to question it?

By the time he got off the phone, he'd promised Anna he would not leave Florida without seeing Lily, no matter how much of a coward he was. He checked on Grace who sat cross-legged in a trance in front of the TV watching cartoons and called the front desk to arrange for Kayla to baby-sit. Butterflies filled his stomach as he thought about how to put his plan into place.

Chapter Twenty-five

**Oh that my request
might come to pass,
And that God would grant my
longing!
Job 6:8**

Lily slumped against the counter after the lunch rush. Not only had she worked the late shift the night before, but she'd also had difficulty sleeping. Knowing that Jack had called her, her mind had not been able to quiet. She was bone weary but at the same time, filled with nervous adrenaline. She needed to call Anna to see if she knew anything, but it was too late by the time she got home last night. She'd planned to call her this morning but was running late. As a result, she'd been wondering all day long about that phone call from Jack. *Could it have really been him?* She thought. *After all these years.*

It had been a busy day and the hours passed quickly. She had just removed her apron and gone to the kitchen to take a break when she heard the bell on the door announcing someone else had come in the restaurant. "Nick, can you check the floor? I'm just about to take my break," Lily yelled to an empty kitchen. No answer. "Uh! I'm never gonna get to sit down." Lily walked back around to the bar. The bright day was shining through the windows, momentarily blinding her. The silhouette of a man stood just inside the door. "Go ahead and seat yourself. I'll be with you in a minute." Lily called out as she rounded the corner back toward the kitchen to retrieve her apron. "Can I bring you something to drink?" Lily had both hands behind her back trying to tie her apron strings as she rounded the corner again, her ponytail flying, in a hurry to get back to her customer.

"I always thought you looked cute with a ponytail." The stranger said with a lopsided grin.

A voice from long ago stopped Lily dead in her tracks; her breath caught between her chest and her throat. Frozen in time and space she stared at him, words completely escaping her.

"Hey Lily," Jack spoke softly as he walked towards her.

She snapped out of her stupor and walked around to meet him halfway. "I can't believe you're here." Lily exhaled the words as her eyes transfixed upon his. Once his steps completed their task, and they were finally standing face to face, the spell was broken, and she nervously gave him a quick hug. But as she started to pull away, his warmth drew her in. He put both of his arms around her and held her tight. She took a deep breath and gave in, holding him too if only for a moment. That familiar electricity radiated between them. She pulled back and looked up into his eyes, standing motionless before him. The wave of emotion so strong it forced her back. Her face flushed as she stumbled and struggled to compose herself. "Um, what are you doing in Florida?" She looked around the restaurant. "Are you by yourself?"

Jack cleared his throat. "Well, I brought Grace for a vacation." At the mention of his daughter's name, Lily looked around the restaurant again. "Oh, I left her back at the hotel." A confused look formed on Lily's face leading Jack to grasp for words. "With the kids' activity director. I wouldn't have left her, but the director actually turns out to be Charlotte's niece," he stammered.

"Charlotte?" she asked. "Charlotte from Texas? Charlotte who used to be my boss Charlotte?" Her words spilled out.

"Yeah, small world, huh?"

"Sure is." Lily smiled nervously. "And Hailey?"

"Not here." His tone warned Lily not to ask.

"So how did you end up here?"

"Well, I remember you mentioning the Jupiter Resort once, and I thought *why not?* Grace wanted to go to Disney World of course, so I thought it would be nice to go to the beach too."

"Disney World isn't exactly close by, ya know?"

"Oh I know. But you don't work at Disney World." His eyes met hers and held them.

Lily blushed and looked down at her shoes. "So, you came all the way from Disney World to see me?" She looked back up at him, her eyes searching.

"No. I came all the way from Texas to see you." He let the implications of his statement set in then continued. "We came here first. We'll be staying here for a few days then we'll drive to Disney World."

"Did you *drive* here all the way from Texas?" Lily asked incredulously. "With your baby?"

Jack smiled at the memory of his and his daughter's road trip. It might not have been the best idea he'd ever had, but flying was not really his thing. "Well, Grace isn't exactly a baby anymore. She's four now, but yes, believe it or not, I did. Needless to say, we made many stops along the way, especially every time Grace saw a sign for Wendy's."

"A big fan of frosties, huh?"

"You wouldn't believe. Anyway, I guess we could have flown, but well, I'm not a big fan of flying anymore."

"Me neither."

Nick rounded the corner and stopped short at the scene in front of him. Lily looked at her boss and took another step back from Jack. Then she introduced them.

"Uh, Nick, I'd like you to meet Jack." Jack held his hand out to shake Nick's.

"Nice to meet you." Jack's grip tightened on Nick's hand telling him exactly what he needed him to know. That he meant business.

"Nice to meet you too." Nick retrieved his hand and put it in his back pocket. "Lily, why don't you go home? I can do your preps for the next shift. Go catch up with your friend."

Lily looked at Nick and then Jack and back at Nick again. "Are you sure?"

"Yeah, go on. You've already done most of it anyway. I can handle it from here."

"Okay. Great! Thanks." Lily looked at Jack and waited.

He smiled and reached for her hand. It was warm and sweaty and still sent heat through his veins.

"Would you like to go somewhere and talk?" Jack asked unable to disguise the hope and excitement in his eager voice. Just then, Lily's stomach growled. Loudly. They laughed at the sound. "And maybe get something to eat?" Lily smiled and nodded her head.

"Just let me grab my stuff. I know this great seafood place right on the water. You're gonna love it. It's amazing."

Anywhere with you is amazing. Jack thought.

They left Lily's truck at work and took Jack's to the restaurant. Once they got there, they each ordered a frozen fruit drink and began to relax. It was a hot day, but not by Texas standards, so they decided to sit on the outside deck overlooking the water. Lily was right, it was amazing. The day was warm, the breeze was soft, the sky was blue, and the water sparkled, and Jack and Lily fell into their old familiarity with ease. They talked and laughed for what seemed like hours. The afternoon was magical.

"Is the weather always this perfect here?" Jack asked.

Lily laughed. "Not exactly. Sometimes we have fierce thunderstorms that come out of nowhere, and it feels like the lightning is right on top of you, deliberately hunting you down. Of course, Texas has some scary storms too, but not like Florida. Plus, there are hurricanes."

"Do hurricanes hit here often?" Jack's curiosity was piqued.

"Actually no, but the threat is here just the same. Needless to say, we keep a close watch on the weather during hurricane season."

Jack had something tugging at his mind, and an uncomfortable silence crept up on them. He didn't come all the way to Florida to talk about the weather. He had never forgotten Lily, not in all these years, but it had been a long time since they'd been around each other, and he wondered how much she might have changed. So far though, they still seemed to fit like a glove. It was as if no time had come between them at all. Jack grew serious. "Lily, how long has Damien been gone?"

Caught off guard at the sound of her husband's name, Lily's smile faded. No one in Florida knew much about her former life. She'd left Damien in the past. She looked over at the water. Reflections of the sun sparkled in the ripples of the waves. "Well, I guess around…almost six years."

"I'm sorry. I shouldn't have brought it up."

"It's okay. It's life." She picked up her drink and took a sip. "Why do you ask?"

"I just wondered how you handled it all? You seem so strong."

Lily knew exactly how she'd handled it and exactly where her strength came from. "God helped me through it." Jack nodded his head in perfect understanding. "It was kinda weird actually. It was like I was in some sort of bubble." She looked away, letting the memory come. "And there was this peace surrounding me, helping me get through all the duties and responsibilities I had to deal with when he was sick…and when he died." Lily looked down at her plate. "After that, I finally had a small break down." She picked up a french fry and swirled it through the ketchup. "There was so much change in my life. I needed to get out of that house and go back to work, but I couldn't move back home and work at Charlotte's again. It would have been too difficult working with you." She looked up at her sudden confession. Jack nodded. "Sorry. No offense. I just knew I had to start over somewhere fresh." She dropped the French fry on her plate and wiped her hands on her napkin. "So, I came back here where the air is salty enough to heal all wounds." She formed a faint smile. "So, what about you? Why are you here with your baby girl, but not your wife?"

It was Jack's turn to release the details of his life. However, he didn't answer, and she didn't push. After their late lunch they decided to take a walk on the pier behind the restaurant, stopping to marvel at the stingray soaring through the clear water. "I can see why you would come here, Lily. The perfect place to mend a broken heart."

She stopped him, took his hand, and looked at him straight on. "Is that why you're here?" she asked bluntly.

"Partly," he admitted.

"So you wanna tell me what happened?"

Jack took a deep breath then slowly released it. "Hailey left us."

Lily was shocked. "Us? You mean she left Grace too?" *How does a mother leave her child?*

"She gave me custodial rights. Which means, Grace lives with me most of the time and visits her mom every other weekend and one day during the week."

Lily tried to hold back her disbelief, but she knew her eyes probably betrayed her. She would have given anything to have a child. How could Hailey walk away from hers? "Well, that's good for you. How does Grace feel about it though?"

"She misses her mom, but she's a strong little girl. This trip is to help with the transition."

"I see. So why'd she do it?"

Jack looked over at the water and released a stifled breath. "She's in love with someone else." He turned to look at her as the irony of his words fell on them. "She's been having an affair for a year."

"Jack, I don't know what to say. I'm so sorry. I always wanted you to be happy. You know that, right?" Lily touched his arm.

"Lily, I know *you*, so yes, I've always known that."

His words warmed her heart. They had both tried to do the right thing, but falling for each other had truly caused some problems in their marriages. Even so, Lily had been able to find happiness with Damien in spite of never getting over Jack.

"Jack, were you and Hailey ever happy?"

Jack shook his head. "Probably not. Not really anyway." He leaned against the railing. "It was my fault. I tried to make it work, but I guess my heart was never really in it. I don't blame her one bit." He turned to Lily. "Ya know, I never admitted to her that I went to the hospital to see you during our wedding reception, and she accused me of lying about where I'd been."

"Wait…what? You were at the hospital?" She glared at him.

"Yeah, you don't remember?"

"No!"

"Didn't your mom tell you?"

"No. No one told me. I didn't even know you knew I had an accident."

"Well, I did know, and I drove to the hospital as soon as I found out. I stayed with you a while until I knew you were okay. Then I had to leave to get back to the reception. I was pretty vague when Hailey questioned me. She accused me of lying to her." He shook his head. "I hate lying," he said under his breath. "Anyway, it wasn't the best way to start our marriage, but I just had to see you, to make sure you were okay." His eyes held hers. "Wild horses couldn't have stopped me."

Lily's mind went back to the night of her accident. She'd had no idea that Jack had been with her. Her mom never told her. Charlotte never told her.

"You *were* okay, weren't you, Lily?" Jack interrupted her thoughts.

"What? Oh, yes, I was. I had a slight concussion, some scrapes and bruises, but that was it. Jack, if I had known that you were with me that night…"

"It wouldn't have changed a thing. Damien needed you, and I had just gotten married. I don't blame them for not telling you. It probably would have just made things harder for both of us."

Lily leaned back against the rail and exhaled. "You're right. I know, but they still should have told me. I was stunned when I heard about your wedding. So, that might have eased the blow a little." Lily looked at Jack with a lopsided grin. "I'm terrible, aren't I?"

"No, you're beautiful. Still beautiful. After all these years." Jack stepped closer, touching her face gently, and leaned toward her. The sun was beginning to set revealing the lateness of the hour. "I need to go get Grace," he said softly, breaking the spell.

"I understand." She took a deep breath and let it out.

"Are you free tomorrow?"

"Actually, I am, why?"

"Well, Grace and I are going to the beach. Would you like to join us?"

"Are you sure you want me to meet Grace?" she asked nervously.

"Of course! It's time that my two gals meet each other." Their eyes locked as they both realized what he'd just said, but it was too late to cover it up. It was out there. "Come on, let me drive you back to your truck." Jack put his arm around Lily and walked her through the restaurant and out to the parking lot. He opened the door for her when they got to his truck. *Always a gentleman*.

As they drove back to Uncle Nick's Bar and Grill, they finalized their plans for the next day, as Lily did agree to meet them at the beach. He walked her to her truck and waited for her to get into the driver's seat. Then he leaned in and kissed her forehead, leaving her feeling all warm and giddy inside.

Lily grinned from ear to ear the whole way home, but once she pulled up to her apartment thoughts of Jayme assailed her. Jayme loved her. He wanted to marry her. He was good to her. He helped her get back into life after Damien's death. He was her best friend, but she'd hesitated whenever he brought up marriage. She cared for him deeply, but marriage? Something had been holding her back, and now she knew what. The Lord was working in His mysterious ways. Was God giving her another chance with Jack? She and Jayme were in a crossroads in their relationship, but did that give her the right to get involved with someone else? However, Jack wasn't just someone else, and if she couldn't marry Jayme, it might very well be due to her feelings for Jack, and now that he was no longer married, this might be their first (and last) chance to find their way back to each other. No, she had to see this through, or she would never know. Unfortunately, she would also have to tell Jack about Jayme, which just might mess up everything. She needed to call Allison, but that would have to wait till tomorrow. By the time Lily crawled into bed, all she could think about was how close her lips had been to finally touching Jack's once again. She fell asleep, her lips curled upward in happiness.

Chapter Twenty-six

**Hope deferred makes the heart sick, But desire fulfilled is a tree of life.
Prov. 13:12**

The next morning, Lily found herself humming a happy tune as she got ready for the day. Baxter meowed at her impatiently wanting his breakfast. She started her percolator and went to the pantry to get the cat food. "I'm going to the beach today, Baxter. Care to take a guess who I'm going with?" Baxter meowed again. "No? Really? The most exciting thing that's happened to me in years, and all you can think about is food, huh?" As if mentally summoning Jack, Lily heard a text come through on her phone.

"Hope I didn't wake you. Just wanted to share this beautiful sunrise with you." Attached was a photo of the sun rising over the beach. It was stunning.

"Beautiful pic! You didn't wake me. Baxter did, begging for breakfast," Lily replied.

"You still have Baxter???" Jack asked.

"Of course!"
"Can't believe it! Still up for the beach?"
"Did you tell Grace I was coming?"
"Yes. She's excited!"
"In that case, yes. I'm excited too, and nervous to meet her."
"Don't be nervous. She'll love you! Poolside restaurant at 11:00?"
"Sounds good. See u soon."

"Well Baxter, I get to meet Grace today." Lily released a long sigh. "I'm scared, but that's not the only thing I'm scared about." She took a deep breath, poured herself a cup of coffee then walked out on the balcony to finish watching the sun rise, marveling at God's artwork, knowing that in a way, she and Jack were watching the sunrise together. It amazed her that even after all these years and all the miles apart, their connection remained strong. She called Allison and filled her in.

"Still having flutters? After all this time? What about Jayme?" Allison asked.

"Oh Al…I don't know…I'm so confused," Lily answered.

"And Jayme is out of town?"

"Yes, for a couple of weeks."

"Well, I guess you should use this time to see what you want. Just be careful how far it gets. You have to think of Jayme's feelings too."

"You're right. I'll be careful. Thanks for the advice."

"Hey, what are friends for?"

REMEMBER ME

Just before 11:00 a.m., Lily walked through the Jupiter Resort's lobby and out the door to the poolside restaurant. The day was bright and already hot. Approaching the pool, she was met with the sound of a festive beach song played by Charlie on his guitar. *Some things never change.* She waved to Charlie, walked over to the bar, and ordered a pineapple juice with a splash of cranberry. She sat down and took a sip. Refreshing. Just then she heard the giggles of a little girl and turned to find Jack striving to keep up with her. He caught her up in his arms and threw her over his head and onto his shoulders in one fell swoop. The sight caused a hitch in Lily's breath as she took it all in. In spite of being without her mother, Grace looked like a happy little girl. Lily watched Jack's eyes scan his surroundings until they finally landed on her. Their eyes met with a wide smile. He walked over to her and gently leaned over to introduce her to Grace.

"Gracie, this is my friend Lily."

"Hi Lilwy. I'm 4." She held up four tiny fingers. "But I'm goin' on 5." She then held up five fingers with pride.

"Hi Grace. Nice to meet you." Lily reached up and shook Grace's hand. "You certainly are a pretty young lady."

Grace beamed with pride at the compliment. "Tank you. Yer pwetty too."

"Why thank you."

"Have you had breakfast?" Jack asked Lily.

"Yes, early this morning...while I was watching the sun rise." Lily winked.

"Mmmmm, what a coincidence. Me too." Jack grinned. "How about lunch then?"

"That sounds good. They have great food here."

"I wanna cheeburger." Grace patted her dad on the head impatiently.

"Okay, Doodlebug. Cheeseburger coming right up. Lily?"

"Ummmm, I'll have a club sandwich."

Jack ordered two cheeseburgers and Lily's club sandwich. They walked over to a table and sat under a large umbrella. Nobody was in the pool yet, but Grace begged to go in.

"Daddy, can we go swimming now?" Grace hopped up and down in front of Jack.

"Jack, I can wait for the food if you wanna take her in for a quick dip," Lily offered.

"Are you sure?"

"Pleeeeeeease Daddy." Grace patted Jack's arm repeatedly.

Lily nodded her head and laughed at the cute little girl in front of her pulling at her daddy's heartstrings. It must be tough to say no to that sweet little face.

"Okay, but just until they bring our food."

"Yaaaaayyyyyy!" Grace squealed with delight.

Fifteen minutes later, the server brought out their food and all three were ready to eat. Jack dried off while Lily helped Grace with her towel. They chatted all through lunch, Jack paid the bill, and they headed out to the beach.

"Lilwy, would you put sunbock on me?"

"Sure, Grace. Turn around." Lily applied the sunblock liberally. There was no way that child would get a sunburn today. Not on her watch.

"Would you put some on my back too?" Jack wiggled his eyebrows at Lily making her laugh.

"Sure, as long as you return the favor." She grinned.

While waiting for their food to digest, they decided to sit in the sun for a little while. Grace focused on building her sand castle while Jack and Lily sat close to each other gazing out to the sea, listening to the ocean waves crash gently against the shore. It was mesmerizing. Jack reached his hand over to Lily's and linked his pinky finger with hers. A jolt ran through her entire body. It was amazing how one little pinky finger could emit so much power. She squeezed Jack's hand. After a while, they got up and walked over to the water's edge. At first, Grace would only get in ankle deep but soon enough they found themselves jumping in the waves hand in hand in hand as Grace squealed with laughter between them. It was a good day. They stayed at the beach for over two hours until Grace started to yawn. Jack held Grace in his arms as they walked back up to the hotel. She was already starting to fall asleep on her daddy's shoulder.

"I'd better take her to the room for a nap or I will live to regret it." Regret already settled in

Jack's mind though, knowing he had to end his date with Lily. It had been such a wonderful day. He'd been worried about Grace's reaction to her, but all his worrying had been futile because they hit it off right from the start.

Lily nodded her head with the same look of regret in her eyes. "I had a really nice time Jack. Thank you for including me." She rocked back and forth on her heels. "Grace is a terrific little girl. You should be proud." As she looked down into her purse searching for her keys Jack gently touched her chin. Lily looked up and gazed into his yearning eyes. In her slumber, Grace stirred, breaking the moment. Jack shifted her to his other shoulder.

"I'll call you later?"

Lily nodded then picked up Jack's hand and without words, kissed the top of it. His entire body warmed at her touch. He leaned down and kissed her forehead, hovering close to her lips.

Lily floated on air all the way back to her truck, but a nagging feeling in the back of her conscience burst her happy bubble. The opportunity to tell him about Jayme never arrived.

That night Lily was in the tub when her phone rang. It was Jack.

"Hey. Whatcha doin?" he asked.
"Soaking in the tub. What are you doin?"

"Well, now I'm thinking about you soakin' in the tub."

Lily laughed. "I had a great time today. Grace is terrific."

"She is, isn't she? I'm a lucky dad. She really likes you too. Couldn't stop talking about you this afternoon."

"Really? That's so sweet." Relief flooded over Lily. She had been worried about Grace's reaction to her daddy's new friend.

"She's sweet," Jack replied. "So are you, by the way."

"Well, you aren't too intolerable yourself."

"Gee, thanks." Jack laughed and asked, "What are you doing tomorrow?"

"Well, I have to work the lunch shift, but then I'm off around 4:00."

"Would it be okay if Grace and I came in for lunch?"

"Yeah, that would be great!" Lily's heart leapt. He wanted to see her again! "So, I will see y'all tomorrow then," she said calmly, masking her excitement.

"Yep. See ya tomorrow. Oh, and Lily?"

"Yeah?"

"You are still so beautiful," Jack said softly.

"Thanks Jack. You better be careful though. You're making my heart flutter."

"Flutter, huh? Well, I guess I've still got it, then."

"Ha ha. I guess you do. Hope you can sleep with that big head of yours. I mean it might be too big for your pillow."

"Oh Lily, you're still a funny girl, aren't you?"

"I have my moments."
"See ya tomorrow."
"Tomorrow." Lily sank into her suds, beaming. *I'm falling in love…again.*

Later that night, Lily wasn't sleepy so she scoured through her book shelves for something that would be intriguing enough to take her mind off of Jack. She landed on a book about the end times. "Well, that should do it," she said to Baxter who meowed at the foot of her bed. She curled up in bed to read the frightening book. It was about Revelation and the end of the world. Even though the book was labeled fiction, it really freaked her out, especially because she was all alone and she knew that Revelation was not really meant to be fiction. As she got to the part where the anti-christ was about to be revealed, her phone dinged. She jumped so high she could've hit the ceiling. It was a text from Jayme, whom she had not heard from in days.

"Are you awake?"
"Yes."
"What are you doing?"
"Reading."
"Reading what?"
"A book called <u>The Days of Noah</u>"
"Is it about Noah's ark?"
"No. LOL. It's about the end times."
"OMG. Get real."
Lily was already frustrated with his attitude.
"Anyway, how are you?" he asked her.

Lily sighed. *"Fine. You?"*
"Okay. I miss you."
"Then why haven't I heard from you?" Lily knew her hostility was unfounded. She just felt guilty about being with Jack, even though they had done nothing wrong, plus his attitude really ticked her off.
"I'm sorry. Just needed time to think."
"Me too. I'm not mad. Just confused."
"Me too. I thought you'd want to marry me. This isn't good for my ego."
"I've been married, remember? Not all moonlight and roses."
"I know. You went through hell."
"It's not just that."
"My age bothers you."
"I'll be signing up for AARP before you even have one gray hair!"
"LOL. Actually, this whole thing is starting to give me gray hair!"
"Just enjoy seeing all your old friends and your family. We can talk about all this when you get back."
"As long as I know you aren't mad at me."
"I'm not. You still mad at me?"
"No. I can't stay mad at you. You and your gray hair are just too cute."
"Ha Ha. Be careful. See you in a few days."
"You too!"

Jayme was a good guy. However, they were not equally yoked. He was a Christian, but a fair-weather one. That was another reason she held back. She didn't want a repeat of a life with Damien. Even though he finally came around to Christ, the first few years had been really difficult, and the next time she got married, *if* she got married again, she wanted Christ to be just as important to her new husband as He was to her.

Her phone dinged again, but this time it was Jack.

"What are you doin?"
"Reading a book about the tribulation."
"Wow. Heavy reading before bed. Hope you don't have nightmares."
"Me too. It's really freaking me out, but it's just too good to put down."
"No reason to freak out. God will protect us—if it happens during our lifetime."
"You're right. He always has, always will."
"Can I borrow it when you finish reading it?"
"Of course."
"See u tomorrow?"
"Yes, tomorrow."

What a difference, Lily thought, then she continued to read late into the night. It was the only thing that could keep her mind off of Jack.

Chapter Twenty-seven

I found him whom my soul loves; I held on to him and would not let him go.
Song of Sol. 3:4

The next day the restaurant was pretty slow. Jack and Grace walked in around noon and sat in Lily's section.

"Hi, Lilwy," Grace waved to Lily with a huge smile on her face. Lily smiled and waved back. She finished taking a food order and walked straight over to Grace, picked her up, and gave her a great big hug.

"How's my new friend?"

"Happy. We goin to Disneyworld tomowow!"

"Wow! That sounds like fun!"

"Can you come, please, please, please?" Grace asked impatiently.

Lily looked at Jack. He nodded and gave her a thumbs up. "Well, I'm supposed to work, but maybe I can get someone to cover for me. I'll try, okay?"

Grace nodded gleefully. "Okay. I hope you can come!" Grace threw her arms around Lily's neck.

"Me too." Lily said, relishing the warmth of a small child in her arms.

"Me three," Jack added with a wink.

Lily made arrangements with Nick to have the day off so she could go to Disneyworld, and Jack and Grace ate their lunch and got ready to go back to the hotel so Grace could go swimming. Lily stared at the both of them wistfully as they walked out of the door. Jack turned around and winked at her, making her heart flutter. She took a deep breath and picked up the money he'd left on the table to pay his bill. There was a note with it. Lily unfolded it, amazed at what two little words could do to her heart. "Dinner tonight?" Lily grabbed her cell phone and typed out the word "Yes". He replied about ten minutes later. "Pick you up at work."

Lily had just finished her shift when Jack walked in. She had been tired, but her adrenaline kicked in as soon as she saw his face. They were walking out the door as Nancy was coming in.

"Hey Nancy," Lily said.

Nancy turned to look at Jack as he exited the restaurant. "Hey Lily. What's up?"

"Not too much. On my way out. You aren't working are you?"

"Not tonight. My baby-sitter is out of town, remember." She pointed at Jack who was already walking to his truck. "Is that guy a friend of yours?" Nancy asked.

"Um, yeah. I gotta run. See ya later, Nancy." Lily made a quick escape, avoiding further interrogation.

Jack followed Lily back to her apartment so she could change clothes. While he waited, he walked around her small living room looking at all the little doodads produced by a woman's touch. Over on the mantle stood a hodgepodge of framed photos. He held up a picture of a teenage Lily and her dad fishing by a pond—Jack wondered if it was taken at the ranch. Next to it stood an old family photo of Lily with a mouth full of braces and her parents. A picture of Lily holding Baxter in front of a Christmas tree finished out the ensemble. There were no pictures of Damien or any other men. Relief swept over him.

Lily came out of her room dressed in a white lace top and denim skirt. He stared at her, speechless. She was beautiful. He was so tempted to kiss her, but not here, not now. They decided on Italian food and went to a small quiet bistro on the other side of town frequented only by locals.

Jack opened the door for Lily and she walked in ahead of him. The lights were dim and candles glowed softly. A single red rose adorned the white linen tablecloths, simple but elegant. The setting was full of romance, perfect. Lily's fragrance of orange blossoms and hyacinth left him feeling both peaceful and wanting. The hostess led them to their table and Jack pulled out her chair, as a gentleman should for a lady. He sat down across the small table from Lily, never taking his eyes off of her as soft music played in the background.

They had white wine, which eased any trace of self-consciousness. They ate their dinner slowly as they talked, completely enchanted with one another. They reminisced and laughed and blossomed in each other's presence.

After the server cleared the table of their empty plates, Jack reached over the table and lightly touched Lily's hand—she, tenderly lacing her fingers through his own. Noticing other couples starting to dance, Jack pulled Lily to her feet and slowly led her to the dance floor. He held her close as they swayed back and forth to the music. Her essence drew him in, intoxicating him. Searing heat from their intertwined bodies left him feeling dizzy. Oh to be within each other's arms again, so warm, so close, so tender—just as they were meant to be.

Lily was enchanting, singing softly into his ear, and drawing him in even closer. Her breath on his skin raised the tiny hairs along his cheekbone. He pulled back and gazed into her eyes longingly revealing what his body felt, what he felt. He leaned in and kissed her tenderly, her lips opening to him in invitation. Fire blazed through his veins. Lily's body responded with a heat that matched his own. She returned his kiss with fervor, wrapping her demanding arms around him, pulling him tight into her embrace. The heat and headiness of their fiery attraction left them wanting. Jack pulled back slightly with heavy breath and declared softly, "Oh Lily, I never stopped wanting you. I never stopped dreaming about you. It's always been you."

REMEMBER ME

He kissed her once again with gentle hunger. They realized too late that their emotional—and physical—display was drawing some attention. Lily blushed, but Jack would not allow a little social discomposure to separate her body from his, so he gently guided her head to his shoulder and they chastely danced the rest of the evening as they allowed the heat of their bodies to die down to a warm flame.

Jack drove Lily home and stopped his truck in front of the steps leading to her door. Relieved, Lily saw that the lights were off in Nancy's apartment. She didn't know how she would explain this scene with Jack to her neighbor, who was also her friend, as well as Jayme's sister. Lily knew she walked a tight rope and had to be careful.

Jack walked around and held out his hand to help Lily down from the tall truck, and then walked with her up the stairs to her door, never letting go. He turned to face her and stepped closer. Anticipation swirled through her as he leaned down and gently touched his soft lips to her own, building up their desire once again. She pulled him closer, deepening their kiss. Jack pressed his body into hers, her back pressing against the door. Her heart raced as fresh air seemed to fill her soul. She wanted him, but she knew him, so she was not surprised when he pulled back, his eyes full of longing. "See ya in the mornin'," his raspy voice whispered to her lips. She felt as if she would melt into a puddle right there on her doorstep, her lips desperate for his touch. She wanted to cry out to him but just stood there, still, as she watched him get into his truck and drive away.

Jack and Grace picked Lily up at her apartment early the next day and then hit the road heading to Disneyworld. It was a warm day but not sweltering, and they rode all the way to Orlando with the windows down, wind blowing through their hair. Jack and Lily stole intimate glances as Grace chattered on continually in the back seat. The moment they walked through the gates, however, Grace was entranced. They couldn't ride any of the bigger rides since Grace was too little, but they had a wonderful time and took lots of pictures together, and of course, the day ended all too soon.

On the way back home that night, an exhausted Grace slept peacefully in the back seat. Jack gave Lily a happy smile and held her hand, but Lily's mood fell as she realized that pictures would be the only thing left after Jack and Grace headed back home to Texas, which would be in only a couple of days. She also realized that she still hadn't found the right time to tell him about Jayme, not that it would really matter if this was only a short fling. That thought broke her heart. It was dark in the truck so Jack didn't pick up on

Lily's sudden mood swing. When they got to her apartment, she leaned over and kissed him tenderly and hopped out of the truck before he had a chance to turn off the engine and walk her to the door.

That night, Jack had a hard time sleeping. He had to go home soon, and he didn't know what that meant for him and Lily. They'd had a great day together, so he couldn't understand what had gone wrong on the way home, but he could tell something was off with Lily when she didn't give him the chance to walk her to the door. Maybe it was just that she didn't want him to leave Grace in the truck, or maybe she didn't want to risk a heated repeat of the night before with Grace so close by. Either way, he knew something was amiss. It was time for them to talk, but he'd been so enamored with her these past few days, he hadn't had a chance to put his thoughts or his words in order. Tomorrow morning he would call the front desk and make arrangements for Kayla to watch Grace so that he and Lily could finally have a chance to talk. It had to be done. He knew exactly what he wanted and it was time he tell her. He reached for his phone.

"You awake?" Jack asked Lily.
"Yes. You?"
"Ha ha. Almost fell for that one."

"I had a great time today. Thanks for including me."

"Me too. What's your schedule tomorrow?"

"Lunch shift. Should be off around 3:30 or 4:00.

"Can I pick you up around 6:30 at your apartment?"

"Sure. What are we gonna do?"

"Dinner on the beach? I can get some food from the restaurant here."

"Sounds like fun."

"Great! See ya tomorrow. Sleep well."

"You too."

The next morning, Jack was able to make arrangements for Kayla to watch Grace that evening. Grace liked Kayla so she wasn't too upset that he was leaving her behind. Jack, on the other hand, felt quite nervous. He knew that this date would determine his future. He knew exactly what he wanted from Lily. He had never forgotten her, had never quite gotten over her, in fact, he'd never stopped loving her, but he couldn't ask her to marry him, it was too soon, and he couldn't expect her to move back to Texas for him if he wasn't asking. *Or could he?*

Jack arrived to pick up Lily at 6:30. She was beautiful. She had on shorts and a blue t-shirt that brought out the color of her eyes. She carried a large straw tote bag.

REMEMBER ME

"I brought some wine. Is that okay? Oh, and some plastic wine glasses." She was nervous, he could tell. "Can't have glass on the beach."

"Sure. Let me help you with that." Jack was nervous too. She was so pretty. Their eyes locked, and he couldn't turn away. Just then he heard a young girl's voice yell Lily's name. He turned as she ran up to them and jumped into Lily's arms.

"Julie! Hey girl!" Lily hugged her back. "Where's your mama?"

"Mama's at work." Julie pointed behind her. "I'm with Uncle Jayme."

With wide eyes, she turned around. "You're back from Louisiana?" She asked Jayme.

"Uncle Jayme got homesick." Julie offered.

Horrified, Lily watched as Jayme trudged up the sidewalk toward Lily and Jack.

"Lily?" Jayme nodded at her. Hands in his pockets, a dismal look on his face.

Jack looked at Jayme and then back at Lily. Lily met his eyes and slowly shook her head, then looked down. He guessed that was his cue to leave. He handed the bag with the wine back to Lily and walked to his truck. He glanced over at her one more time, but she was focused on Jayme. He got into his truck and watched them. Jayme was standing close to Lily, *his* Lily. Jealousy sprang up like a wildebeest, territorial and protective. He wanted to punch that guy, but why? It wasn't his fault. In fact, Jayme should probably punch him. They walked into her apartment...together. Anger took hold of Jack's heart. He hated this feeling. Jayme turned back and looked at Jack, paused, and glared at him, then he closed the door, the door to Lily's apartment. It occurred to him to wait to see if he came out, but he thought better of it, so he started his truck and drove away.

Jayme schlepped into Lily's apartment with his head down. He stood by the sliding glass door leading out to the balcony, his back turned to her.

"Would you like something to drink?" she asked.

He whipped around. "Drink? That's all you can say? Do I want something to drink?"

"Okay. Sorry." Lily threw her hands up and traipsed across the small living room.

"Is he what you've been doing while I was away?" Jayme pointed at the door.

"Jayme, it's not what you think." Lily sank to the edge of the sofa.

"Really? I never took you for a liar, Lily."

"Okay. It is sort of what you think, but nothing's happened." Lily crossed her arms over her chest.

"It didn't look like nothing to me. Geez Lily, I thought if I went away for a while, you'd…"

"What? Come to my senses and marry you?" she asked, brows furrowed.

"Well, I sure wasn't expecting this!" Jayme scowled at her. "How could you, Lily?" He started for the door. "I guess we're done here, aren't we?"

"Jayme wait." Lily stood up and went to him. "Don't go like this. Sit down. Please. Let's talk."

Jayme turned to look at her. She thought he would walk out, but he shuffled back over to the armchair and sat down. He put his hands over his face and leaned forward. Baxter looped through Jayme's legs, meowing, then jumped up into his lap. Jayme turned all his attention to Baxter, petting him as Lily talked.

"Why did you come back early?" Lily asked quietly.

"Nancy. She called me. Said I should cut my visit short."

"Oh." Lily felt like a liar and a cheat. She looked down, filled with shame. "I'm sorry Jayme."

"Is he the reason you won't marry me?" He looked at her with such pain, it tore her apart.

"In a way."

"So you've been seeing him behind my back?" Tears emerged in his eyes. "For how long?"

"No. It's not like that. He lives in Texas. He showed up here a few days ago. We...reconnected."

"Reconnected. Right." He sniffled. "Doesn't make you less of a cheater though, does it?"

"No, I guess it doesn't."

"Damn Lily, I really loved you. I wanted to marry you. Have kids with you. I've never felt that way about anyone before."

"I loved you too." Oh, this was so hard. She hated hurting Jayme. He didn't deserve it.

He gave Baxter a big hug and set him down gently. "Bye Bud. I'm gonna miss you."

"Just because two people love each other, doesn't mean they would be happy for the rest of their lives together," Lily said.

Jayme stood up and went to Lily. He softly gripped her shoulders and looked down into her eyes. "I would've been." Then he walked out, closing the door on her, and their life together.

Lily watched him through her window as he walked down the steps and got into his little red car. He hit the steering wheel then peeled out of the parking lot. She turned away and curled up on the couch, holding close the throw pillow that had been a gift from Damien their last Christmas together, just a few short years earlier, a lifetime ago. Through her tears she read the inscription, "And we know that God causes all things to work together for good." Baxter jumped up beside her and curled his warm body into hers as she let the tears flow.

Jack felt sick, but he couldn't go back to the hotel. He just couldn't put on a brave face for his daughter right now. He decided to go to a bar, but the only one he knew of was the place where Lily worked, and since he knew she definitely wouldn't be there, that's where he went. He walked into Uncle Nick's Bar and Grill and sat down at the bar. Nick walked up to him from the other side of the bar and asked, "What's your pleasure?" Recognition hit him all of a sudden as Nick realized who he was. "Hey, aren't you Lily's friend?"

"Yep."

"You okay, man? You look like your dog just died."

Jack wasn't sure what he could share with Lily's boss, even though he could use a friend right now, so he kept his feelings to himself. "I'm okay. I'll have a beer. Wait. No." Jack stopped Nick before he had the chance to open the bottle. "I'll have a whiskey and coke." Jack's next mistake of the evening. Nick nodded and poured the drink. After drink number two, he opened up to Nick and told him what happened at Lily's. By the time he'd finished his fourth drink, Jack had told Nick the entire story of everything he'd ever been through with Lily, and then Nick cut him off, as he'd obviously had too much to drink.

"Jack, I'm going to give you some advice, from bartender to drunk, okay?" Nick leaned on the bar across from Jack.

"Sure." Jack folded his arms and rested them on the countertop, his eyes half closed.

"Look, I've known Lily for a while now. She's one of those women…well, she's special. Honestly, I'd kill for a chance with her." Jack glared at him. "Don't worry, I've never had a chance with her, but what I'm saying is you better not let her go. It's obvious how she feels about you."

"Really? How does she feel about me?" Jack asked.

"Let's just say that Lily doesn't ever look at Jayme the way she looks at you."

"Is he her boyfriend?"

"Yeah man. He is. Sorry."

"What am I supposed to do about him?" Jack smacked his palm to his forehead and leaned heavily on his elbow.

"She doesn't love him, at least not enough to marry him."

"Marry him?"

"He's asked her several times, but she keeps putting him off. Now I think I know why."

"Why?"

"You, dummy." Nick threw a hand towel at Jack, landing on his head.

"But we just met up again a few days ago. I can't just ask her to pick up and move across the country. I can't just ask her to marry me."

"Why not? How long have y'all…ya know?"

Jack gave him the eye, "I've *loved* her for nearly a decade."

"Well then, seems to me like it's long overdue."

Nick promised to keep Jack's secret and put him on the cot in the back to sleep off the whiskey.

"What! He's where?" Lily let out a deep breath. "Thanks for calling me, Nick. I'll be there in a few minutes." Lily was exhausted. Yesterday she was the princess of Disneyworld, today she was Chicken Little and the sky was falling. Her life was such a mess. She pulled into the parking lot of Uncle Nick's and then around back to the delivery door. Nick opened the door for her and led her to the back room where Jack was still sleeping.

"I wouldn't have called you, but it was creeping up on closing time and I knew he wasn't in any shape to drive. All he's done is sleep and snore, sleep and snore."

"Help me get him in my truck, Nick. We'll just have to leave his truck here for the night."

"Why don't we try to get some coffee into him first? You can't take him back to his hotel like this."

"You're right. Okay. Let's get him to a booth." They each took an arm and lifted Jack up to drag him to the cushioned booth where he promptly fell over. All the customers had gone, so Nick locked the front door and put out the *Closed* sign. "Thanks Nick. I know you probably want to get home."

"Hey, anything to help the broken-hearted."

Lily looked at him, stunned. "Broken-hearted? What do you mean?"

"Lily, really? You don't see it? He's got it bad for you. He came here for you, not Disneyworld."

"How do you know? Did he tell you that?"

"Well, four whiskeys for a man who obviously can't hold his liquor, plus a broken heart? He may have opened up a little." Nick grinned and winked at Lily. She was embarrassed but had no time to worry about that now.

Lily made coffee while Nick helped Jack sit up. He felt like death warmed over. Lily walked toward him with a coffee cup in her hand. He bowed his head in shame and refused to look at her. She put the steaming cup down in front of him then slid into the seat across the table. He took a sip, ran his hands through his hair and smiled sheepishly. She raised an eyebrow at him and gave him the look. She waited until he'd finished his first cup of coffee, then stood up to go get him a refill. She brought herself another cup back with her. Apparently they would be up for a while. Jack was still somewhere in between sick and impaired, but he was quite conscientious of his situation.

"Lily," He looked up at her, his eyes meeting hers, "I'm sorry."

"I know," she replied softly. "It's okay. I don't blame you. After all, you did get stood up." She grinned at him as she put her hand over his. "I should have told you about Jayme. It was my fault."

"No. It was mine. I couldn't exactly expect that you would be sitting here waiting for me."

"What do you mean?

"Lily, I didn't come here to go to Disneyworld. I came here, to Florida, to see you." He paused, waiting for her to respond, but she didn't, so he began again. "Lily, I know you've moved on with your life, and you'll probably end up marrying that young guy, but I just have to tell you how I feel."

"Jack, I..."

"No Lily! Let me finish. I didn't want to come here and disrupt your life. We haven't even seen each other in years. I can't ask anything of you, but you need to know I never forgot you. I never stopped caring about you. I never stopped lov..." He took his hand away and looked down again. Bracing himself with the table, he stood up and walked over to the wall and leaned his hands against it for support. He stared at the floor for a few minutes then turned back to look at her. She watched him quietly. "Lily, I never stopped loving you."

Her eyes widened at his words.

"There. I said it. So, if you want, I will just go on home to Texas and you will never have to see me again and you can go on with your life and marry that young tan surfer dude and live happily ever after and…"

Lily stood and faced him, "Jack! Stop!" He stopped his ranting and looked at her as if just now realizing she was there. Lily let out a deep breath. "How about, instead of me planning a wedding, which I am in no place in my life to be planning right now, and no one to plan it with, by the way…How about if we just go on that picnic you promised me instead."

Jack's mouth gaped open. "Wait. What? Say that again? You aren't gonna marry that guy?"

"No. Don't get me wrong. Jayme is an incredible guy, but I just can't marry him."

"Why?"

"Because I want to love the man I marry, and I want to marry the man I love."

It took a minute, but Lily's words finally tunneled through the fog to his brain. "You don't love him?"

"I should, but no, not the way a woman should love the man she's gonna marry."

"And…wait! Who is the man you love?"

Lily walked up to Jack, threw her arms around him and said, "You, you big dummy!" then kissed him.

Nick cleared his throat from the other side of the bar. "Can we close up now?"

Jack and Lily pulled out of their embrace and blushed, nodding their heads.

"Great! I'm exhausted. Lily, take the next two days off and figure out the rest of your life, would you?" Nick said.

Lily smiled and nodded her head. "Thanks Nick. I'll call you in a couple of days."

Jack sent Kayla a text, letting her know that he would be late, and they made arrangements for Grace to spend the night with her. Lily drove as she and Jack headed to the beach to finally have their picnic, only now it would be under the moonlight, instead of the sunset...and coffee instead of wine.

They parked near Juno Beach. The moon shone so bright they had no trouble seeing their way down the path to the ocean. Lily spread out a blanket on the sand and marveled at the moonlight glistening off the water. They plopped down next to each other and admired the view.

"Jack, can I ask you something? I don't mean to bring up the past, it's just, I've just always wondered."

"What, Lily? You can ask me anything."

"Well, when you got married," She stiffened.

"Yeah?"

"Well, why didn't you invite me?" She exhaled, wrapping her arms around her knees.

Jack cleared his throat and grinned, "Well, to be honest, because I loved you."

She understood. It wouldn't have been fair to Hailey. "Jack?"

"Yeah?"

"Did you love her?"

"Who? Hailey?" Jack stared out at the water for a silent moment before answering. "Yes. Just not in the way she needed me to."

Lily leaned her head against Jack's shoulder and they talked and talked until the sun came up.

It was early in the morning when Lily drove Jack back to the bar to get his truck. He looked completely disheveled, but sober.

"Can I see you tonight?" Jack asked.

"Well, since I have the next couple of days off to figure out my life," Lily laughed, "I guess you have me until you head back to Texas."

"Great! Go home, take a nap, then come back to the resort."

"Sounds like a good plan, but on your last night, I want to cook dinner for you at my place." Jack agreed and kissed her good night.

Chapter Twenty-eight

**There is no fear in love;
but perfect love casts out fear.
1 John 4:18**

Lily woke from a long nap feeling rested and happy. She stretched her arms over her head and looked at the clock. It was 1:00 in the afternoon. Staying up all night was something she hadn't done in years. She started her coffee then jumped in the shower. She fed Baxter and curled up in the chair on her balcony with her coffee and phone in hand. She dialed her mom's number.

"Hello, Sweetie." Her mom answered on the first ring.

"Hi, Mom. How've you been?"

"Great. I love this California weather, and the houses are gorgeous, but really expensive and—"

"I'm glad, Mom. Listen, I was calling to let you know that I'm thinking about going home to the ranch for a while. Would that be okay with you?"

"Of course, Honey. It's your home. Is everything okay with you and Jayme?" she inquired. "Won't he miss you?"

Lily took a deep breath. "I broke up with Jayme, Mom."

"Oh. Guess you could use some time back home, then. You okay?"

"Yeah, I just feel bad for him. He's a good guy."

"Then can I be nosy and ask why you broke up with him?"

"Well," Lily sighed, searching for the right words, "if I can't be sure after five years with him, then I'm fairly certain God is trying to tell me to move on."

"Are you sure that's what God is telling you? Or do you think maybe you might be scared?"

"Mom, I've been married. I know what it's all about—the good, the bad, the ugly. I don't think it's about the fear of marriage."

"Okay, then what is it? Don't you love him?"

"Not the way I'm supposed to, no."

"There are all kinds of love, Honey, not just one. I hate to see you pass up a chance at happiness."

This conversation was not going as Lily had planned and was quickly moving in the wrong direction. "Mom, it's fine, okay. I want to go home. Jayme isn't home."

"I just hate seeing you alone."

"Well, I don't think I will exactly be alone. Jack and I have been…well, I'm not sure what you call it."

"Jack? Wow. Well, I heard he got a divorce, but fairly recently, right?"

"Yeah, I guess you could say the ink has barely dried on the paperwork."

"So what does Jack have to do with this? Have you two been corresponding?"

"He came to Florida, to see me."

"Wait. What? Say that again."

"Yes, Mom. He came to Florida. To see me."

"Well, I'll be."

"We've been spending some time together recently. In fact, he's still here, but he's going back home soon."

"So you're following him back?"

This conversation was becoming exasperating. "Mom, I'm going home to Texas. If it works out with Jack, great. If not, well, I've been through worse. I think I can handle it."

Lily's mom sighed. "Just be careful, Honey."

"I will, Mom. Either way, my time in Florida is over, and it's time for me to go home to the ranch. I miss it."

"I know what you mean. I love California, but there's no place like home, right?"

"Right. I'll let you know my plans once I figure them out. It will be a few weeks before I can make the move."

"Okay, Sweetie. Let me know if you wanna talk. I'm always here for you, you know that."

"Thanks, Mom. I miss you so much!"

"I miss you too, Daughter. Take care."

Lily hung up the phone and wiped her eyes. She wished her mom didn't live so far away, but such is life, and she had to move on with hers too. Lily couldn't blame her for that, especially since her dad was gone. Still, it didn't make it any easier. Lily went to the kitchen, poured herself another cup of coffee and fixed herself a sandwich. *Texas. I can't wait to get home!*

Jack woke up and looked at his clock. "Oh crap!" It was already lunch time, past actually. He looked over at the other double bed in the room and saw Grace sitting Indian-style, watching cartoons, shoving handfuls of dry cereal in her mouth and all over the sheets. Kayla had brought her by earlier that morning, but Jack was so tired, he had gone right back to sleep. He groggily stumbled out of bed and walked over to Grace and kissed the top of her head.

"Hi Daddy. Want some cerweal?"

"No Sweetie. Daddy's gonna take a shower, and then we'll go down to the pool and get a hamburger. How does that sound?"

"Can we go swimmin', please?"

"Yep. You get your swim suit on, and we'll go right after my shower."

"Yay! Swimmin'!"

Jack let the warm water rush over his head. He was hung over from his night of self-pity, but glowed at the memory of watching the sun rise on the beach with Lily. He quickly got dressed and sent Lily a text.

"We're goin to the pool. Meet us there?"
"Sure. Gimme about an hour." Lily responded.
"Great! See you soon."

Jack still couldn't believe he was in Florida and he and Lily were finally together. Really together. No Damien, no Hailey, no Jayme—Nothing stood in their way! Well, except for maybe a few states. But that could be worked out. He opened his suitcase and rummaged around until he finally uncovered the small box containing his grandmother's wedding ring. Years earlier, she had given it to him before she died, in hopes that someday he would give it to his bride to be. It never once crossed his mind to give it to Hailey. He must have known in his heart that she wasn't the one.

He had run across it when he'd opened the gun safe he kept in his office. One couldn't take any chances on the roads these days, so he'd decided to take a weapon with them on their journey. The door to the safe opened, and there it sat on the top shelf, presenting itself to him—his grandmother's brilliant diamond ring. It sparkled, just begging to be picked up, admired, on someone's finger once again, but not just someone—Lily's. He'd packed the ring at the last minute…just in case. Nick's words came back to him, "Don't let her go." Well, he wouldn't. Not this time. This time, he would do all he could to make Lily his. They'd had such long lives without each other, but God finally put them together and he would be eternally grateful. He sent up a silent prayer of thanks.

Lily arrived at the pool just as Jack and Grace finished their lunch.

"Lilwy!" Grace ran and jumped into Lily's arms. She was still wet from swimming, but Lily didn't mind. She loved having a child in her arms. "Can you go swimmin' wiff us?"

"I'd love to, but shouldn't you finish your lunch first?"

"Yes, Ma'am." Grace jumped down and ran back over to her seat to finish her burger. Jack stood up and gave Lily a lingering hug. He was dripping too, but she didn't mind that either. Feeling his wet, half clothed body pressed up against her however, was a little disconcerting, but she was finally in his arms, where she'd always belonged. They decided to go to the beach where they sat down on a blanket and watched Grace play in the sand.

Jack's happy expression faded. "We have to start home day after tomorrow." He held her hand in his and looked at her longingly. Lily's grin stretched from ear to ear. "Why are you smiling? So eager to be rid of me?"

"No, it's just that the sooner y'all leave, the sooner I can start packing."

"Packing? For what? Are you goin on a trip?"

"Yep. A long one."

Jack frowned. "Well...where are you goin'? Who are you going with?"

Lily realized what he must be thinking. That maybe she'd changed her mind about Jayme. She pointed to the west. "A few states that direction."

"Wait. What?" Jack asked.

"Jack, I'm going home, back to Texas."

Jack's face lit up, his eyes widened. "Texas? Really? By yourself, though, right?"

Lily giggled. "Of course by myself. I'm moving back to the ranch." Silence met her declaration. Lily stiffened as she waited for Jack to reply. "Well, what do you think?" Lily started to get nervous. What if Jack didn't want her to move back to Texas? What if she'd been a fool and misread the situation?

"Moving??? You're MOVING back to Texas?" Jack stood up, pulling her along with him, then picked her up and swung her round and round. Lily's worries disappeared.

By then they had gotten Grace's attention and she ran over to them and jumped up and down laughing and giggling with them both, though having no idea why. After they had all calmed down, Jack explained to Grace that Lily was moving back to Texas. Grace was delighted.

"When Lilwy? When?" Grace asked over and over again, clinging to Lily's legs.

"Yeah, when Lily? When?" Jack repeated.

"Well, I'm not sure yet," she said to the two expectant faces. Lily counted down with her fingers. "First, I have to get out of my apartment lease. I need to put in my two weeks' notice at work, pack everything I own, and rent a moving trailer. All that might take, uh, I don't know, a month, I guess."

"Then I will be back in three weeks with my truck to help you."

"Jack, you don't have to do that. I made it here on my own. I can make it back on my own too." Lily declared.

"Yes, but now you don't have to, do you?" He pulled her close to him. She sighed inwardly. For once she wouldn't have to do it on her own. The relief she felt overwhelmed her. Not that she couldn't live her life on her own, or with the help of God, handle everything by herself. She'd been very independent for a very long time.

She'd had to be independent all these years. She was always the one who had to take care of everything, even with Damien, *especially* with Damien. Letting go of some of that independence and leaning on someone else released a burden she'd long been carrying. It felt good to share the weight with someone else, especially when that someone was Jack. Lily hugged him tight and agreed to accept his help. She could get used to this. Jack kissed her right there in front of Grace.

"Daddy has a girfwend." Grace laughed and sang over and over and hugged them both around their legs.

"Yes, Daddy does." Jack and Lily said in unison.

"Hey…what's goin' on over here? What's all the commotion? Are we celebrating something?" Kayla caught Grace midflight as she jumped up and flew into her arms.

"Daddy got a girfwend and she movin' to Tesas!" Grace exclaimed with obvious delight.

"Really? That's great!" Kayla extended her hand to Lily. "I'm Kayla. Nice to meet you."

"You're Charlotte's niece?" Lily asked.

"Yep. The one and only."

"So nice to meet you."

"I really just came over to get Grace. It's activity time. What d'ya say Grace?"

"Daddy?" She looked at her father with pleading eyes.

"Sure, it's okay with me."

"Great! We finish today around 5:00. We'll be in the banquet room. You can pick her up there."

"Sounds good. Bye Grace. Be good." He reached over and gave her a quick kiss on the cheek, and then Grace reached for Lily. The beaming smile on Jack's face showed his joy and relief that Grace liked Lily so much. They stood for a moment watching Kayla and Grace walk away then he turned to her, "Wanna go swimming'?"

Jack's hand reached for hers, and they ran and jumped into the rolling surf. Waves crashed all around them as they emerged from the water clinging to each other. Lily kissed him with salty fervor, enjoying the feel of his taut muscles against her. She wanted him body and soul. Unchaste desires built inside her like the flood waters of a dam threatening to burst its walls. Her passion for him was boundless and overpowering, the exposed setting being the only thing containing their steamy appetite for one another. They broke apart, reluctantly, wet and breathing heavily, then headed back to the sand and landed with a thud on the beach.

"We need to talk," he exhaled with laborious breath and laughed.

"I'm all ears," Lily grabbed a towel to dry her hair.

"Ohhhh, I want you so bad I'm ready to explode. When I touch you...it's like..."

Her fiery eyes blazed. "I know. I feel the same way." She leaned over and kissed him, remaining close, her forehead fondling his. She whispered longingly with heavy breath "I want you. All of you."

His husky voice replied, "I want you too, Lily." His fingers wound through the back of her hair and pulled her to him. He kissed her tenderly, searing heat through her veins. Then Jack pulled away, taking a deep breath.

Lily sat back, putting some distance between them. Quiet moments passed before she spoke. "We've waited so long, but I just don't want to displease God. Jack, I know it won't be easy—God's been so good to us, giving us back to each other—we need to wait."

"I know. You're right. And I know we can't go on like this forever because, well, I'm just not that strong." Jack sat up straight and turned to Lily. His eyes focused on hers. A look of determination crossed over his face. He squeezed her hand. "Lily, I'm vowing to you right now, I won't have you until I make you my own... legally... before God...and our family."

Lily looked away, staring into the ocean waves. "You're right." Lily shook her head, still clearing out the steam his kisses created. "We can't be alone together. I don't trust myself— Wait..." Lily looked into his eyes. "What did you say?"

Jack stood, pulling Lily up with him.

"Are we going somewhere?" she asked.

He stepped close, his eyes fixed upon hers, and gently brushed the wet salty hair out of her face. As they shared the space in each other's realm, salt, sand, sun, and surf all faded into the background, and he gazed deep into her eyes, revealing a soul eternally connected to her own.

"Lily, I loved you then, back when I wasn't supposed to." He picked up her hand and kissed it. "I love you still." He kissed her other hand and held onto them both. "And I will love you till the angels take me away. Then I will love you all the more in God's perfect presence."

"Oh Jack." Lily's heart swelled. She wondered how she had ever lived without this man.

Jack took a deep breath. "Lily, I've lived a life without you that I will gladly cast aside in the hopes that you will begin with me a new life, with God as our center. I don't want to walk this earth unless you are the one beside me, to be my friend, my helper, my lover." Jack cleared his throat. "Though we've only been back together a few days, there is a place in my heart where we have loved and held each other for a decade. Lily, I will never let you go, and I will never love another." He broke into a smile. "Please put me out of my lonely misery and love me forever. Will you?"

Jack dropped down to one knee right there on the beach, drawing the attention of other beachgoers. "Will you be my wife, Lily? Please?" Tears flowed from Lily's eyes at the sound of the most beautiful words she had ever heard. She only hoped he wasn't being hasty in this impromptu proposal, but those fears were quipped when he reached into his bag and pulled out a ring and placed it halfway on her ring finger. Before he completed the task, he stopped and looked up into her eyes, pleading for a response to the declarations of his heart, open and bleeding and exposed to the burning sun and the pain of an unanswered request.

Lily dropped down to her knees and met him eye to eye. "You are my one and only, my soulmate, the love of my life. I never dared to hope for this day to come, but in my heart, the dream was always there, holding on against all odds, surviving. I love you. It's always been you. I belong to you and I always will. Now finish putting that gorgeous ring on my finger!" Jack laughed. Joy flooded over them like the ocean tide only feet away. He wrapped his arms around her, and they fell back to the sand, laughing and kissing. Lily held up her hand to admire the ring Jack had just given her. "Thank you, Jack. It's beautiful!"

"It belonged to my grandmother. Now it belongs to you."

"Then I'll treasure it all the more," Lily promised.

With sand stuck to her skin, the platinum, three-stone diamond ring glistened in the sunlight with the promise of a bright future.

"I can't wait to tell Grace!" Jack said.

"Do you think she'll be happy about it?"

"Are you kidding me? She loves you as much as I do. Well, almost." His eye twinkled and he leaned over and kissed her lingering and longingly. "I can't wait to make you my bride."

WALKER LANE

That night, Lily cooked dinner for Jack and Grace. They gave Grace the news and she was thrilled. Jack did not go home as he'd planned and instead extended his vacation until Lily could pack up her things and they could drive back together. Two weeks later, she had everything packed up and ready for him to load up in the trailer he had rented to pull behind his larger truck. Allison stopped by to say her good-byes and joyously agreed to be Lily's maid-of-honor. Lily would miss her, and she would miss Florida, but Texas was home—where Lily belonged. Nancy and Julie also came by. Julie hugged Baxter for so long, Lily wasn't sure she would give him back. Through more hugs and tears they said good-bye with promises to keep in touch. The only thing left to do was pack some books left on the shelf and that wouldn't take long. After her friends had gone, Lily sat alone on the floor and pulled each book out one by one and stacked them into the last box. A letter fell to the floor from Damien's bible. She picked it up gingerly as if it might disintegrate. She stood up and went over to the window, and this time without tears, read through it again, his last letter to her. She realized in his own way, he was giving her his blessing on her new marriage. She reread his last words to her once again:

> *Thank you for loving me. Now, go find happiness. I will always be with you, watching over you.*

"Go find happiness." Damien wanted her to be happy. "Thanks Dame," she whispered to the sky.

Jack appeared in the doorway with Grace in tow. "You almost ready?"

"Ready," Lily said wistfully.

Jack picked up the small bookshelf and carried it out. Lily put the letter back in the bible and placed it into the box…the last box. She picked it up, placed her apartment key on the counter, and walked out the door without looking back. She kissed Jack and Grace then hopped into her own truck, ready to follow him back to Texas, to home. She had so much to look forward to.

Chapter Twenty-nine

My beloved is mine, and I am his. Song of Sol. 2:16

The early morning sun shone through the upstairs windows boasting the promise of a bright beautiful day. Outside, bluebonnets and orange Indian paintbrush covered the grounds with cheery excitement. Joy sparkled in the air. Lily opened her window and leaned out, marveling at the beauty all around her. The perfect place for a wedding. The perfect day for her and Jack to become man and wife. Oh how Lily had longed for this day. The years of sadness and confusion had finally come to an end. Today, she would commit the rest of her life to Jack and his daughter Grace. Today would mark the beginning of happier years ahead.

Lily reached her arms up then leaned down and stretched over each leg. She walked downstairs to the kitchen, nearly tripping over Baxter who was meowing for his breakfast. The sun poured in through the bay windows, but the kitchen was empty. Her mom must still be sleeping. She took advantage of the peaceful moments and said a prayer, thanking God for all His blessings, then made the coffee, fed Baxter, and headed back upstairs. She crawled back into her cozy bed and opened the bible sitting on the nightstand. She turned to the book of Ecclesiastes, chapter four:

> 9 Two are better than one because they have a good return for their labor. 10 For if either of them falls, the one will lift up his companion. But woe to the one who falls when there is not another to lift him up!

Finally, Lily would have someone who could and would help her up. For too long, she had been on her own, taking care of herself. It was hard, but God was always with her, holding her and helping her up. Now God had sent Jack, her very heart's desire. *What did I ever do to deserve such a gift?* At this thought, Lily thanked God and prayed for Him to help her to be a good wife and a good mother to Grace. Lily continued to read on about the benefits of having a partner in life, and sighed with inner peace and happiness.

The next few hours flew by in a flurry of excitement as Lily and her mom delegated orders and direction to anyone who happened to be standing close by. Charlotte was catering the event, the photographer had arrived, and the D.J. needed direction. The florist's job was actually pretty simple since the wedding would take place in the front yard with a vast view of blue and orange colors bursting like the brushstrokes of an artist: *The Artist.* The two-tiered wedding cake had arrived and was set up in the formal dining room, overlooked by a portrait of Lily's dad. Lily's mom took over and sent her to her room to get dressed. She was glad for the escape. Weddings were just so chaotic, and she wanted to feel calm and peaceful when she finally walked down the makeshift aisle.

"Mom, I have one more thing I need to do before I get dressed."

"What's that Honey? Nearly everything is done. Now go get ready!"

"I can't. Not just yet." Lily reached for her bridal bouquet sitting on the kitchen counter. She gently removed a white rose and headed for the door.

"Where are you going?" Her mother called.

"I'll be back." Lily ran out the door among the throngs of people left staring.

Bob picked up Jack and Grace from their house. They arrived at the ranch about an hour before the ceremony but stopped at the barn to wait there. Jack's mom, Patricia, was waiting for them and quickly gave Jack a hug and a kiss and whisked Grace away to get her dressed in the main house. Jack was nervous, but happy, happier than he'd been since the day Grace was born.

"Well, it's finally happening!" Bob slapped Jack on the shoulder and gave him a big grin.

"I can hardly believe it! I've loved Lily since…" Jack hung his head sheepishly. "Well, since long before I was supposed to."

"Hey, nobody's perfect. You both did your best to do the right thing. God knows that."

"Do you think it's enough, though?"

"Course not." Bob grinned.

Jack looked at Bob with confusion.

"We all fall short. That's why we need mercy," Bob reminded him. "Remember that bible verse that says to deny self?"

"Yeah, but I'm not denying self. I'm getting exactly what I want," Jack pointed out.

"But you did. And she did. You both denied what you really wanted because it didn't fit with God's word or God's will…at the time."

"And now?"

"Now is your time. Don't screw it up."

Jack shook his head. "Lily met her commitment 'till death do you part'. I didn't. I got divorced."

"True, but Hailey left you, remember? For another man, at that!"

"Thanks for reminding me. Not that I blame her. She wasn't stupid. She knew I wasn't all in. Sometimes I feel so guilty." Jack looked down at his new boots, their shine glinting off the sun's rays coming through the window. "I loved Lily even when I was married to Hailey."

"Look, you can't restrain what's in your heart. You can try, but the heart is free, even when we aren't. The heart will love who it loves, and there's just no way around it. But you both denied self, just as we are called to do. Jack, God is merciful. He's given you and Lily a second chance."

"Okay, I guess you're right."

"You wanna make up for all your past sins? Then make this marriage work, till death do you part. Make Lily happy, because if anyone deserves a happy ending, it's that girl."

Jack shook his head. "She's seen too much pain in her life, and some of it, I caused."

"Look, dude, we are all a bunch of messed up people, but God knows that, and He helps us make our paths straight. If we could do it on our own, He never would have sent His Son to die for us."

These were just the words that Jack needed to hear. "Dang Bob, for a bartender you really know your stuff. Maybe you shoulda been a preacher."

"Uh Jack, preachers don't serve drinks. But maybe in my next life, huh?"

They laughed and embraced then Jack walked over to a desk in the corner of the barn. He opened the drawer and found exactly what he was looking for, a bible. A feeling of rightness filled his heart when he opened it up and saw Lily's dad's name in the front. Then he turned back to Bob and asked, "Will you pray with me?"

Brimming with new spring leaves, a canopy of tree branches welcomed Lily as she drove through the old cemetery gate barely hanging on by its rusty hinges. The smell of freshly cut grass led her down the narrow lane solemnly past ancient headstones so faded by time, the names were illegible. She parked near the family plot, spotting a hand-written sign warning to watch for copperheads. Great. That's all she needed on her wedding day. Lily envisioned hobbling down the aisle all bruised and swollen from a poisonous snakebite. She shook the thought away and decided to heed the warning.

The heavy truck door swung open and back towards her before she could put her foot out to stop it. It slammed shut. Taking a deep breath, she opened the door once again, clamored out of the truck and reached for the flower she had removed from her bridal bouquet. She carefully stepped over the residing graves until she reached her father's headstone. She cleared off fallen sticks and cleaned up the area as best she could. It had been a long time since she'd been here. She needed this, this quiet moment with her father before she took the next biggest step of her life. The concrete bench her mom had placed near her dad's grave beckoned her. Holding the flower close to her heart, she sat upon the bench in silence, its coolness seeping through to her skin. Her father needed no words to understand all that Lily felt. She just needed to be close to him once again. Oh, how she wished he could walk her down the aisle, but he would be with her.

Once again peaceful in mind and spirit, she placed the rose on her daddy's grave then walked the short distance to Damien's headstone. "Beloved husband, son, and child of God." That's what he'd wanted engraved on his stone, "child of

God," and he was. She knelt down over Damien and said a prayer for his peace on this day, the day she would give her life to another. She kissed her fingers then touched his stone. "Bye, Dame." Her life with him seemed an eternity ago. Now, she had done what she came to do, and she was ready to begin a new life.

John Walker walked into the barn looking for his son.

"Dad, hey! Bob and I were just about to say a prayer. Would you join us?"

"I'd be honored to, Son, especially if you let me lead it." All three men bowed their heads and clasped hands in a small circle. John Walker asked God to bless the marriage of Jack and Lily and to help his son be a good husband. He thanked God for giving them the desires of their hearts and the patience to wait for His timing. When he finished the prayer all three men looked up with tears glistening in their eyes then Bob raced out the door to go get Lily, leaving Jack and his father with precious moments alone.

"Dad, do I have your blessing? Your approval means the world to me," Jack asked.

"Lemme tell you something, Son. You have more strength and resolve than I've ever had. You've been through a lot. Don't know if I could've been so strong. I'm proud of you." John placed his hand on Jack's shoulder and looked him square in the eye. "God is giving you a gift. I know you appreciate it all the more for having to wait."

"But, I know it was a long time ago, but you seemed so disappointed in me when I first told you how I felt about Lily."

"Easy for me to talk. I wasn't the one in your shoes, now was I? Besides, God gave me the words you needed to hear. I was just the messenger." John Walker slapped his son in the back and embraced him.

"I love you, Dad." Jack held his father tight.

"I love you too, and don't you forget it." John pulled back and looked proudly at his son. "And yes, you have my blessing. Now, let's go have us a wedding, shall we?"

Lily gazed at the long white dress in the mirror. It's simple, scooped neckline led to sheer lace sleeves. White lace covered the bodice extending to an A-line waist lightly adorned with shimmery silver and white beads—simple, yet elegant...and perfect. She had decided to forego the train and veil, and instead had weaved little white gardenias into her hair braided back from her face. The back of her hair hung down, wavy and free. She proudly wore the pearl drop earrings her mother had given to her that morning and the gold cross necklace that had belonged to her father. Wanting to be a beautiful bride for her perfect groom, she was checking her make-up for the tenth time when a soft knock interrupted her primping. She turned to the door as her soon-to-be mother-in-law peeped in.

"Lily?" The door opened wider and Jack's mom hesitatingly leaned inside. "Oh my!" Patricia's hands went to her cheeks as she stopped and stared. "You are stunning."

Lily smiled and released a deep breath. "Please, come in." She hated the formalities, but she was still somewhat uncomfortable around Jack's mom. Patricia Walker, a regal woman, entered the room then turned to close the door.

"May we talk?" Patricia asked.

"Of course." Lily pulled up a chair "Here, sit down."

"Oh, I'm too nervous to sit." Patricia gingerly stepped up to Lily and placed her hands on her shoulders. "I just needed to say this before the ceremony starts."

"Okay, what is it?" Lily's stomach churned.

"Lily, I'm so very sorry for hurting you that day in the hospital."

Lily blinked away her surprise at Patricia's words. Maybe she wasn't so bad after all. "No, you were right. You were just being God's messenger."

Patricia looked at her, confused. "What do you mean?"

Lily turned her back to Jack's mom and walked across the room. Looking down at her hands, she turned her engagement ring round and round on her finger. "I don't regret being at the hospital with Jack," she confessed. "He needed me." Lily took a deep breath then turned to face her. "But I was married, and once you got there, it was time for me to let go."

"Nevertheless Dear, I want to thank you for being there for my son. You helped him to hold on." Patricia looked at Lily with compassion in her eyes. "I heard about what you went through after that with your husband. You are very loyal and it's to be commended. What I'm trying to say is that I'm sorry, and I hope we can start over." Patricia walked over to Lily, took her hands and held them in her own. "You are marrying my son, and I want you to be my daughter."

Tears filled Lily's eyes as joy and relief filled her heart. "Of course we can start over."

"I know how much you and my son love each other. I know Grace loves you too. Thank you for being so good to them both." Patricia took a deep breath. "Do you think you could consider calling me Mom?"

"Yes…Mom." Lily put her arms around Jack's mom, now her mom.

Patricia pulled back. "I almost forgot. Do you have something blue?"

"Oh no. I sure don't."

Patricia went over to her purse and pulled out something wrapped in tissue paper. "My mother gave this to me on my wedding day. It's not much, but it's blue. I want you to have it." Lily held out her hand. Patricia placed in it a small handkerchief embroidered with tiny blue flowers and the name Walker stitched across.

Lily gently studied it, admiring its handiwork. "It's beautiful. Thank you."

"You keep it, and maybe give it to your daughter-in-law someday."

"I will treasure it."

Just then, Bob rapped at the door, startling them both.

"Come in."

"You ready to get hitched, Little Lady?" he asked.

"Yep, never readier!"

Angelo peeked around Bob's shoulder into the room at Lily. "Uh, may I have a minute with the bride?"

Lily was stunned at seeing Angelo again. Though they had kept in touch through the years, she hadn't seen him since she'd moved to Florida. "Please, come in."

Angelo walked into the room and Bob and Patricia stepped out closing the door behind him. He reached for her hands and clasped them tightly. "Oh Lily, my beautiful daughter. Damien would be so happy for you today."

"You really think so?"

"Oh yes, Child. He hated that he was unable to give you children. He once told me how he'd prayed for God to someday give you the family you'd always wanted."

Lily smiled. "Well, I don't know about that. I'm not exactly a spring chicken anymore, but I know I will love and care for Grace as if she were my own."

"Yes, and you will be a wonderful mother, but Lily, it's not too late for you to give Grace a brother or sister. God has given you another chance."

"Oh Angelo...Dad. I hope so. I've wanted children ever since, well, ever since I was a child."

"Well Lily," He squeezed her hands. "I know this sounds strange, but I had a dream about you last night."

"Really?"

"Yes. Damien and I were standing in a doorway of a hospital room. You were in the bed, holding...well, you were holding two babies."

Lily's eyes widened. "Twins?"

"I guess so." He laughed.

Lily's hands flew to her face. "Oh my goodness!"

"Anyway, I just wanted to say how happy I am for you. Is he a good man, Lily?"

"Oh yes! He's a Godly man and we really love each other."

"Then I'm so happy for you, and I know my son is too."

"Thank you." Lily's eyes glistened. "I'm so glad you're here."

Angelo kissed her lightly on the cheek, but Lily knew that it wasn't his kiss she felt. She looked up into the heavens and whispered, "Thanks, Dame."

Lily stood impatiently and waited behind the front doorway. Her maid-of-honor, Allison, stood next to her in a long blue chiffon dress. She gave Lily a quick hug then stepped outside. Lily peeked through the window watching as Allison stepped gingerly on the makeshift aisle of white fabric placed over the grass in the front yard. Grace threw red and white rose petals down the aisle and all over the yard on her way towards Jack. Lily's mom looped her arm through hers and asked, "Are you ready for a lifetime of happiness?" Lily fought the tears forming in her eyes.

"Mom, I've been ready for this day for longer than you could ever imagine." Lily stepped out the front door, onto the porch and down the three steps, looking down—as was her habit—at her shoes sparkling in the sun.

"Lily," her mom whispered, "are you looking for snakes, or what? Look up." Jack was waiting for her under the twin live oaks, their branches lovingly reaching out to each other creating a natural archway where a rose bush had intertwined and proliferated, cascading red blooms down from overhead. Her eyes found his and they locked in on each other. An invisible bridge instantaneously connected them in love—openhearted, no holds barred, always-existing, never-dying love. Jack couldn't have looked more handsome in his dark suit, crisp white shirt, and bolo tie. The walk down the aisle seemed to take forever. The traditional wedding march led her finally to his side as her mother gave her away one last time. Jack's eyes filled with adoration as he reached for her arm.

Lily glowed. He had never seen anyone more beautiful. He took her arm in his, her beaming smile reflecting his own. He gave her a wink then they faced the preacher. Brother Tim began the ceremony and spoke of the importance of a marriage with God as its center. He already knew the result of a marriage without God as its center. No doubt about it, this time would be different. This time Lily would be his wife, and she loved the Lord as much as he did.

After the preacher spoke, Charlotte read the scripture:

> Song of Solomon 8:6-7: "
> Put me like a seal over your heart,
> Like a seal on your arm. For love is
> as strong as death...Many waters
> cannot quench love, Nor will rivers
> overflow it.

The sweet voice of Patsy Cline sang the promise of "Always" as they each raised a single candle to light one together in unity. Happiness filled the atmosphere as they promised to love and cherish one another for the rest of their lives.

"You may now kiss the bride." Jack's hand reached out and softly grazed Lily's cheek. It was calloused and strong yet capable of pure gentleness. So like Jack. His soft kiss became one of restrained passion, leaving her slightly dizzy. Cheers went up from the crowd filled with their loved ones, and Grace, clapping her small hands together, jumped up and down yelling out "Yay!"

Jack and Lily laughed as he picked up his little girl and the three embraced as a family, the family Lily had always longed for.

They had each been married once before. They'd each had their challenges and tribulations and heartbreak, but this was a new start for a new life, together, and together they were herculean. God was giving them a second chance at happiness. This marriage would hold God as its center. This new life held inexhaustible promise—the promise of God.

Just after the wedding, they quickly set up for the reception. The food was put out buffet style in the house and tables were placed in the front yard. The wedding party quickly donned them with white linen tablecloths and centerpieces of tea roses in metal tins, baby's breath, and burlap ribbon. Hanging lights swung overhead shining brightly in the trees. Allison, Charlotte, Bob, and Jack's father each gave comical yet emotional speeches and toasted the happy couple. The D.J. spread out his equipment on the porch and they danced on the driveway. For their first dance, they swayed together to the sultry words "At Last" by Etta James, oblivious to the world around them. At the end of the evening, they changed into a casual wardrobe of jeans and boots, said their good-byes, gave Grace several hugs and kisses leaving her in the care of Jack's parents, and headed down I10 to a much-anticipated destination reaching the cabin just before midnight.

Chapter Thirty

**Consequently they are no longer two, but one flesh.
What therefore God has joined together, let no man separate.
Matt. 19:6**

Back in Florida, Jack and Lily had promised to wait until they were married to consummate their union. It had been a trying time in the few months that led up to their vows, but they were so grateful to God for finally bringing them together, they'd felt they owed it to Him to be faithful to His Word. The wedding had been magical and the time had finally come. It was time to become one. Excitement and nervousness overwhelmed them both. After all these years of wanting each other, denying themselves, choosing right over wrong, they could finally be together with God's blessing.

For their honeymoon they had chosen a cabin in a pecan orchard on the Frio River only hours away, and Jack was delighted. He loved the river. The river would be icy cold this time of year, after all it was named *The Frio*, which did mean *cold* in Spanish, but they probably wouldn't spend much time in the water anyway.

Jack unlocked the door and turned on the light. He'd made Lily stay in the truck until he could come back and pick her up and carry her over the threshold. They both burst into laughter when he accidentally slammed her feet against the doorjamb. He kissed her and put her down to the floor and then went back to the truck for their bags while Lily scoped out the cabin. It was rustic, built out of cedar, but clean and fairly new. She walked over to the little coffee table in front of the leather sofa and picked up the bottle of Dom Pérignon that had been left chilling in a galvanized metal bucket. A dozen red roses and two Arthur Court champagne flutes lay in wait beside it. Lily put the bottle back in the ice then picked the card out of the fragrant blooms and opened it. "To my wife, at long last. I love you. Always, Jack." She looked up as Jack walked in the door carrying all of their bags in one trip. "In a hurry?" she teased.

"Are you kiddin' me? Patience has its limits, ya know." She did know. In fact, Jack had been the stronger one in their efforts to wait.

"These roses? Not store-bought, are they?" She gently touched the blooms and leaned over them, inhaling the aroma of their natural fragrance.

Jack dropped the bags down on the floor. "How could you tell?"

"They smell heavenly, and they have so many blooms. How?"

"I asked the lady who owns the cabin where to find real roses. She actually has some growing out back."

"And the card? It's your handwriting."

"Yeah. I wanted to write the card myself. I mailed it to her." Lily smelled the roses once again, marveling at his thoughtfulness and attention to detail.

As she turned toward him, their eyes locked across the tiny living room. "Thanks Jack," she said softly, "They're beautiful."

"Like you." He went to her and kissed her gently. Lily wondered if anyone had ever died from happiness. As he reached around her to pick up the champagne bottle off the table, she could feel him—not his touch, but something beyond touch, as if his warmth and light coincided with her own. Jack popped the cork and filled two glasses with champagne bubbling over. She could not take her eyes off him as he toasted to her of love, eternal loyalty, and thanks to God, then they quickly finished their glasses. He reached for her empty glass and put it down on the table next to his then took her hands into his own and bowed down to one knee. He looked up at her with an intensity that blazed in his eyes. With a pledge of unwavering honor, he placed their intertwined hands over his heart and vowed, "You—are mine. You belong to me—and I, you." Lily thought she might swoon right there in the small living room, but then he swiftly stood, picked her up, and carried her through the doorway to the bedroom setting her down on the bed with gentle urgency. She could feel his heart racing. No more words were needed.

REMEMBER ME

    The weight of him lay gently upon her, the confines of their bodies verging upon immortal bliss. He kissed her softly, a kiss that quickly built up in ardor. "Wait!" She told him as she pushed him away and hopped up from the bed leaving him in a state of heavy breathing. He rolled over onto his back and groaned, feeling as if someone had just ripped off his life jacket in the middle of a roiling sea. He heard her rummaging around in her bag and caught a glimpse of her as she streaked into the bathroom. Moments later she reappeared in a long white silky gown, thin and clinging. He sat up abruptly and stared muddleheaded. She slowly ambled over to him and stopped, suspended in time. He swung his feet to the floor and quickly pulled off his boots then sat on the edge of the bed taking her small hands into his own. He looked up at her with intent eyes fixed upon hers and fiercely declared with a whispered vow, "Soul of my soul." She pulled him to her chest and stroked his hair, then leaned over him, her body compelling his downward into the sheets. He felt her warm breath on his tingling skin as she in turn declared the vow, repeating his words, and they kissed with a heat and desire that had been locked deep inside them for an eternity. All these years they had wanted each other, their own forbidden love, locked away in a secret place in their hearts of what could never be, but now God had given them the desires of their heart. Their union was now blessed by God Himself, and with a love forbidden no longer, from embers that had once been smoored, passion reignited, and their bodies and souls unleashed the fire of their unwavering love…and in the early morning hours, at long last, they became one.

Chapter Thirty-one

**And we know that God causes all things to work together for good to those who love God,
to those who are called according to His purpose.
Rom. 8:28**

Lily sat curled up on the couch wrapped in an old afghan made by her grandmother. She stared out the window at the frisky squirrels chasing each other. They ran along the top rail of the fence, scattering in their wake an avalanche of snow flurries. The yard and the pastures beyond were covered with a blanket of white snow. Three days before, the Texas air was hot and humid, today cold and crisp. Texas had encountered a freak, unexpected snowstorm of that which even the weather forecaster had no previous knowledge. The cats daintily stepped through the snow as if wondering what on earth this cold wet stuff could possibly be. But they seemed to enjoy it. It was an unexpected gift from God, a white Christmas in Texas. It had to be a miracle—a sign of promises of a future yet to be.

Five-year-old Grace sat under the Christmas tree with her legs curled up under her investigating her neatly wrapped presents. "Lilwy, what time does Santa Cwaus come?" she asked as she focused on the gift with the big red bow.

"Well, he comes at night, on Christmas Eve, that's tonight, but not until little boys and girls fall asleep."

"So he won't come if I don't go to sleep?" she questioned.

"Well..."

"But what if I *can't* fall asleep?" Tears began to well up in her big green eyes.

"Oh well, don't worry about that! Boys and girls *always* fall asleep. God makes sure. After all, He wouldn't want you to miss out on Santa's visit, would He?" Grace's smile lit up the room. She hopped up off the floor and ran over to Lily and hugged her tightly. Lily's heart melted. She had waited all her life for a moment like this one.

"So when do I get to open my pwesents?" Grace asked.

"Well, tomorrow morning you get to open Santa's gifts, but tonight, after we get home from the candle-light service at church, we'll eat supper, open our family gifts, and watch Christmas movies. Which Christmas movie would you like to watch, Gracie?"

"Mmmmm...Charlie Brown. The one where he gets the little tree and they decorate it real pwetty." The bright lights on their tall Christmas tree seemed dim compared to the way Grace's smile lit up the room.

"Okay, sounds good to me. Your dad loves that one too." As if on cue, Jack walked in from the kitchen with a tray of hot chocolate. He gently put the tray down on the coffee table all covered with garland and homemade decorations. Handing a cup to Lily, he bent down and kissed her on the cheek.

"You feeling okay? You haven't been off the couch in an hour."

Lily was tired. She had spent all morning cooking and baking for tomorrow's Christmas dinner. Her mom and new step-dad were flying in from California to spend Christmas with Lily and her new family at the ranch, the ranch where Lily grew up and had always dreamed of raising her own children. "I'm all right. I've been watching the animals outside play in the snow."

"It's hard to believe...a white Christmas in Texas. It's like a miracle. Like you." Jack leaned in to kiss her again.

"Ewwww. Yuck! Stop kissing!" Grace exclaimed. "Let's go play in the snow. I wanna build a snowman like on Frosty the Snowman! Can we Daddy? Please?"

Jack looked at Lily with a lopsided grin, and said, "Welcome to parenthood." He turned to Grace and said, "Sure Doodlebug, but drink your hot chocolate first."

Lily had never been happier. She and Jack were finally together. They were back in Texas, married, and living on her family's ranch. Their spring wedding here had been perfect, overlooking rolling pastures full of bluebonnets and orange

Indian paintbrush. She had always felt her dad's presence at the ranch, and that day was no exception. Lily thought of all the people that had attended their wedding, friends and family surrounding them with love. She'd never felt so lucky in her entire life. All the years of trials, heartaches, and death were behind her, and a happy, promising future full of love and family lay ahead.

Life couldn't be any more perfect, except for one thing. Lily wanted to have a baby. She loved Grace with her whole heart, but she wanted to give Jack another child. She wanted to carry their child in her own womb and experience motherhood from the very beginning. Lily had her suspicions that maybe, just maybe, she might get her wish. After all, it was a miracle that she and Jack were finally together, so why not this miracle too? Even though she was in her late thirties, she still held onto hope. She'd bought a pregnancy test at the store yesterday, but wanted to wait until after Christmas to use it. She didn't want their first Christmas to be ruined in case she was wrong. However, she also knew that her mother would bring wine to Christmas dinner tomorrow and would be suspicious if she declined. So, out of necessity, she needed to know for sure. At least, that's what Lily told herself.

Christmas Eve would be special, just the three of them tonight. Tomorrow there would be a whole house full of family—Lily's mom and new step-dad, Jack's parents, Charlotte and Bob, and even Anna. So tonight, they would just cherish each other and their first Christmas together.

The night proved magical, celebrating Jesus' birth by candle-light at church, driving through the neighborhoods to view all the Christmas lights on decorated homes, and the ride home where Jack explained the story of Jesus to Grace and watched her child-like faith come to life. Grace had a blast ripping off the shiny wrapping paper to the discovery of her first gifts, the ones her dad and Lily gave her, and watching Charlie Brown love that little Christmas tree. Jack gave Lily a heart locket containing a picture of himself with Grace. Lily gave Jack a chain watch that had been her father's, only she had added an inscription, "Love has no boundaries of time. Love, Lily." Together they both tucked Grace in with promises of a visit from Santa. She was so exhausted, she had no trouble falling asleep after all. Also exhausted, Jack and Lily curled up in each other's arms and slept the whole night through.

Jack woke early to make coffee and make sure Santa's gifts were ready, and Lily ran to the bathroom. A few minutes later, she slowly walked out with her head down and tears spilling over. Jack was under the tree rearranging Santa's gifts when he looked up and saw her coming into the living room crying. His heart hurt for her, wondering if she was thinking about Damien or missing her dad.

"Lily?"

"Jack…" Lily choked back a sob.

"What is it? You're scaring me. Are you okay?"

Lily walked over to Jack and slowly lowered herself to the floor to sit next to him. He reached for her hand. "It's just that…I have to tell you something. I thought that maybe…Lily took a deep breath to control her voice. Okay, here goes… I have one more present for you."

Jack breathed a sigh of relief. "Oh good. Is that all? You had me worried for a second. Okay, what is it?"

"Well, I've already given you my love."

"Yes, and I've given you mine."

"And you've given me Grace."

"Yes, and you are a magnificent mother."

She paused for a moment before continuing. "Well, I was thinking…" Lily danced around a grin.

"Yes…" Jack's patience was wearing thin.

"Well, I was thinking, if it's alright with you, that is,"

"Lily! What is it???"

"Okay, I was thinking that we could call this gift…Faith, or maybe Hope?" Lily took Jack's hand and placed it tenderly on her stomach. "If it's a girl, that is."

Jack stared at Lily. She was glowing. Wide-eyed he glanced down at his hand on her stomach. His heart seemed to stop beating. He couldn't believe it. Lily pregnant? It was more than either of them had dared to hope for.

"Really Lily? Really?" Jack stood and pulled her up off the floor, threw his arms around her, and swung her around. He halted, realizing his actions, and gently put her down. He cupped her smiling face with his hands, leaned in, and kissed her softly. "You know, twins run in my family."

Lily's eyes widened and her heart sprung with hope as Angelo's dream came to mind.

"Well," Lily beamed, "Faith AND Hope then. I always wanted a houseful of children." Finally, after all these years, their dreams were finally coming true.

For I know the plans that I have for you, declares the LORD, plans...to give you a future and a hope. Jer. 29:11

The End

Made in the USA
Monee, IL
04 October 2022